ÉILÍS NÍ DHUIBHNE was born in Dublin. She has written novels, collections of short stories, children's books, and plays, as well as television scripts for RTÉ's *Glenroe* and Teilifís na Gaeilge's *Ros na Rún*. She has received an Arts Council Bursary in literature, and won various awards, including the Bisto Book of the Year Award and the Readers' Association of Ireland Award.

Her short stories were first published in the *Irish Press* in the 1970s, and have been translated into several languages and selected for many anthologies, including *Best Short Stories 1986*, *The Picador Book of Irish Fiction*, *Irish Comic Writing*, and *The Blackstaff Book of Short Stories* (1988 and 1991).

She has studied Old and Middle English and Irish Folklore at University College Dublin and at the University of Copenhagen, and has worked as a curator in the National Library of Ireland for many years. She lives in south County Dublin.

The Inland Ice
and other stories

ÉILÍS NÍ DHUIBHNE

THE
BLACKSTAFF
PRESS

BELFAST

ACKNOWLEDGEMENTS

Thanks to the Head of the Department of Irish Folklore, UCD, for permission to adapt 'The Search for the Lost Husband' from a version of that
folktale included in the department's manuscripts collection.

Thanks to Bernard and Mary Loughlin, Tyrone Guthrie Centre,
Annaghmakerrig, where some of the stories were written.

Thanks to Blackstaff Press for their patient and helpful editing.

Thanks to my family, for their love and patience.

First published in 1997 by
The Blackstaff Press Limited
3 Galway Park, Dundonald, Belfast BT16 0AN, Northern Ireland
with the assistance of
The Arts Council of Northern Ireland

Reprinted 1998

Typeset by Techniset Typesetters, Newton-le-Willows, Merseyside

Printed in Ireland by ColourBooks Limited

A CIP catalogue record for this book
is available from the British Library

ISBN 0-85640-596-5

For Bo,
with love

CONTENTS

THE SEARCH FOR THE LOST HUSBAND

L ONG LONG AGO THERE WAS A FARMER who had an only
daughter. And every day a little white goat came to her
door. She became accustomed to his visits. And eventually
she fell in love with the little white goat.

After a year or so the goat stopped coming. She asked if anybody had seen him. And an old woman told her that he had
gone over the road to the east. When the girl heard that, she
set off after him.

GWEEDORE GIRL

MRS McCALLUM ASKED, 'CAN YOU COOK?'

I said, 'Yes.' This was not the whole truth.

'What can you cook?'

I thought for a moment before answering. 'Most things.'

She looked me in the eye and I knew she did not believe me. 'Most things?'

'Eggs. Porridge, potatoes. I can fry,' I said. 'Bake bread. I can churn.'

'It will not be necessary to do that,' she said, and closed her notebook. It had a dark red cover and later I found out that it was her accounts, listing every penny spent, which she showed to Mr McCallum on Fridays after tea.

I got the situation as a general. I was to have twelve pounds a year, plus board and lodgings. Supply my own uniform. When she asked I said, yes, I had my own uniform, new. It was not new and it was not a uniform. I had an old cotton dress, blue-and-white striped, which I'd got in the pawn in Falcarragh for three shillings. It was tight around the chest and short in the skirt, but the colour was fresh and suited me. My three aprons I made myself from flour sacks. I washed them ten times and bleached them in the sun until they seemed white as snow. Then I sewed them, finishing them off with frills. I thought they were beautiful, until I saw Mrs McCallum's apron, bought from the shop. It looked like a white lily. Nothing you make at home is as good as the thing you buy in the shop.

My mother said, 'I don't know why young girls are so mad to get married.'

'You did,' I said. She married my father when she was eighteen. (He was thirty-six then, but it was not a made match. I know that much.)

'You'd be wiser off staying single and bettering yourself. You'd have a good life, away from this place.'

I thought she was telling me this because she knew, or suspected, that nobody would want to marry me – the reason being that I am not pretty enough. My mother is small and stout, with a thick bolster of a bosom and brown bulging cow's eyes. She was the best-looking girl in the parish. I know this because she has told me so herself – more than once. She does not use the word that means 'pretty' or 'nice' to describe her youthful good looks, but a word that sounds more like 'elegant' or 'gallant'. When she says that word I see her as a girl made of polished, golden wood, like the curved leg of a fine sideboard, and not a woman made of soft, hot, smelly stuff.

'I was the best-looking girl in the parish,' she says, sighing, looking wearily at me. She is always weary. There are so many of us to look after.

We all look different – some of us like her, some of us like my father, some of us like both of them, some of us like neither. I am more like my father, big made and jet-haired. My eyes are blue and I've a mouthful of slab teeth, horse's teeth.

'Your father looks like a bull,' my mother says sometimes. 'And you take after him.' She hasn't got a lot of time for my father or his side of the family, which is a cut below her own.

My mother says: 'Moya Devanney had great go in her.' Moya Devanney is her first cousin. She went to Derry and worked there for thirty years and they thought the world of her. When her missus died she left her the house and a thousand pounds. 'She'd great go in her and she did well for herself.'

We own our own farm, ten acres, and we own a boat and a seine net. Also twenty hens and ten ducks. Geese before Christmas. We sell the eggs to Hughie the Shop or exchange them for tea and sugar. Only at Easter do we eat eggs ourselves, and on Shrove Tuesday we use some for pancakes.

In the winter my mother sits by the fire and knits socks. The man from Falcarragh comes every Friday to collect them. Tuppence a sock. I helped her knit before I came here but I didn't enjoy that much – the hairy wool scratching my skin, the endless, dull stitching in the half-dark kitchen.

I am allowed an egg for breakfast. I have my breakfast in the kitchen, when Mister and Missus have finished theirs in the dining room and when he has gone to work. I like best being alone for breakfast but often she is in with me, heating milk for the child and telling me all I should do and how I should do it.

She is very small. I am like a giant beside her. She likes this, that I make her look even smaller than she is. My mother liked it too. Small women are usually very proud of being small, I have often noticed – as if being small means that they are very clever and good babies, who normally could not be expected to do a single thing for themselves. 'And the size of her!' my father would say proudly when my mother had given a hand with the hay, or baked a big stack of scones for a *meitheal* – something as ordinary and easy as buttermilk scones, that size had no bearing on one way or the other. And she'd smile, as full of herself as a bonny boychild after a bowl of poundies, all thirteen stone of her, wee pet!

That's what himself calls the missus. Sometimes I am beside her in the kitchen when he comes in in the evenings. And over he comes and kisses her and says, 'My wee wee wee pet.' Three wees, like the three wee piggies. And gives me a look as if to say, You big ould heifer, you. And this even though the missus is expecting and has a huge tummy on her like a turnip. But all that does is make the rest of her look tinier. And to be honest, the rest of her is very slight and thin, not swollen up at all. I believe she's delicate, although they'd never let on.

She wears nice clothes – a dark blue skirt and a frilly blouse, snow white, starched (by me), a fresh blouse every second day. She sits in the kitchen and chats. 'Don't you miss your family?'

'Sometimes.'

'How many brothers and sisters have you?'

When I tell her – twelve – she gasps and smiles.

'Are they all still at home?'

They are. I'm the eldest.

'It must be strange for you, living in the city.'

'It's different.'

It is different. Every single thing about it is different, so that when I first came to Derry, first got off the train, first came into the McCallums' house, different from any house I had ever been in, I felt completely lost and very tiny, like a little spider or a fly. But I was still myself. I was myself, only smaller. That is the thing that I have found out. And after a few days I began to grow back to being my big self again, and the strange things all around me shrank back to being their own size.

'It's exciting,' I added. 'But you get used to it.'

'Exciting?' She could be as nice as you like when she was interested in something.

'Yes. It is all so different and that makes it exciting.'

'Maybe it is like going to a foreign country, where people speak a different language, and wear different clothes, and where everything looks strange?'

That's it to a tee. It was just like that. Foreign. Foreign language, foreign clothes, foreign place. But, you know, I don't think she knew what she was saying. When she said 'like a foreign country' she was laughing; she meant it was not, of course, really a foreign country. That's where she's wrong. She didn't seem to know at all that at home we speak a different language and that the houses are different and even the people look different. If she knew this, she thought it was unimportant, that they were differences that didn't count. She had never been to Gweedore. Or, maybe, anywhere.

'Have you been to a foreign country?' I asked.

'Och no. We go to Portrush on our holidays. That's it.' She wanted to go to France. Her friend had been there last year, staying in Paris. And she wanted to go to London. That's what she meant by foreign. 'No harm in dreaming,' she said. 'I'll never see further than Portrush. Or Dublin, if I'm lucky.'

I wondered what Portrush was like. She tried to tell me. There is the sea and a beach and a place for men to bathe and women to bathe. There is a promenade and a lot of hotels, and brass bands playing along the seafront in special stands, like merry-go-rounds. (What is a stand? What is a merry-go-round?) And people on holiday, walking about. There are children making sand castles and old men paddling. Sometimes I thought it sounded like Derry, sometimes like Gweedore. Sometimes I just could not picture it at all. I hoped she'd say, You'll see it yourself when we go in the summer, but she never did. It was January when I started with them, and I thought she would be having the baby at maybe Easter, if not sooner. Maybe they would not go to Portrush at all.

I had to do everything in the house. Clean everything, scrub everything, cook everything, wash everything, and also mind the baby. Missus did nothing, really. Nothing worth mention-ing. She was too small, too delicate, too tired. At first I was tired too, very tired. I felt homesick because I was so tired. I would lie on my bed, when I finally got there at about eleven o'clock, and cry from tiredness. It was, I thought, as if I had come into a lovely place, a place like the Eastern world, the shining kingdoms I knew about from old stories, but had to work so hard there that the magic world turned into a nightmare.

After a while I became accustomed to the work and managed it better. And I must say that from the start I loved the house. It astonished me. The storytellers never described the insides of the castles and palaces the princes and princesses lived in at the end of the tale. They just said they were full of good things to eat and drink, and fine golden goblets and cups of silver. But they must have had other things in them. Lace cloths, silver vases of carnations, brass bowls with green plants growing in them, cabinets full of white china painted with roses. Mirrors, curly-legged tables and chairs. They must have had beds covered in silk sheets or snowy linen trimmed with crochet. Mrs McCallum's house was so cluttered up with such things that I felt I would never get to know them, and I could hardly imagine that she had ever had the time or the strength, let alone the money, to get them all.

But I did get to know them, soon, because I had to dust them all three times a week. I got to know them intimately, the china shepherdesses, the green cat on one side of the fire-place and the white dog on the other, the silver cruets, like bas-kets lined with blue glass, the twisted candlesticks. First it seemed like a treasure cave, or a shop crammed with things, confused, unknowable. And I was moving around, wonder-ing. And then I knew them every one. Liked some. I liked the shepherd, who was pale pink and blue, and had a harmless smiling face and a wavy crest of yellow hair, not like any boy or girl I have ever seen. Hated some. The green cat, which was the colour of York cabbage, crinkled like that, with a wild angry snarl. Why would anybody like a thing the like of that?

Mrs McCallum did. 'I love my green cat,' she said, when I once criticised it. 'It is so artistic.'

Artistic. A new word for me. Like arthritis. The cat was like gangrene, arthritis, bitter cabbage, and I thought that is what artistic meant, except it was good, like France. Flat plain 'France'. It reminded me of bedsprings, springy steel things. I did not like the sound of it much but it sounded much better than 'artistic'.

She went out a lot, the missus, even in the state she was in. I realised that is how she came by so much stuff – she went to the shops every day and bought. Sometimes she showed me the things. A blue shiny plate. A new silver instrument for beating eggs. More often she got clothes for herself or for the child. Ribbons, stockings. Also hats, jackets, dresses, nightgowns.

'He'll murder me if he finds out,' she said.

What could I say? I did not think he would murder her. I did think he would be cross. Sometimes, I think, he did not find out. She showed him her red book on Fridays and they shut themselves into the room, locking the door, all important. She was nervous – for good reason – and he bossy and stiff like a sergeant major, even though normally they were not like this to each other. It was as if they both decided to become different people, on Fridays. And they did this because they liked it. I could see it when they came out, they kept glancing at each other, their eyes looking teasing and dangerous. And they went straight up the stairs afterwards, always.

She did the real shopping too, and that was her excuse for being out all the time. She called every day to the baker's, the dairy; several days a week to the butcher's, the greengrocer's, the grocer's. She only sent me to the shops when she was so tired she could not get outside the door, or when it was raining very heavily, or when she had forgotten something. Mostly she left me with the baby and the house while she was out.

I did not get to the shops but I met the delivery boys who carried the things she had bought to the house in the baskets of their bicycles, or under their arms. The baker's boy and the milkman, the grocer's lad and the butcher's. They came and banged on the window of the kitchen and left their parcel on the sill. All except the butcher's boy. He came to the door, knocked, handed over his brown parcel stained with blood. If he left it outside the cat would have got it.

The butcher's boy was Elliot and he came of a Tuesday, Wednesday, Thursday and Saturday. Mondays we ate cold meat left over from Sunday and on Fridays, fish, since they were, like me, Catholic, although they looked Protestant. Elliot looked Protestant too, like all the other boys. He wore a brown jacket with patches everywhere and a big peaked cap covering his head and his eyes. The only different thing was that he always had a white shirt. You could see the snowy collar sticking out over the jacket.

He was full of cheek. 'There you are, wee pet,' he said on the first day, and ran off.

'How is my wee fairy today?' he said on the second day.

'Cheek of you,' I said, or something like that. 'None of your lip.' I'd learned some of these expressions from school and from Mrs McCallum. 'Cheek of you calling me wee pet and me old enough to be your mother.'

I thought he would say something like, And big enough to be my father – in Gweedore boys teased me about my height.

But he said, 'You don't look it', in a serious and nice voice.

All of a sudden I felt like crying. I did not know what had come over me. 'Go away out of that,' I said. 'Haven't you a job to do? Like meself.'

In the morning I get up at six and light the range and bring them tea in bed. When I go into the bedroom Missus is awake, lying against the white bolster with her fair curly hair frizzed out against it, some of it falling down over her shoulders. Her dress is lying on the chair beside the bed and her clothes, her white underclothes, sometimes on the chair and sometimes on the floor, so that I have to pick them up as soon as I've left down the tray on her knees. He is asleep beside her. All I see are his big brown whiskers sticking out over the edge of the quilt, wiry and thick, funny beside her soft fair face and her soft white nightdress. The room smells of them and of bedrooms, that thick, skinful, shameful smell. As soon as I open the door I get it and then I am walking through their smell as if it were a soup. The smell of their sleeping bodies, lavender water, soap, the smell of their chamber pot under the bed (I would have to empty it later, carrying it, covered by a bit of newspaper, out to the lavatory down the back). The child is with them in his cradle near the bed and always cries when I walk in.

I leave the tray and get out as quickly as I can from the room. As I go out I know she is stretching out for the baby and his eyes are opening and looking at me. He was just pretending to be asleep. There is always a difference, between people who pretend to be asleep and people who really are. Maybe it is that people who are asleep can't pretend anything, and you can see that on them. They look so foolish, often, their faces doing things they wouldn't let them do if they could help it.

'Any chance of a cup of tea?' he said.

'The missus doesn't let me give tea to people.' She hadn't
said that. But it was just because it never occurred to her that I
would. She had said in the interview, 'No followers', and Mister had glanced at her and smiled, as if to say, We don't have to
worry about that.

'She's not here,' he said. 'I just seen her down in the
Diamond.'

This was after I had been with them about three weeks. It
was the beginning of February.

He came in and sat at the table while I wet the tea. When I
had my back turned to him he took off his cap and when I
turned around I saw his hair for the first time. It was a big fair
bush, curly gold, standing out in a crest around his head. I had
never seen such hair on a boy before and could not take my
eyes off it.

He took bread and butter and dipped it in the sugar bowl.

'She'll be raging,' I said, 'if she finds out.'

'You're allowed to eat,' he said. 'What time do you get up
in the morning? When do you go to bed?'

My bedroom is a room at the back of the kitchen, cosy and
warm in winter, at least. It used to be a storeroom and there
are shelves along one wall still, containing broken crockery,
old basins and jugs and chipped potties, that she doesn't want
to throw out yet, but can't use. There is no window, so I have
to leave the door open or light the candle to see anything. A
bed, a chair. On the wall is a little mirror without a frame. It
has brown freckles all down one side but, if I light the candle, I
can see myself all right. I can see myself but I can't do my hair
or anything at the same time, because there is nowhere to put
down the candle.

Nevertheless, I spend a long time looking at my face in the
mirror, because at home we hadn't one and I do not really

know what I look like. Now I still don't know. That is, I know, but I do not know if I am pretty or not. The face in the freckled mirror looks nice to me. The cheeks are pink, the eyes are blue, the mouth is red, the hair is black and curly. It is not a bit like Mrs McCallum's face, of course, and maybe there are all kinds of things I do not see, in the dark, and because I am trying to make it out to be better than it is. How can you know these things? Maybe I look nice to myself, and to everyone else, ugly.

Before Elliot comes, I go up to her room if she is out and do my hair in the mirror on her dressing table. After a while I use her brush with the silver back, and I dab a bit of her lavender water behind my ears, and a little of her powder on my nose, which is shiny because I am so hot from all the work.

He asked me if I had a half-day.

Wednesday. I get off after the lunch, and I'm allowed off until nine at night. What do I do with the time? I walk around. I walk around and look in all the shops. I walk around the walls and look at the river. I walk by the harbour and look at the boats. Walk and look is what I do. I love that.

He could meet me at six. I'd like to go to a show? There is a music hall on the Strand, but the show is not over until half past ten. Then we'll just go for a walk.

Since this is what I do all the time I am pleased enough.

It is better walking with him than walking alone. People don't stare at me when I am with him, looking me up and down, as if they despised me or as if they liked me. When I am with him they just glance at us and look away again quickly, or else stare at him. It is better, because he talks to me and makes jokes, and because he knows the place inside out, tells me who lives in what house, tells me stories about every place we see.

What sort of stories? Stories about women who were murdered and chopped up into small pieces and served up in pastry for dinner. Stories about the devil appearing at card games and about ghosts who come back to repay money they owed to usurers or to landlords. A story about a bailiff who was cursed by a widow and taken off by the devil in his bag. The bailiff had met a man who turned out to be the devil. The devil said he was walking around, planning to take whatever would be offered to him from the whole heart on that day. A woman cursed her pig for digging up her potatoes, saying, 'The devil take you!' And the bailiff said: 'Take that pig now!' 'I will not,' said the devil, 'because she did not offer it from the heart.' Then they see a mother chasing her son across the road. 'The devil take you!' she says. But the devil will not take him, because the wish was not sincerely meant. Then they come to the house where the bailiff is going to issue an eviction notice to an old widow. She comes out and begs him for mercy. But he won't give her any. 'The devil take you!' she says. And the devil takes the bailiff off to hell, because the widow's wish came from the heart.

Elliot laughed a lot at this story, which I did not think so very funny. A lot of his stories were about money, or bailiffs.

He had other stories, though, some concerning himself.

He found a baby in a bag on the Strabane Road once when he was a little boy. I was walking along collecting blackberries, he said, and I saw this bag with two legs sticking out of it. I thought it was a wee cat or a dog or a doll maybe. And I went over and took off the bag and it was a little baby. No clothes on her or nothing. What did you do? I asked. Went to the police, he said.

He asked me questions as well. Not questions like Mrs McCallum's how-many-brothers-and-sisters-have-you-don't-you-miss-them? He really wanted to know things. He wanted to know how many of us slept in the same bed and what sort of cover we had on the bed, and how many cups and saucers we had. He asked if I could swim or if I went fishing on the shore or in the burn. He wanted to know how many new dresses I had had in my whole life and what sort of dress I would buy if I had all the money in the world. He wanted to know what my mother looked like and my father, and what I got to eat at the McCallums', and what Mrs McCallum wore in bed, and how many pairs of shoes she had, and what he worked at, and how many pairs of shoes he had, and how many shirts and did I iron them? Everything? The tails and all?

I wanted to know everything about him, too, but I did not ask questions. Why, I don't know. Maybe because so much of the time went talking about me, about Gweedore and about the McCallums. I didn't know there was so much to say, but now I found out there was. My life turned into a big long story that went on and on and I kept finding new things in it that I hadn't ever thought about. He even asked me about my dreams, so that when I was finished talking about things that really happened there was all that stuff that happened when I was asleep to tell him as well.

He wasn't backward about talking about himself either and I found out things. He lived with his mother who was a widow, his father had been a driver, driving a horse and cart for a coal merchant and now his mother worked at the shirt factory. He had only one sister and she was also at the shirt factory. Her name was Victoria. She was a card, he said, and he told me a lot of things about her, about the funny things she said and did.

Being with him was like being in an egg, I thought. The two of us in one shell. When I was not with him I thought about all kinds of things – I was worried about what Mrs McCallum thought of me, I wondered how they were getting on at home, I thought that maybe I would not have a job next year, and also that I would still be in this job and that I could not stand it. Worries and ideas. But when I was with Elliot it was as if all that stuff was not in the world. It was as if the world stopped moving, and there was only one whole thing, me and Elliot, one whole, bright, perfect egg, with the light shining on it.

Missus had the new baby in March. There was a midwife in and a nurse for a week, but the bulk of the nursing and the work fell on me. I have seen many babies being born and I knew that this birth was not difficult. A short confinement and a healthy baby. She made the most of it, however, her being so little and delicate and all.

'She is so fragile,' she said. The baby was a girl, tiny, only five pounds, but of course that was because Missus is tiny herself. I told her this but she ignored it. She wanted the baby to be delicate. 'Isn't she tiny, a tiny little doll? Her head is like an eggshell! I am afraid she will snap under my fingers if I am not careful.'

She would not feed her herself, her breasts were small and anyway she wouldn't want to. A woman like that. Too much trouble for her. She'd sooner let me do the work and lie there reading books from the library that he brought home for her. I was up to my eyes boiling bottles and boiling milk and nursing the baby as well, and there was the other wean to mind, the wee fellow, with his wee nose out of joint because of the new arrival. His mammy paid little attention to him now that she had her new pet, a wee girl. For a month she stayed in bed playing with her – Molly, she started calling her. I was up and down the stairs a hundred times a day.

'You are a treasure,' Mr McCallum said.

We were alone together a lot of the time now. The whole house was through-other thanks to wee Molly. Sometimes he ate his dinner in the kitchen to help me out a bit. More often he ate it from the tray with herself up in the bedroom, which did not help me at all, just made matters worse. Up and down with the soup, up and down with the dinner, up and down with the sweet, up and down with the cup of tea. I was getting thin.

He patted my shoulder. He patted my head. He patted my bottom. Nothing more. And I didn't mind him much.

He was bigger than me, which was nice for a change (Elliot was barely the same size, and a good bit thinner). And I felt I knew him so well. Knew his shirts and his underclothes, his socks. I knew his thick sleeping smell, his sleeping whiskers. I made his food for him and threw out what he did not eat in the pig's bucket. I knew the smell of his piss. He was as known to me now, really, as my own brothers or sisters. Better known, in fact, than most of them.

I got used to it and I started to wait for it, to tell the truth. The feel of his big hand on me. I missed it if he forgot, but he didn't usually. He'd just rub me, wherever, just once, and then we'd go on with whatever we were doing as if this hadn't happened. It meant we looked each other in the eye in the morning, amused. I wasn't afraid of him at all.

He rubbed my breasts, standing beside me, asking me to put down a bigger fire than usual, his mother and father were calling to see Molly. My body leaped to life when he did that and I wished he would go on. I had to catch my breath. But he just said: 'They'll come at seven o'clock just after tea. Please see to it, there's a good girl. And we will have some biscuits and cocoa at about ten.'

'Very well, sir,' I said.

Elliot rubbed me, too. My legs, my breasts, down there, between and inside. A sin, I supposed, but I never bothered much about sins one way or the other, and I liked it quite a lot, especially if I did not think about it while we were doing it. And I loved to kiss him. We kissed all the time. After the first month or so we didn't walk around much any more. The evenings were getting longer and we went outside the city to the banks of the river, or to fields, and we sat and kissed, or lay in the grass and kissed, rubbing our bodies hard together. I knew that to do anything else, any of the tame, calm things we did at the beginning, would have been a waste of our short time together: the time we had now was meant for lying in the grass and kissing, for that alone, and there was never enough time, for kissing Elliot, for feeling his body, hot and sweet and pounding, press into mine. I always left him with huge reluctance, unable to believe that I could continue to exist away from his arms and his mouth.

When I came home from these evenings I was dishevelled, with my stockings torn as often as not, and inside I felt strange. Ripped. I was with him, wrapped up in him in every way, and then I was ripped away from him, so that I felt torn like an apple that has been broken in two. I'd want to cry and even scream for a while. I could not bear being without him – even though I knew that tomorrow I might see him again and in a week I would lie in the grass with him again, and taste his mouth and his skin, and draw his heat and his strength into me. Knowing it all did not lessen the pain a bit.

That was strange. But even stranger was the fact that gradually my own world would come back around me, would close over me like skin growing over a scratch on my arm. Elliot would fade away, and the house and the babies and the shepherd on the mantelpiece would swim around me once more, and take over. Her yellow hair that I combed for her sometimes. His big hand on me.

For a day or two after Wednesday I hated the hand, Mr

McCallum's hand. I put up with it. I had to. But it made me
angry and disgusted. And the funny thing was, after Wednesdays he was worse. He never missed Wednesday night,
although I was not home until nine o'clock. He'd be there
waiting for me. As if he knew. Well, he did know – not that I
was with Elliot, but that I was with some boy. I don't know
how. Maybe people can smell it off you? And that annoyed
him and made him touch me not once, on Wednesdays, but
three or four times. Made me wish I could lock the door of
my room, but I could not.

On Easter we go up the hill behind the barn with the Friels and
the McGettigans and build the house. We call it a house but it is
a circle of stones, a pretend house, a doll's house. And inside the
house we build a fire and boil the eggs on it. As well as eggs,
we have bread, butter, cake, boiled sweets – anything we can
get. We have pandies of cold tea to drink. The lambs are calling and the grass is that sharp green that makes you want to
laugh and cry at the same time. The ditches are smothered in
primroses. It is Easter and the sun is starting to dance after the
winter. We act the fool and eat our picnic, we play hide-and-
seek and blind man's buff, we sing songs. Full of laughs. I think
we are full of laughs, like the sun is full of sparkles, the burn full
of babbles and giggles, the ditch full of yellow stars. The sun
dances and we dance.

Easter is when people get married.
    Elliot came to me the week before Palm Sunday. It was not
a Wednesday. I no longer saw him every Wednesday because
on some Wednesdays he had to work, or to be with his
mother. Also the McCallums did not want me to have my
half-day every week now, because of Molly.
    This was a Tuesday. He called around, with the meat, and

came in for tea. She was in bed. I was worried that she would
hear anyway, and come down, as she sometimes did, in her
wrapper, but I had not seen him in ten days and I let him in.

'Little Biddy' – this was his name for me. 'We could get
married.'

I hadn't expected that. I had thought about it and I wanted
to marry him but I did not think he would ask me yet.

'Glory be to God,' I said.

'You want to, don't you?'

'Yes.'

'I think we should. You are fond of me?'

'Yes. You know that.' I was more fond of him than I ever
had been of any other human being. It is amazing how fond I
was of him. Fonder than of my mother and father and twelve
brothers and sisters put together, or of the McCallums or the
babies, or my pal at home, Sava. It is astonishing that you can
be that fond of somebody you haven't even known for long. It
is not sensible. Still, that is how it was with me, I might as well
be honest.

'Well then.'

'My situation . . .'

'You are not their slave. Maybe you can stay on for a while
anyway. You don't have to tell them.'

'No? Wouldn't I live with you? Where?'

'You could live with me and my mother. Or you could go
on living here. It would mean we could . . . Biddy, I don't
want to wait.'

He meant, stick it in. That's what he was saying to me. We
had not done that. I hadn't let him because I know what happens next. And we had such a nice time not doing it anyway,
pressing hard together. I thought that would be enough for
him, since it was for me. For me it was all I thought I could
get. That is what I thought then.

'Well . . . when would we?' I said.

'Palm Sunday.'

'But that is next Sunday!'

'Yes. I know someone who will marry us then, and I can get a licence quickly.'

'Is it a priest?'

Elliot was a Catholic, he told me when I asked him. But I thought you could not get married on Palm Sunday if you were a Catholic. I felt a shiver running down my back. Someone walked on my grave.

'Yes, yes, a priest.'

'All right then,' I said. I was so fond of him, I could not imagine not marrying him sometime anyway. I knew perfectly well that it was the only right thing and the only possible thing in the world. On the other hand, I could not imagine marrying him now. So suddenly. I thought all that would take a long time and that lots of people would know about it and be part of it. 'I will go on living here for a while until we find our own place.'

'You're a treasure,' he said. He had not said that before. 'But there is one thing. I need a pound to buy the licence now, and I will need a pound for the wedding on Sunday. Can you give me the pound?'

I didn't like parting with one of my pounds. I only had three altogether. But I gave it to him. I knew he gave most of his money to his mother.

On Wednesdays when I was not with Elliot I stayed at home and worked, or else walked around, as I used to do before I had started courting him. For that is what it was, courting, although I had not called it that earlier. I had not called it anything. I didn't need to, since nobody knew about it apart from the two of us and when we were together we were like one person. It is only when there is another that you need to put names on things.

The city was familiar to me now, and the shops and everything less surprising and smaller than they had seemed when I first came. I felt somehow impatient with them, tired of them, fed up with them. They had seemed so glittering and grand and now I had no interest whatsoever in them. Dusty, they seemed, full of useless gimcracks, stupid clothes that cost more money than I would ever have. When I was on the street I found myself thinking of home, home in Gweedore, and of the shore, and of the burn. I wished I could be at home for a day or two and see my friends, and see the chickens and the ducks, and talk the way we talk there, and see the cats. The children, my brothers and my sisters. I missed them now, whereas before, I had not thought about them much. I missed my father. He would be turning the field near the house, putting in the seed potatoes and the cabbages. I thought of the clay, brown and thick and wet and stony and smelling of the dead and the living – the Gweedore clay.

I took to going down to the harbour and looking at the boats. It is not, of course, like the harbour at home. There are a lot more boats, big ones and small, and more going on, in Derry. I thought the seagulls and the waves would remind me of home but they didn't. They were the same, really, as the seagulls and waves at home, but they didn't remind me of them. The waves broke against the wall, plop plop plop. The seagulls wheeled and screamed. But to me they were all flat, like pictures in a paper or a book.

Something was being built at one end of the harbour. Later I found out what it was – a factory for curing fish. I liked to stop there and look at the muddy building site. Men swarming all over it, men in dirty old clothes carrying big stones, bags of mortar, hammering and sawing and breaking up the ground

with huge axes. In McCallums' I had only seen Mr McCallum
and the delivery boys, the postman, sometimes the men in the
shops. They were pale men with white soft hands, men that
were indoors most of the time. Not like my father or the men
at home. Now I saw where the other kind of men were. They
were at the harbour. They were on the boats and they were on
the building sites. Their bodies were different from Elliot's and
Mr McCallum's. They were wider, broader, stockier. Strong-
er. They had red skin, leathery, and their hands had thick fingers. They were always covered in clay or mortar or dust and
they smelled of that sort of thing. They smelled of clay and of
work, not of themselves. Like my father. Those men were part
of their work and part of the earth, like animals, I suppose.
Real animals. Elliot and Mr McCallum were like women, like
the pussycat, soft, sleepy. Well looked after.

Aye. Still, watching the men at the harbour, I would think
how superior Elliot was, with his white face, his long fine
hands, his mop of angel hair. I would think how strange it
was, that I, a Gweedore girl, would fall in love with and marry
such a boy as Elliot.

On Palm Sunday he called for me at four o'clock. Where were
they? I don't recall. I think they were out visiting, for once,
themselves and the older child. I had the baby with me, in the
cradle, and we were together in the kitchen. I had a new dress,
because he had asked me to be fine for the wedding. The dress
was lilac and white, with a lilac sash. I'd done up my hair with
a matching ribbon. Over it all I had a new white apron, just to
fox Mrs McCallum.

'You look lovely,' he said when he saw me. I had the kitch-
en neat as a pin. My big lovely kitchen.

'Thank you.'

He was wearing his Sunday clothes. He also looked lovely.

But he always did. He was the most beautiful boy I ever saw.

'Something terrible has happened. Sit down there, will you?' His mother was being thrown out of her house. She couldn't pay the rent because she'd been sick during the spring and had fallen behind. 'I had to give her the pound to fend off the bailiffs,' he said. 'There was nothing I could do. But we can get married next week. That is all it means. I'll need another pound, though.'

'It's my last pound,' I said, as I gave it to him. I'd spent fifteen shillings on the dress and the apron and things. I was crying as I said this, because of the pound and because I was so disappointed.

'I'm so sorry, my dear darling. But what could I do? I really couldn't do anything else. It is only another week and you'll like it better on Easter Sunday anyway.'

'Who are the witnesses?' I hadn't even thought of this before.

'Two butties of mine. Douglas Hamilton from the shop and his girl. Victoria will be there, too, and my mother.'

'Is she better?'

'What?'

'Your mother.'

'She's a bit better. She might be able to come, or she might not. But she knows about it.'

'I never met her.'

'You'll meet her next Sunday. Or would you like to meet her before that? I could take you home on Wednesday?'

'Yes. I think I'd like that. I think I should see her before the wedding, don't you?'

'If you want to. Grand. I'll call for you on Wednesday then, at about four o'clock.'

'Don't call for me. I'll meet you somewhere. Say somewhere.'

'I'm going to be so busy on Wednesday. But all right. I'll meet you under the clock at Austin's the draper's on Wednesday.'

'At four o'clock.'

'Four o'clock. I've got to run now. Bridget' – he took my head in his hands, he kissed me on each cheek and then, quickly, on the lips – 'I love you very much.'

He'd never said it before. I believed him. I still believe him.

You know how this story ends.

I was under the clock on Wednesday from four o'clock until six. Staring at the sky. It was a strange sky, with streaky clouds and fluffy clouds mixed together, and sharp blue patches with white streaks racing across them. I watched the fluffy clouds turn black and the streaky clouds race across, across, across, for two hours, and the seagulls wheel and the starlings flock and chatter on the shiny gutters.

Then I went home, all dressed up in my finery. I knew his address but I thought I'd wait until he came for me. I still thought he'd come for me.

By Sunday, Easter Sunday, he had not come, not even with the meat. Another boy left it on the windowsill, liver, dripping blood. When I asked him where Elliot was, he said he hadn't a notion.

On Sunday I went to his house, leaving the baby alone. This was at five o'clock, the time we were supposed to get married at. It was on Ross Street. Fifty-three Ross Street, a little two-storey house with no garden.

A girl about my own age answered. She was much smaller than me and had fair hair.

'Victoria?'

'I'm not Victoria.'

'Is Elliot there?'

'What do you want with him?'

'I'm a friend of his.'

'Well. I'm his wife.'

I screamed and shouted and pushed into the house. Into their sitting room.

'Go home,' he said when he saw me. He did not use my name, then, or ever again. He looked weary, as if I were a bold wean that had to be humoured. 'Go home. Just go home.'

'But you're supposed to be marrying me,' I said.

'I got married last week. To Louise.'

'You asked me.'

'Leave this house. You are trespassing.'

'And you took my money. You took my two pounds on me.'

'If you don't get out, I will call the police.'

'Two pounds. You owe me two pounds.' I shouted about the two pounds. There were lots of things to shout about but that is what I latched on to, the thing that mattered least to me.

'If you were a man, I'd knock you down.'

'I'm not a man. I'm a girl.'

'You're as big and awkward as any man, any old ape of a Paddy digging his way through the muck.'

He put his arm around Louise. She was as small as Mrs McCallum, although not, really, as pretty. To tell the truth, she was like me, a smaller version of me, if the reflection in my foxy mirror is anything to go by. He did not press her tightly to him, but handled her lightly, as if she were fragile and easily damaged.

I had to go away. I had to go home without my two pounds and without Elliot.

I reported him to the police for taking my two pounds, and

promising to marry me, and threatening to strike me if I were a man.

It was Mr McCallum who told me to do that.

When I came home he was waiting. They were wondering where on earth I'd gone, leaving the baby alone and unattended. I hadn't even thought of what I would tell them if I'd been off getting married, much less what I would tell them if I'd been off not getting married. And I felt so confused. I felt I was not in the world at all, that the world had turned into a new place that I did not recognise, where nothing was where it should be or what it should be. If the baby had jumped out of the cradle and bitten me, I would not have been surprised.

Mr McCallum put his arms around me and patted me on the bum.

'Sue him,' he said, 'for breach of promise, dear little Biddiebums.'

He lead me into my room and put me on the bed. And licked me. He was full as an egg and could do no harm but he did rather a lot that I could have done without. I didn't care. I didn't have the strength to do anything about him, and I don't know what I could have done anyway. I felt that I was all heart. I could see my heart like a big cow heart, the kind they have in the butcher's, red and livery and covered in a lacy veil of white dripping, and I could see it throbbing, I could feel it throbbing, big and ugly and bloody and torn, inside its veil, inside me. It felt as if it would burst out through my ribs, as if I were filled up with it. And sometimes I felt empty as well, as if I had been tipped upside down and poured out. Either way, I didn't care what happened to me and I let him slobber all over me from top to toe and then fall asleep at the end of my bed.

The next day I was dismissed by him, for having been away from the house without permission when I was supposed to be minding the baby.

★

I met Elliot in court. He looked better than ever, in a starched white shirt and a black jacket, and when the judge found against him he nodded curtly and left the courtroom without looking at me. In case it would do some good, maybe. As much as I wanted my two pounds, I wanted him to look at me and to say my name. Bridget.

I dreamt of him that night, and on many other nights.

I dreamt I was to meet him in a town by the sea, not Derry or Gweedore or anywhere I know. One of the places that I go to when I dream. This is a flat place with sand dunes and a lot of rushes. In this particular dream it was near Derry.

I was in this place with Elliot and I knew that Louise was not far away. I arranged to meet him in the sand dunes, near a house that stands there.

When I came to the sand dunes a woman approached me and asked me to walk with her to the corner of the road. The woman was not any woman I know but she was very tall and she looked like someone I knew. My mother maybe, or some woman I see often but do not talk to.

I did not want to miss Elliot and I knew if I was not there that he would not wait for me. But I did not want to disoblige this woman. I decided I would try to do both things.

I walked halfway down the road with the woman. Then I said, 'Is this far enough?'

'No,' she said. 'It's not far enough. You must come the whole way with me.'

But I didn't.

The next thing Elliot appeared, with Mr McCallum. Elliot signalled to me, with a knowing, sly face, his head down in his collar, that he could not talk to me now, and Mr McCallum looked at me and then looked away, as if he did not know me.

I looked at the woman. She was lying on the ground. I picked her up. She had turned into a piece of paper. She was a large cut-out doll, drawn in heavy black ink, with an old ugly face like a witch. She was folded in two on the ground and I opened her up and spread her out and read her.

Elliot was gone and I had to run after him, as in all my dreams about him, knowing I could not catch him again that night, but that I would meet him, some other night, in some other dream.

They wrote about me in the paper:

GWEEDORE GIRL DECEIVED AND RUINED.

That was not right. I was deceived, but not ruined (by which they meant, up the pole).

I had got my two pounds back, and had another job by then, not as a general, but in a shop, which was much better. I lived in a room over the shop with four other girls who worked in it, and was free much more than I had been with the McCallums. I'd even got a new boy – a carpenter from the yard down by the docks, with black hair and thick hands, twinkling eyes. His name is Seamus and he is a good boy, kind, and funnier than Elliot, and earning much more money. I know I can marry him any time I want to.

It is amazing that I know that Seamus is good and kind and honest and will never mistreat me; also I will never love him. Or maybe that is not amazing at all. Maybe those two know-ings are the same, two different knowings in the same shell, or one and the same knowing, bright as an egg with the sun dancing on it.

THE SEARCH FOR THE LOST
HUSBAND

She saw him ahead of her and she followed him. She followed him for days. And then the little white goat spoke to her.

'Musha,' he said. 'Which would you prefer? Me to be a goat during the night and a man during the day, or a man at night and a goat during the day?'

'I'd like a bit of company at night,' she replied. 'I'd like you to be a man at night and a goat during the day.'

And that's what happened.

They set up home in a big fine house. And he was a goat by day and a man by night.

LOVE, HATE AND FRIENDSHIP

Fiona is flying to france. She is going to attend a one-day conference on Literature in European Minority Languages, to be held in Bordeaux. She is not especially interested in this conference and has never planned to see Bordeaux, although its associations with wine, of which she has always been aware, and with Rome, of which she became aware last night when she looked at a holiday brochure the conference organisers had sent to her office, are certainly attractive. She decided only a week ago, however, to use all her conference allowance on this trip, because just then she felt a pressing need to escape from Ireland. She believed if she placed herself in a fresh environment, even for a day or two, she would change the relationship she was having with the empirical world in general.

The plane is filled with holiday-makers, returning home after trips to Ireland; their tourist status manifests itself in the bags they carry, plastic, stuffed with woollen jumpers and bottles of whiskey.

The girl sitting next to Fiona has an Aran jumper folded on her lap. Her boyfriend's hand is in the jumper, fondling its ropy hairiness, whenever he takes a break from fondling the girl's shoulders, bare arms, face. The face is soft and loose, the sort of face for which the word 'louche' might have been coined. It has, however, a perverse attractiveness, dimly perceived by Fiona. Its very flabbiness and laziness, its carelessness about the standard rules for beauty, lend it a power which brighter, more alert faces could not achieve. Her awful clothes have the same odd appeal. They might have been selected with a view to killing the French reputation for chic once and for all, although Fiona has noticed before that many French people depart radically from the national stereotype in their dress. The girl wears a print frock in some shiny synthetic material, shapeless in cut and of that length which reveals all flaws but is determinedly unsexy. Its colours are brown and purple. Around her shoulders hangs a thin cardigan in one of the murkier shades of pink, rather dirty. The Aran jumper is clearly destined for another day, or another wearer.

Fiona herself has a tidy, well-structured face, and an expression which is simultaneously sweet – or perhaps just shy – and penetrating. Her blond hair, freshly tinted by the hairdresser, is cropped close to the head with only a ragged fringe softening the harsh style, popular at the time. Fiona hopes it suggests femininity, but, of course, what it implies is something different: childishness, or even vulnerability. Her clothes, by contrast, could not be smarter. She has a short grey skirt, a grey, collarless, Chanel-type jacket, a stiff, crisp, snow white blouse. She has read in a novel that grey is correct for Paris and hopes that what is correct for Paris will also be correct for Bordeaux. Besides, grey and white suit her. Edward liked her in her grey dress. 'You look like a Quaker,' he said, whenever she wore it. He liked girls to look like Quakers. 'It's lovely.' He has not seen this suit, and perhaps will not.

They are practically making love, that pair. Both their faces wear the oblivious, abandoned expression of people who have recently enjoyed blissful sexual union. Fiona sighs enviously.

Tears prick her eyes. She thinks if she were another type of person, a more noble and altruistic person, or maybe just a slightly older person, she would be pleased by this frank manifestation of love. She would smile benignly and avert her eyes, recalling fondly, without rancour, that as they are now so was she, once. More than once, to be honest, and with more than one man. True love is rare, but not as rare as you believe when you are in it. Even if she could accept that much with her whole heart, she would probably be less irritated than she is at this moment.

She closes her book, which she has been unable to concentrate on, and takes a writing pad and Biro out of her bag. She starts a letter to Edward. She has no trouble at all in concentrating on that.

She met Edward Matthews at a prize-giving ceremony for novelists a little over a year ago. She was not getting a prize; she was there because of her job as a public relations officer for a publisher of books in Irish (she edits, typesets, keeps accounts, and drives around the country with piles of books on the back seat of the car, as well as being public relations officer). Edward is not a writer, either, but a literary agent from London. Fiona had met him a few times before, at book launches and similar events, but he did not remember that.

He approached Fiona and a woman she was talking to, a protégée of his, called Carol. Carol was very dramatically dressed that evening – as, indeed, she usually was – in a long, clinging purple dress. She had several strings of imitation diamonds wound around her neck and her lips were painted a startling scarlet.

'You look like a cardinal,' said Edward.

Carol immediately moved away and joined another group.

'Would you look at that man!' said Edward to Fiona. He

had had three glasses of wine and was indulging his habit of staring at people and passing remarks on their appearance, a habit which Fiona shared. Fiona wondered why he and Carol did not get on. 'Can you believe that he is fifty-eight?'

Fiona turned her gaze to the novelist who had won the award. He was tall, with a trim white beard and matching hair. 'Well,' she said. 'What age are you?'

Edward was slim and not very big. He had an intriguing fringe of gingery hair falling over his forehead, and a thin veil of greyish hair bravely scraped across his naked crown. 'Take off twelve years or so,' he said sheepishly.

'Those Americans!' said Fiona. 'They all look like that. I used to think they got face lifts but now I believe it's the kind of cornflakes they eat. They send the dross to Europe. All that stuff about riboflavin and vitamin B is just a cover-up. That's what I've heard.'

'Get away!' Edward smiled and his eyes met hers. Behind his glasses, his eyes were a surprising shade of green, moss colour. His skin was very clean. Fiona understood that he did not think she looked like a cardinal.

'It's true. And I don't like that man's looks, either. I think he looks as if he lives in Salem, Massachusetts. I think his name could be Judge Hathorne.'

Edward moved an inch closer to her.

'I can picture him sending old women called Goody this and Goody that to the stake, can't you?'

He did not take Fiona home that night. He couldn't, because his wife was at the reception, too, circulating in the crowd. But two days later he rang her office and asked her to have lunch with him. He wanted to discuss a few ventures on which they might co-operate to their mutual advantage. Fiona knew what the invitation meant. She knew, because her stomach gave a little silly flip of pleasure when she heard his voice. And also because the one kind of Irish literature Edward, or any London agent, could have no interest whatsoever in was the kind she published, Irish literature which is not written in English.

The air hostesses bring around trays of food. Dinner, even though it is four o'clock in the afternoon. The couple had stopped kissing when Fiona had started writing her letter, casting uneasy, suspicious glances at her writing pad. Now they fall upon the little bits of salmon and potato salad with gusto, picking up things and examining them in the light, commenting on the taste of every item. Fiona eats, too. She is not hungry, but she does not know when she will get an opportunity to have a meal again. So she munches her way through everything, from baby tomatoes to blackcurrant tart, and begins to think about the food that will be available in Bordeaux. Food with a taste. It will be good to eat food with a taste, the kind you get in France. Surely that will change her perspective.

The couple begin to have a quarrel. The boy has spilt some red wine on the Aran jumper, and the girl is berating him. She is not shouting, but talking in a fast, furious whisper, while she rubs at the wine with a tissue. Rubbing it in.

'Try some salt.' Fiona leans over. She does not like this girl but she can't resist giving advice. Before she worked for the publisher she was a teacher.

The girl looks at her angrily. Her face is not louche now. It looks alert and edgy. Like an Irish face.

'*Du sel!*' says Fiona, picking up a little white package and dangling it in front of the girl's nose.

'Fuck off!' says the girl.

She is still fighting with the boy when the plane lands in Paris and when Fiona sees the last of her she is stomping out of the baggage reclaim area dragging an enormous suitcase,

without wheels, across the floor, while he waits nonchalantly
for his bag to appear on the carousel.

Fiona arrives at her hotel at about ten o'clock that night. She
checks in, puts her bag in her room, and has a shower. The
room is tiny and functional. Its only decorations are two
framed tracts on the walls. Maxims by La Rochefoucauld.
Funny things to put on walls, but cheap hotels often express
eccentricity in this way, she has noticed before. 'Love and
Hatred are more akin to one another than Friendship' is in
one frame. 'We can forgive those who bore us, but we never
forgive those whom we bore', the second proclaims. Fiona
wonders if somebody else has used that, after La Rochefoucauld. Oscar Wilde or somebody?

She takes off the grey suit. The only other outfit in her bag is
a pair of black velvet leggings and a long blue silk shirt, put in
at the last minute, in the event she would need them for some
exciting and unplanned social event. Fiona has been abroad on
trips of this kind often enough to know that such occasions seldom arise. She has never, on a plane or at an airport, met a
wonderful, charming, delightful man who has invited her to
dinner. Not since she was about twenty, anyway (and then
she mistrusted them, quite sensibly). But she always travels
with clothes to date in, something silk or something velvet.
Just in case. Now she puts on these things in order to go for a
solitary walk. She cannot bear to go to bed before she has
had a look at the neighbourhood. This impatient curiosity she
recognises as a good sign, and its indulgence well worth the
risk of rape or murder, which for all she knows she may be
taking, wandering around this strange city in the middle of
the night.

The hotel is situated on a seedy street lined with office
blocks. Like most office buildings, they present at street level a
variety of shaded foyers, dark entries, secluded porticoes. And

in some of these threatening caves Fiona notices stirrings and signs of life. A drunk snoring with his back to a pillar. A young, dark-skinned man emerging suddenly from a porch and diving into a taxi.

This part of the walk is unenjoyable but soon she is in a much better part of town: the old part, where the houses are flat fronted and locked up or else pedimented with brightly lit cafés, from which strains of music and talk emerge onto the pavement. She examines a menu or two, peers into interiors with oilcloth and candles on the tables, sees Chinese faces, Algerian, Turkish and French (she thinks). Soon she arrives at what has to be the cathedral. It is a big medieval chunk of a building, shaped like a brick and made of crumbly blocks of sandstone which are the colour of tabby cats in the flood-lights. She walks right around it, looking at the statues which project from the pavement, taking pleasure in the big wood-en doors, barred with iron, like the doors of a fortress. She imagines mail clad soldiers galloping up to these doors, ham-mering on them with their swords. We are the king's men. And the reply, from the shadowy, cosy sanctuary: We are all the king's men.

The cathedral is dedicated to a saint whose name reminds her of Edward's. That is not the reason for Fiona's impatience to see it. She believes. On the contrary, that coincidence puts her off. She is surprised that she can look at this cathedral and enjoy its unpretentious contours, its friendly medieval air, even though it has this association. Surprised, and glad. His power must be diminishing, as she hoped it would, now that she has put water between them.

Edward colonised her territory. Everywhere she looked in Ireland reminded her of him. He had taken over every place and every object in her life.

First he did this systematically. 'I want to know everything about you, everything!' he said, eagerly. 'Do you have glass in your hall door? Do you drink red or white? Do you shave under your arms?'

All too soon his curiosity was satisfied. What there was to know, he knew. It is hard to resist men like Edward, men who overwhelm you initially with the intensity of their need for you. It is hard to resist them even if you know from experience that such men will, and must, cool off just as abruptly, and almost as emphatically, and there will be nothing you can do about it. Because there was nothing you did in the first place, either, to start the whole thing off. Except acquiesce. Gladly, in this case – which means the acquiescence was more than that. Edward was so attractive. This cliché suited him eminently well. Summed up the mixture of gentle manners, good humour, clean skin and light colours that constituted him. Summed up his easy gossipy conversational style, his interest in everything that was ordinary: clothes and people and food. Talking to Edward was like talking to a woman. It was that easy and that intimate. And at the same time you could sense that there was some hard and masculine characteristic at his centre, some barrier you would have to crack in order to reach him.

She could not remember when she had stopped thinking he was monkish and started thinking he was sexy. She could not remember when she stopped indulging him and started needing him. She could not remember when she had started loving him more than he loved her. She could not remember when he had stopped loving her altogether. Or if he had. She was tired. Not of him, but of the way he claimed her world, the world that should have been her own.

First, when he loved her and she did not quite love him, she saw everything exaggerated and crystallised. Objects acquired a hard, polished look; they were like reflections in a highly buffed mirror. She moved through this looking-glass world like a high, haughty queen, letting her hand flutter along surfaces, not condescending to touch anything.

Then, when she loved him and he still loved her, the world disappeared. She was not dismissive of it, she just didn't see it. Not at all. There were only two people. Everything else became a blurry, dim backdrop for the reality that they represented. Time disappeared then, too. This was the flash-of-lightening phase, the road to Damascus. The gate opens, just a chink, but that is enough to eliminate everything that is ugly in the world.

The third phase was the bad one. Is the bad one, because it is still going on. When Edward became complacent, then indifferent. Her attempts to hold him met with polite but stunning rebuffs: that hard masculine part of him was no longer a secret centre, but a suit of armour which gleamed menacingly whenever she saw him, through the feminine polish of his chatter.

She saw him less and less often. But his absence was more powerful than his presence. It drained all objects and at the same time invested them with an astonishing potential to inflict pain. Trains, trees, cups and saucers stabbed her. She could look at the sun shining on a field and think, Oh God, I can't bear it. She could not stand the sight of flowers, dustbins, children playing in the street. Young lovers, mothers, elderly, tottering couples.

Self-pity, this sort of thing is called. Fiona knows its name. She knows its nature, too, and she knows it will eventually pass. But none of this makes it easier to put up with the onslaughts when they are at their worst. They are at their worst when Edward says he will phone her, and does not, or when he can't at the last minute make it to a lunch date, and leaves her waiting for him in a restaurant or on the side of the street.

He has done this more than once. She has let him away with it. She has no self-respect where he is concerned. Even when she decides that she can't take it any more, she gives in. His excuses always seem reasonable. And he is always so penitent, there can be no question, as she suspects when she is standing in the porch of some pub, her stomach gristled with rage and despair, that he is trying to get her to leave him. After standing her up, he reverts to being just what he was in the early days. To being desperately in love with her, clinging like a child who has been naughty and needs absolute forgiveness. She strokes his hair. She brushes his warm, light skin. She grants him absolution.

She knows the line of thinking which maintains that this is self-destructive and masochistic and the line of thought which maintains it's plain silly. But she feels, at these undignified, pride-shattering times, that she is getting to know Edward's secret. It is at these times, only at these times, that he seems to let her in.

She dreams that she is standing on a beach, watching the waves approach the shore. They are large navy blue breakers, and she enjoys looking at them. One wave, in the middle distance, gets bigger than the others. It swells and swells as it rolls in. She stares, unable to believe that it is really getting so huge, on what is a little, familiar, predictable Irish beach. Suddenly she notices that it is dangerously high, higher than a house, a great tidal wave of a thing. She runs away behind the beach, stands in a car park among sand dunes, waiting for it to crash. The wave pursues her, sweeps over the edge of the high dunes, splashes down around her and the cars, drenching everything but not harming her.

The dream does not frighten her. It is accompanied by a pleasant sense of security and delight, and she wakes from it smiling.

★

The conference is not taking place in the city, but on the coast, about twenty miles away. Delegates are transported there in a bus. The bus deposits them in a car-park in a big evergreen forest. The conference centre turns out to be a variety of marquees, dotted like mushrooms in a clearing. Fiona begins to wander from tent to tent. There are a number of lectures going on simultaneously, and, it seems, more than one conference. Fiona notices a crowd of men in cotton suits tasting wine, another crowd watching videos of Donald Duck: that tent has a sign saying 'Vidéothèque' outside. Most of them do not have any signs, however. You are supposed to be divinely inspired, it seems, or else just to check out everything until you find what it is you should be at.

The ground is covered with pine needles and here and there are huge, outsized cones. Fiona picks up one, then throws it away when a big insect creeps out of it. She is feeling very hot. The grey suit is not at all correct, it could not be more inappropriate for this suntrap. Everyone else is wearing shorts, or little strappy dresses. It is only ten o'clock in the morning but the sun is throbbing in the sky. Fiona feels her head begin to swim.

She retreats from the clearing where the tents are pitched and goes into the forest. The trees from which those huge cones fall are themselves huge. They stretch like skyscrapers into the burnt blue heavens. Their scent is strong and sweet, and the wind hisses and roars through their branches. Everything here is big, and energetic; there is a sense of tremendous fertility. The trees, the tables in the cafés groaning with food, the vines bent by their thick loads of fruit. Loads of sun and light and growing things. You can't ignore the world here, because it is bigger than you. It is a giant which stoops over you, overwhelms you. Not like the little, watery, cool nature of Ireland, totally dependent on the observer. Being human seems less of a big deal, here, and is probably more fun in consequence.

If you're dressed for it. It is horribly hot. She takes off her stockings, shoes, and her jacket, and puts them under a stone by a tree. Then she walks through the forest along a little path. She comes to a signpost which says 'Plage'. It does not mention a distance, so she assumes it is not far away. And sure enough, after about ten minutes she reaches a stretch of water.

It is not the sea, but a lake. The beach is a little shelf of shingle. Lake water flirts with it, lapping against the shore with lacy gestures, butterfly strokes. She had been thinking she would find herself up against the Atlantic. She had been thinking of huge navy blue breakers, pounding against the shore, ranting and raving in her ears. The lake is big but it sounds like a baby. Its baby waves plash on the sand. Plup plup. Gurgle.

What type of man is Edward? It is unreasonable to classify people, but Fiona, who wants to think about him all the time, anyway, finds it comforting to categorise him. Labelling gives her the illusion of control, a control she feels she lacks entirely in reality. He is this type: a childish man, with a child's enthusiasm for new things and a child's diffidence. And a child's dependence. He is the type of man who falls rapidly in love, pursues the beloved with utmost energy, almost with aggression, and then, just as quickly, falls out of love again. After that a few things can happen. If the circumstances are right, and if the woman wants it, he could marry her. If the circumstances are not right, or if she doesn't want him desperately enough, he won't bother. He is not going to push himself, one way or the other. He is not going to raise storms, shatter lives. Or even rock any boats.

He will not leave his wife and marry Fiona, because his wife wouldn't like that. But he will not leave Fiona, not if she doesn't want him to, and not if nothing unpleasant happens. For instance, if his wife finds out, he will probably abandon Fiona. He will then feel that hers is the lesser right. But if she doesn't, or if she does and doesn't mind too much, he won't abandon her.

Fiona has not seen Edward for more than a month. He has probably not been in Ireland during that time. Sometimes his work takes him there one week out of three, sometimes less frequently. An absentee landlord. Still, her imagination has surrendered her places to him, territory which he certainly doesn't want. Half the streets of Dublin are in his fiefdom. That is why she needed to get out, to fly to France, a wild goose. (Which reminded her of something else: get some of that Château Lynch wine when the shops open, for her boss, Molly Lynch. She liked to get drunk on wine bearing her own name on the label, and so did Fiona.)

She could ring Edward herself. If she does, he will be gentle and understanding. He will ring her soon anyway, even if she doesn't get in touch with him. When he visits Ireland again, when he feels he should check to see that she is all right. He is a considerate man – too considerate, if anything. Why should it be so hard to forget all this romantic stuff, and simply accept his friendship?

She walks into the water. It is warm, as she hoped it would be. Not warm like a bath, of course, not even quite lukewarm, but much, much warmer than any natural water in Ireland, or any place she has been before. She paddles around, enjoying the comfort of it on her feet, watching the motor boats rip through the lake. It would be lovely to swim, to feel this warm soft water all over her skin, to wallow in the south, in its generosity, its blessedness. But there are people not far away, and she has no swimsuit, no towel, nothing to wear except that hot grey skirt and starched blouse. So she keeps paddling around, letting her toes have a holiday.

THE SEARCH FOR THE LOST HUSBAND

A year passed. And she was expecting a baby.

The little white goat spoke to her when she was close to her time. He told her that something might happen to her baby after it was born. And he warned her to make no protest, nor to shed a tear, if anything happened. Because if she did, she would lose him, her husband.

The baby was born. He was a grand baby, a boy. But soon after he was born he was snatched from his mother's bed. He vanished. And she was very sad. But she remembered what the little white goat had told her and she did not shed a single tear.

The little white goat came up to her in the bed.

'I see that your baby has been taken away from you,' he said. 'But that shouldn't worry you one way or the other. Haven't you me for company?'

That's how it was.

SUMMER PUDDING

WE CAMPED AT CAER GYBI FOR THREE DAYS waiting for Father Toban. Two tinkers we'd met in Llanfair told us he was on his way there from Bangor. But although we'd kept an eye out for him on the road we had not seen him, and we had not heard tell of him either. When we asked about him people laughed, or gave a useless answer or no answer.

We camped on a patch of ground above the beach, close to the harbour, where we could see the packet sailing in and out. The weather was dry and calm, and the tides were quiet for April. We'd missed three sailings in the three days.

'We should go,' I said, 'without him. We can say our own prayers.'

Naoise did not believe this and neither did I. The truth was, I did not want to say prayers at all any more. But he did. He would not go. He had it in his head that Father Toban would come and that was that. I was getting to know him, and already I knew that he was stubborn as an ass. He had told me that anyway, proudly, and warning at the same time. I was proud, too, when he told me, and I knew that his stubbornness was good for me, a gift for me. Now I could see it could have another side.

There is sharp marram grass on the ground and it is not

comfortable to lie on, or to love on. It is dry, however. The
dunes are alive with rabbits and we have had a good stew every
day – I have onions that I lifted from an old one in the town. I
go in during the day for a few hours and sell tin cans. The
Welsh here are not as bad as in other parts, being used to us, I
suppose, by now. They should be.

Father Toban. Who is he? I have heard him talked about
ever since I came but I haven't seen him and everything I have
heard about him has a hollow ring to it. Maybe he is an old
piseog, like the banshee.

'Do you believe in the banshee, Naoise?' I asked him.

He did.

'She must have been busy during the last couple of years. Or
does she have helpers?'

'Go away out of that,' he said. He didn't like it.

I didn't tell him that I thought Father Toban was like the
banshee. Somebody only your friend's friend has ever laid
eyes on.

In July I came over with my sister Mary and a band of people
from Kildare. Dunnes and Connors mostly, who had been on
the road for years and already knew the tinsmith's trade, as we,
of course, did not. Our father was a farmer outside Kilkenny
and had just died a few months before we came over. Our
mother had died the year before that and all our brothers. We
pledged their clothes in a pawnshop in Naas, where we were
not known. We had been told we should burn them because of
the fever but we needed money and the clothes were good –
trousers with no patches, two good frieze coats, a pair of
leather shoes and two pairs of wooden brogues. I washed them
in the river and dried them two days in the sun and I do not
think there could have been any fever left on them. With the
money we got for them and for some pots and pans and the

blankets from our beds, and the one week's wages our father had got on the Relief, we had enough money for the two tickets. The tinkers we met at the docks and took up with there.

Mary did not like them. 'They are wild animals,' she said. Not 'they are like wild animals', which is what I thought at first. Long scrawny things, with loose arms and legs – loose tongues, loose other things as well. They have bushes of frizzy red hair or fair hair, never combed, sticking up on top of their heads or just tumbling down any old way around their shoulders. The strangest thing is their eyes. The men have mad eyes, that don't seem to blink, like the eyes of cats or foxes. Maybe it is from the *poitín*, which they drink whenever they can – they carry a still with them, on a handcart, so they can make more whenever they camp anywhere for any length of time. The women throw their bodies along the road rather than carry them like Mary does and, I suppose, me as well, as if we were jugs of milk that might spill if we didn't take care. They spread their legs when they sit by the fire and suck in the heat of the flames. Right in. No underpants. They laughed at the way we looked and at our dresses.

'What have you your hair pulled out of the roots like that for?' they said, pulling it down. 'Who do you think you are anyway?'

We have flat black hair, which falls lank down the sides of our faces when the bands are off. Our dresses are plain grey calico.

'You are a sight,' they said, 'for sore eyes.'

They did not ask where we had come from or why we had joined them. They could guess. The surprising thing was that they let us stay with them, and they gave us some of their food.

'I want to leave them as soon as we land,' Mary said. 'I can't stand them.'

We were eating half a loaf of bread we'd got from them.

We had not had bread in months.

'How can we do that? We don't know our way around. We don't know the language.'

'Do you think that lot of eejits know any language apart from their own Paddy bad language?'

They did, some of them, speak Welsh and English, because they had been over before. More importantly, they could get food wherever they went. They could snare rabbits and hares, grouse and pheasants, they could make whiskey and tin cans. And they could beg and sell, they could steal and frighten people into giving them things. They could erect a tent that kept out the rain. We couldn't do even one of these things.

We soon learned.

'Into the town and come home with your dinner,' Molly Dunne, the one who talked to us most, said. She had grey hair, curled like carrageen moss, down to her waist nearly, and a huge beak of a nose.

'Will we sell something?'

'What have you to sell?'

'Well . . .'

'You can sell yourselves if you like but I don't think you'll get much of a price with the cut of you. Do what you see the rest of them doing.'

We went off down the road from the camp with nine or ten of them, women and a few men. The women all had their striped cotton dresses on and big blue cloaks flying around them, and their red hair flying, and the men had white shirts and black coats and carried thick sticks on their shoulders. They moved in a strung-out group along the thin road from the sea to the marketplace, and we were among them. I thought they must look like the wind, blowing into the place. People scattered before them as if they were – the wind, or a band of bad mischievous fairies. The little Welsh women in their black clothes, with their little white lace bonnets close to their faces, fled.

Not all of them saw us, or got away in time. The tinkers cornered any who stayed on the street.

'Ma'am, will you buy a pot from me? A good little pot?'

The Welsh women looked terrified and said in their sing-song voices, '*Dim Sasenig*', although the tinkers were speaking Irish. The men stood close by, staring at the frightened women with their cat eyes, rubbing their sticks thoughtfully. All the women bought a pot or a pan or a mug and then ran into some shop. I heard the word '*Gwydellion*' for the first time. '*Gwydellion Gwydellion Gwydellion.*' It was a whisper, a whimper and a curse. Also a warning and a plea for help. I knew what it meant without asking.

I stole a loaf, not from a stall or a shop, but from a woman's basket. She put her basket down on the grey slabs while she tested some apples on a stall. In the basket were eggs, butter and something I did not recognise, a thick wedge of red stuff, like butter, as well as the loaf of bread. I pretended to be looking at the apples and pears which were heaped on the stall. The woman behind the stall looked suspiciously at me and muttered '*Gwydellion*' under her breath but not aloud. She wasn't sure, maybe. I did not look quite like the other Gwydellion, with my black hair, which I had tied back again behind my neck, and my plain dress.

It was easy to snatch the bread and then I ran away like the hammers of hell.

'Good girl yourself,' Molly Dunne said. 'I didn't think you had it in you.'

Neither did I. I was as proud as punch, and Mary was as downhearted and disapproving as you would expect her to be, a girl who had spent a year studying with the nuns and who might have been some sort of a kitchen nun herself, if things had gone different.

When we camped near a town we were often attacked. People came and tried to set fire to our tents. Often fights broke out because the tinkers were quick to defend themselves. The Welsh men were smaller than ours but they were strong; they had plenty to eat and did not drink whiskey, only their own sweet ale. Once, one of our lads was killed in one of these battles. What Molly said was, 'Just as well it was not the other way round, or we'd all be on the way to Van Diemen's Land, if not worse.'

That was the first time I heard about Father Toban. It was actually the first time I heard about religion from the band, but now it turned out that they wanted Father Toban to bury the dead boy, one of the Connors. They wanted him to get a Christian burial and Father Toban was their only chance of that. 'He is the only Catholic priest in all Wales,' they said.

'Where is his church?' This was Mary. She'd want to know, so she could visit it and get Mass. That she had not got Mass in weeks and weeks was a great heart's scald to her.

'Oh, be quiet, you fool! Do you think he'd have a church in this place?'

'I see a lot of churches.'

'Not one Catholic church.'

'What is their religion, then?'

'They are Protestant, and worse than that.'

'What is worse?'

'They are heathens like the blacks of Africa or the wild men of America.'

'They look like Protestants to me,' I said. And they did. I had never in Ireland seen anyone that looked half as Protestant as the Welsh women, not even in Dublin or Kingstown.

'They are Centers. The Centers is what they call themselves, they are worse than the Protestants.'

We did not find Father Toban and Tadg was buried in a bog

on the slopes of the mountain called Wydfa, where we camped after the fight that killed him. It was a remote place, not too close to any town, and there we felt safe. Some villages, Llanberis and Beddgelert, were about an hour or two's walk away, and during the day we could visit them, sell tin cans or steal. I never begged. I couldn't, although Mary became quite good at that. I stole all before me, preferring that, even though I knew what would happen if I got caught. I stole from farms as well as from towns – eggs and milk, bread sitting out to cool on windowsills. I took the red stuff called, I knew now, cheese. Once, I lifted a lamb from under the nose of a boy on the side of Wydfa. Naoise, whom I had got to know by then, killed it for me and we all ate it, roasted over the fire, for supper.

We were at Wydfa for a long time, for months. The tents bleached in the sunshine as the summer wore on, and I lay on the short grass, smelling thyme and gorse, and all the summer smells, and felt happy. There were hares and rabbits in the mountains, carrots and even potatoes on the farms, everything you could think of in the shops of the village. I felt my face getting plumper, browner, and saw this happening to Mary, too, although she was very thin otherwise. I liked, as well as all this, living in a tent. I liked to feel the sun heating the canvas in the morning when I woke up, or even to hear the rain pounding against it, as if it would wear it away with its beating. I liked to know that I could pull it up in a few minutes and pack it on my back and move. Although we did not move, once we found the valley near Wydfa, and the band stayed there for a long long time, so long that the Welsh people came to know it and to call it the Valley of the Gwydellion.

Mary met the Ladies of Llangollen. Of course she did. She had heard about them at home. For weeks she had been trying to drag me to Llangollen to meet them. She hated the Gwydellion with a vengeance, hated them as much as the

Welsh did, if not even more. And they hated her, too, because they were not stupid and could see her hatred. She was above them all, always thinking of her convent and our father's house and our family. She could not forget. If it had not been for me they would have thrown her out, or they would have starved her or maybe killed her.

She met one of the Ladies on the main street of the town less than an hour after we had arrived there. How did she know who it was? She knew because the lady was the richest-looking old woman walking along the main street on her own, and also because she was wearing trousers. A black coat, black trousers, a high stiff white collar. A man's black hat. Everyone knew that that's what the Ladies wore as soon as they got away from their families (before, in Ireland, they wore silk dresses, pink and yellow, ball gowns, lovely hats, just like all other fine ladies).

Was the Lady of Llangollen delighted to meet a sister Irishwoman? She was not. The country was crawling with them. 'Here is a halfpenny for you now,' she said to Mary, and turned away from her.

'I am not begging, yer hanner,' said Mary, speaking English. 'I am not a tinker at all but a respectable Irish girl looking for a place, yer hanner. I have read the Sixth Reader and was a monitor in my own school in Kilkenny.'

Mary said that because she knew the Ladies of Llangollen were from Kilkenny. She thought it would arouse some neighbourly sympathy, although we hadn't been neighbours, exactly, with the Butlers of Ormonde. Still, it worked. The lady in the black trousers invited Mary up to her house the next day. I went with her, at her insistence.

It was the strangest house I ever saw. It was perched like a bird's nest set on the side of a hill, shaded by big oak trees. The roof was thatched, high and pointed like a cock of hay, and it had tiny black windows set into it, like shiny black eyes. The doors were also black, and when you came close to them you could see they were carved all over with angels and devils and mermaids and foxes and birds and fishes. The walls of the house were white stone, crossed with thick oak beams like the cross on Calvary. Inside, the house was packed with things: furniture, books, ornaments, musical instruments, brass flowerpots. The walls were so thick with pictures that you could not see any wall at all. The furniture was made of the same kind of wood as the front door: black oak, heavy as lead, knotted and curled all over with engravings. Everything was as cluttered up as it possibly could be.

We sat in the kitchen, of course, and talked to the cook, in Welsh – we had learned enough now to have a little conversation. The lady in the trousers came and talked to us in English and then we ate scones and jam and drank some coffee.

Naoise looked different from the others. All the other men looked the same to me, with their wild eyes and skin that looked as if a fine sack cloth had been draped across it, their hair sticking up like straw on their heads, or like bushes of gorse. Naoise had tidy hair, and his skin was clean and glossy, like an ordinary Irishman's, except that on the side of his face he had a birthmark. It was a small purple patch, between his cheekbone and his ear, shaped like a potato, a port wine stain.

The mark was small and you would hardly notice it but it is that that made him quiet and good. Even when he got drunk, as they all did, from the Welsh beer, stolen from farms, as often as from their own *poitín*, he did not shout or swear or fight with his stick, but looked contented and became sleepy. Maybe he did not drink quite as much as most of them. He didn't beat his wife, not that I could see, but sat with her and talked to her, and sometimes he played with their baby, counting her toes and singing, 'This little piggy went to market', or carrying her on his shoulders as he walked about, showing her things.

When I needed pots I went to him rather than to anyone else, because he was the only man in the band I wasn't afraid of. He didn't mind helping me – I gave him some of the money I made, and bits of anything I got. I gave his wife some blue ribbons I stole from a stall in Betws-y-Coed once, and she took them, although she had not much to say to me. Jealous. Naoise and I were fond of one another, we all three knew it.

One night I caught him alone, behind the encampment, where I was fetching water from the stream. He stood still beside me while I filled the pandy and when I stood up he was right in front of me, his face close to my face, his stomach to my stomach. I put my free hand on his face and caressed it. I couldn't stop my hand going up to his face, he was so close to me, it was dark and silent in the middle of the mountains, so that I felt everything in the world had stopped moving. We kissed.

After that he didn't speak to me for a few weeks and made a show of being fond of his wife, putting his arm around her when I was near them. I let on I didn't care. His wife was pregnant again, yellow-skinned and dirty, with her clothes hanging off her, and smelly and old-looking. She was the way the tinker women are as soon as they are married any length of time at all. Scrap.

Poor thing, poor thing, poor scrap. He had kissed me for three minutes, hard, and his heat and his man's smells had gone right into me and stayed there.

We were scullery maids. They had a scullery maid already, a little Welsh girl called Gwynn, and they did not really need us but took us out of pity for Mary, who begged. Mary is a good begger. We were to get our keep but no wages at all. Our bedroom was in a hayshed in the garden.

'It's better than that tinker camp,' Mary said, stretching in the straw.

Old dry dust tickled my nose and the straw scratched my skin. 'Oh yes indeed,' I said.

All day long we worked in the kitchen. Mary washed up, standing over the sink, scrubbing pots and dishes, glasses, cups and plates. I got up at six in the morning to light the fire and make the early morning tea for the cook and for the ladies. I scrubbed the front steps and the flagged floor of the kitchen. I brought the rubbish to the dump around the back and I emptied chamber pots from the bedrooms and I hung washing out to dry and brought it in. I gathered vegetables from the garden.

Most of the things I did were hard and unpleasant, the things none of the others wanted to do. But after a while I learned how to cook some things. I learned how to brew beer. I learned to spin flax and wool, and at night in the winter I sat by the fire with a candle burning and hemmed the linen sheets.

The scullery maid hadn't much work left. She peeled vegetables, she brought stuff in from the garden. Sometimes she went off to the town to market. We never did. Never left the house at all. In eight months we never walked outside the gate.

The scullery maid did not talk to us much. None of the maids did. The kitchen maids were Welsh and the upper maid was English. The English maid never talked to the Welsh ones, not because she did not know their language, but because she felt so high and mighty. And now the Welsh maids had someone to look down upon themselves. Us. It impressed them not a bit that we could speak some Welsh, as well as English and Irish. But it did impress the Ladies, a little.

'Why did you not go to the workhouse?'

'We tried to get into it but it was full. Hundreds of people were turned away, not just us.'

'You did not think of going to America?'

'We had not the price of the ticket. Maybe . . .?'

But we would not get the price of the ticket from here either, since we never got a penny.

'Did your family die?'

'They all died.'

'Of the fever?'

'The fever, yes.'

'It is the fever that kills people, not the hunger, isn't it?'

'Yes, ma'am.'

We were hungry and that is why the fever got us. It would not have got us if we had had enough to eat. When we cut through the lumpy potatoes in July, through their browny-purple, warty skins, and saw them black and sticky inside, soft and sweet, we saw the fever. Their sweet sickening smell was the smell of the fever. The hunger and the fever were the same thing, although people like to think they were different.

Mary had let on we had had a good farm.

'The hunger was not bad in our village,' I said to the lady. 'Everyone had enough. There were a lot of fish in the river, and we had bread and milk, butter. We had corn. The people worked hard and had enough to eat. It was not like other places, in our village. It was the fever that killed people, not the hunger.'

She nodded, her blue eyes sparkling, her little glasses sparkling. 'Yes, yes, the fever is the tragedy. We sent what we could.'

The girls in the kitchen thought this was a joke. They thought the Ladies were a joke. You could tell this from the way they called them the Ladies of Llangollen when it was not necessary to do so.

'Ellen, go and empty the Ladies of Llangollen's pots,' the cook would say.

'The Ladies of Llangollen like their beef rare,' she laughed. 'Oh yes, they do. Rarer than any man, rare as rarebit.'

Mary got cross when this sort of thing went on. She got so cross that she cried, because she was so grateful to them for rescuing her from the tinkers. 'We could be dead,' she said. 'They have saved our lives.'

'Yes,' I said.

'Look at the food we get.'

'Yes.'

'And the dry place we have to live.'

'Yes.'

Mary thought she would be rewarded for her hard work by being promoted and getting paid. She thought she would become a lady's maid here in the cottage, and then become a lady's maid somewhere else, and live in a big house, with her own bedroom and her own sitting room. That was her dream. The cups and the plates gleamed, she polished them so much. They were like lakes in the summer sunshine, each white china plate, or like valleys full of hard snow. Every saucer shone on its shelf, shiny as a new dream.

The scullery maid told us the Ladies were not from Ireland at all. They were not the real Ladies of Llangollen.

'Who are they, then?' we asked.

'They are Englishwomen, queer Englishwomen, who have bought their house and wear their clothes. And carry on in the same way. The Irish ladies died long ago.'

We did not believe them. We thought they were saying it to annoy us, because we were Irish like the Ladies.

'And we are ladies, too,' Mary said. She said it when we were alone.

'Ladies, but not like them.'

'Why not?' she said, pretending not to know.

I blushed, inside anyway. The thought of what the Ladies did confused me completely. They had one bed in their dark, lovely, oaky room, where there was plenty of room for two.

'They are kind. They love one another. What's wrong with that?' Mary said.

At the back of the house was an orchard, with apples, pears, greengages and plums, and there were many fruit bushes and vegetables. I had never been near so much food, even in the convent. Every day we had chops or boiled mutton, bread and cheese, apples, plums, sweet cake, beer.

One day soon after we arrived the cook made summer pudding. I watched her doing it, because I had brought in the berries from the garden and because I wanted to see how she made something with a name like that. She put slices of bread into a bowl, then filled the bowl with blackcurrants, redcurrants, blackberries. Then she put more bread across the top of the bowl and weighed it down with a pound weight from the scales. She carried it to the coldest place in the house, the dairy, and left it there to cool, beside a basin of silent cream.

The next day she carried in the pudding to the big wooden table in the kitchen. When it was turned out on a plate it looked funny, white with red-purple blotches. She cut into the skin with a knife. Inside, it was black and purple, soft, sticky, sweet. She gave us each a slice and poured yellow cream over it from the blue jug.

It tasted like the sun on the white wall in the garden. It tasted like the smell of white cotton that has dried on the line. It tasted like Naoise. Not like his mouth, which was soft and salty, like all men's mouths, but like his name and like his face.

I closed my eyes and said to myself, 'Please, Naoise. Please.' I wished I had a salt herring to eat, so that I could dream of him.

But there were no salt herrings in the house. I dreamt of him anyhow.

One of my jobs was to help the washerwoman who came on Mondays to boil the clothes. I helped her wring, in the hot steamy washroom, and I hung the clothes out for her. When they were dry I carried them into the kitchen and put them on the table and then someone from upstairs came and took them away.

I liked to be out in the yard where long lines were strung between trees, and I liked the feel of the clean cotton against my face. All the lovely white clothes, the nightgowns and frilly blouses, the aprons, the sheets and pillowslips, smelled of the wind, and of something else, grass maybe, or leaves. I let my nose into the heaps of white cloth, and let the sheets flap around me like clouds.

I was there in April. We had spent many months in Llangollen, autumn and winter, dark days in the hot kitchen. Mary was still washing up. Her hands were big and red, and the skin on her arms permanently puckered. I was still in the scullery, doing everything.

The garden was full of daffodils. They had thousands, all along the stone wall, under every tree. The sun danced. Soon it would be Easter. My arms were full of white clothes and I had a white apron on and a white cap.

Someone was standing by the wall, beside the green door leading onto the lane outside. A man, taller than a Welshman. He had a black soft hat, a black coat with tails, and a thick stick. He was standing very still and quietly, looking at me. I knew he had been there for a while, because I had heard nothing at all except the wind rustling in the clothes on the line.

I put my heap of clothes on the damp grass and went over to him.

'I thought you were a goose,' he said, opening the gate.

I went out with him onto the road.

A man with grey curly hair and a tweed jacket, a gentleman, passed close to our tent.

'That is Father Toban,' Naoise said. This was the fourth day in Caer Gybi.

'How do you know?'

'I know by the cut of him. He wears that sort of coat. I will speak to him and see.'

Naoise spoke to him in Irish and he answered in Irish. He said: 'I am not Father Toban.'

'You are,' Naoise said. 'I know you are Father Toban. You will give us a blessing now before we sail for Ireland, since we do not know what is in store for us.'

'If I said I was not a priest but a Protestant and an Englishman, would you believe me?'

'I would not, Father.'

'If I said I could not bless you, would you hit me?'

'I might, Father.'

'If I said I would not give you my blessing, would you kill me with your big shillelagh?'

'I would, Father.'

'Kneel down there the three of you.'

I would not kneel for him. The little girl could not kneel, but Naoise held her in front of him so the blessing would land on her. I watched him, bowing his head and closing his eyes, to the man he believed was the priest.

My father said to me and Mary, the only ones left, after he, and everyone else in our parish, had lost their work on the Relief: 'Kill me and eat me. I will die soon enough anyway.'

It was the beginning of July, hungry July, the beginning of

summer. We had dug the first potatoes early. He knew it would be hungry July, hungry August, hungry winter. Again. Half the people in the village were dead. The landlord had sent others to Canada on a ship from Cork but we had heard terrible things about that journey, and about Canada.

'Get a passage to America,' he said, 'as soon as you can.'

I said yes. I knew I would not go to America, because I would never get the money for the fare together. I knew if I had half a crown I would get to Wales and the poorhouse there would feed me.

'*In nomine Patris et Filii et Spiritus Sancti. Vade in pace. Amen,*' the man in the tweed coat said.

We sailed that afternoon for home.

THE SEARCH FOR THE LOST
HUSBAND

A year later she gave birth to another baby. And once again the little white goat warned her not to shed a tear if anything happened to that child, because if she did, she would lose him, her husband.

And this child was also taken away from her. He was taken away from her in the bed. And she was heartbroken. But she remembered the words of the little white goat. She realised if she shed a single tear, he would be off. So she kept her tears to herself, and the little white goat stayed with her.

BILL'S NEW WIFE

ONE MORNING CATHERINE WOKE UP, as usual, to the clotted-cream richness of a radio voice delivering news. Quickly she stretched and depressed the repeat button on her radio alarm clock. Then off she drifted, around the corner of the house, to a field yellow with swatches of broom. A dog of ugly but harmless appearance bounded out from behind a mountain near the wardrobe. A high thin animal, he sprang towards her on nimble legs. His body was the body of a greyhound, mottled black and white. But his face was round and wrinkled like a bulldog's; his demeanour was inane, almost half-witted. Catherine watched him with mild interest for the brief moment it took him to leap from the wardrobe to the bed. Then, to her immense surprise, he bit her on the hand. At that the radio alarm went on again. 'Carolan's Concerto' flooded her brain and banished the dog and whatever had accompanied him to the great underground realm of forgotten dreams. Was her hand bleeding? Sweetly the harp music assaulted her as she tried to retrieve the hound, spots and mug and bite and all. Give me your hand, oh give me your hand! Carolan means it's *Sunday Miscellany*. *Sunday Miscellany* means it's Sunday.

Sunday!

Catherine pressed the button which gave the alarm the final notice to quit and closed her eyes once again. The music continued. She did not sleep but switched on her sexual fantasy, a serial which had been running in her head for twenty-five years now, almost as long as the radio programme although not by any means as miscellaneous. In fact, even she had to admit its monotony and complete lack of originality as to character and to plot: invariably the same two people up to the same old tricks. But apparently its sameness held some deep comfort for her. Whenever she had tried to replace one of the characters with a fresh model, the fantasy hadn't worked. Like *Coronation Street*, it had a magic, the nature of which she did not quite understand.

This is what Catherine did not see when she closed her eyes: two empty coffee mugs, a copy of *Shoot!*, a broken troll watch with shocking pink hair, a cheque for thirty pounds dated two years ago, three floppy disks which had long lost their cardboard enclosures, an ugly penis-shaped brown candle in an ugly dustbin-shaped pottery candlestick, somebody's idea of rustic craft. And that was just the bedside table.

She was likewise not seeing the dirty clothes basket flooding the dusty carpet with stained underpants, smelly pyjamas, old knickers, grey bras, muddy football shorts, and clean new tracksuits that the children had stopped wearing ages ago because they were of a brand no longer acceptable to children in their class at school. She did not see the mountain of books that lay on the floor at the side of the bed – paperbacks, hardbacks, new, speedily read and abandoned novels and old tattered favourites, self-help books and *Sophie's World* and the collected poems of Lord Byron, and, most alarmingly, books from the library. She did not see the mountain of shoes, pathetically suggestive of the most vulnerable aspects of the human condition, like shoes in a jumble sale or outside a Nazi laager, that pocked the floor space near the wardrobe. She did not see the dressing table, the condition of which I leave to your imagination.

She kept her eyes shut and played with her secondary-school boyfriend.

When *Sunday Miscellany* offered an account of a year spent at the missions in Nigeria as an antidote to 'Carolan's Concerto', she decided to wake up and face the day.

The first thing she saw was the cat, Ginger. She stood on her shins, glaring at her, begging to be fed.

Bill reached for her and murmured 'Hello, Pussy!' in the silly high tones he reserved for children and cats. Who knows, perhaps Nature knows what she's doing when she prompts people to hit such pitches? Perhaps babies and cats have defective ears?

Catherine did not move, not so much gripped by paralysis or laziness as by a sudden overwhelming desire to pretend to be still asleep. Through narrowed eyes she observed Bill slip yawningly from bed, throw on a dressing gown with languid movements, and gesture to the cat to follow him. The pair left the room. Catherine listened to the steps on the stairs, Bill's heavy, slow steps and Ginger's smart pitter-patter, soft as the tinkle of snowdrops on a conservatory roof. What a comfortable sound, she thought, snuggling under the duvet. And how comforting, too, the creak of the back door as it opened and the click as it was closed! The knowledge that Ginger's needs were being met, that her disgusting food was even now being scraped from a can and heaped onto her plate, lulled her.

'Where's Daddy?' Catherine's son, Timmie, stood at the end of the bed. He was wearing Manchester United pyjamas. His face was rosy with sleep but dangerous with irritation.

'Downstairs, I think,' Catherine replied.

'Why did he go downstairs without tellin' me first!' Timmie yelled, his little high-pitched voice rising to a final crescendo.

Catherine tried to think of some acceptable reply. But luckily Timmie left the room. She watched in wonder as his red-and-black back retreated. Clump clump clump, he went, down down down the stairs.

'Daddy!' A loud roar shattered the Sunday quiet of the house. 'Where's my breakfast?'

Timmie seldom demanded attention from his father first thing in the morning. Shrugging, Catherine pulled a book from the stack, the rather neat stack, on Bill's side of the bed. *A Grammar of Ancient Greek*, the first volume was called. She opened it and read examples of nouns of the first denomination. The alphabet, which she had been accustomed to regard as difficult, gave her no trouble at all. From alpha to omega it all was clear as day. Quickly, very quickly, she became absorbed in the work in hand, and the chaos that surrounded her seemed to disappear, subsumed, or perhaps vanquished, by the greater order of the neat ranks of nouns and verbs, declensions and denominations, all redolent of the glory that was Greece and not the mess that was the dysfunctional, disorganised, late-twentieth-century home of Catherine and Bill and Timmie and Paul and Ginger the cat.

She had learned the present tense of the verb *blepo* – her absolute favourite so far – when Bill re-entered the room.

'Here, darling!' he said, placing a mug of coffee beside the mug of cold coffee on her bedside table. 'Don't spill it, it's hot.'

'Thank you, darling,' said Catherine. 'Did you put any sugar in it?'

'Yes, yes, I remembered,' Bill answered shortly. He hated any hint of criticism, and yet he often did forget the sugar.

Catherine continued to read Greek. Bill drank his coffee and dipped into a novel by one of those dreadful women authors he persisted in pursuing against all better advice – life is so short, why waste it on inferior literature when there is so much good stuff to be read and so many languages to be learnt? Then he left the bed once more and walked over to the wardrobe. He remained hovering in front of it for at least five minutes.

Catherine glanced at him from time to time.

He pulled out garment after garment: the wardrobe was crammed with them, some old and much worn, many old and hardly worn, some brand new. Trousers, skirts, suits, dresses, blouses, shirts, clothes for which there is no name: black, white, red, green, black, black, black. After many minutes of agonised determination he selected a pair of black jeans, a black T-shirt and a black jumper. He put them on, and turned to the mirror, where he examined his rear end. He frowned deeply and patted his bottom, then removed the jeans and returned to the wardrobe.

This time he selected a black mini skirt. There followed a frantic rummage in one of the drawers: socks and stockings and tights and underpants and scarves and bras were pulled out, often in long wreaths, entwined together like daisies in a chain. He salvaged a pair of black tights. Into both legs he plunged a hand and reached to the distant toe of each. A ladder was discerned in the left leg. The rummaging resumed. Eventually a potentially unladdered pair of tights was discovered. The hand plunge failing to discover any fatal flaws, he stuffed his feet into the strange receptacles and rolled them up, slowly and carefully, over ankle, calf, knee and thigh, taking particular care to smooth them out at the top of the thigh where leg joined hip. 'They're too small,' he muttered. 'Those one-size are always too small.'

As he pulled his skirt over his head and let it shimmy down his body to its designated position, Catherine could see that the tights were already in a state of slippage. The crotch was positioned below the hem of the skirt, at a half-mast point between knee and thigh top.

Dressed at last, Bill was not yet finished. He sat down at the dressing table and scrutinised his face in the looking glass, turning this way and that as he brushed his hair. He plucked a few hairs from his eyebrows, teased a blackhead and then squeezed flesh-pink cream from a tube onto his chin and began to rub it into his skin. This he followed with a swift brushing of his eyelashes, and a scraping of red lipstick on his mouth.

Catherine thought he looked better without all this gunge but said nothing. She sighed. Turning on her walkman and sticking earphones in her ears, she listened to Dvořák's *New World* symphony: it was too difficult to learn Greek verbs while Bill was in the room, disturbing its peace and equilibrium.

Bill left the dressing table soon enough, and began to pull clothes from the dirty clothes basket. His arms overflowing, he left the room with a deep sigh. Catherine also sighed, in relief, closed her eyes and switched on her fantasy again. She and the lover were by now in a bedroom in the Portmanteau Hotel, a room where, she believed, adulterous assignations often occurred. Indeed, Dublin popular lore hinted that that had been the primary motivation for building the hotel in the first place, so conveniently situated in the middle of bureaucratland and so suggestively named after a type of suitcase. Her lover had just forced her to remove her clothes and was demanding, in a tone that brooked no contradiction, that she spread herself on the floor like a sheepskin rug. He gathered up her clothes in his arms and, adding his own to the pile, flung them onto the bed.

Bill's arms were crammed with clean clothes, pungently scented with Tumble, the piece of perfumed paper he used in the drier because the manufacturers of the drier advised him to do so. He dumped the heap on the foot of the bed and began to classify them: boys' socks, boys' underpants, boys' sweat shirts, boys' jeans, boys' school clothes, anything belonging to

Catherine, anything belonging to Bill. He ran in and out, making trips to the boys' room with two categories at a time. Then he stowed away most of Catherine's things in the chest of drawers, and hung her blouses in the wardrobe. 'I'll iron a few of them later,' he said, 'if I get a chance.'

'That'd be great,' said Catherine sleepily. 'I have a meeting with the director tomorrow. It'd be nice to have a decent blouse.'

'This one is the best, really.' Bill took one blouse, the whitest in the collection, from the wardrobe, and dangled it in front of her.

'Yes, that'll do fine,' Catherine responded. The topic was beginning to bore her. She considered opening the Greek grammar again but decided that it was time to get up. The alarm clock indicated that it was now ten past eleven, although the last time she'd looked it had only been half past nine. What had happened to the time in between?

She went to the bathroom.

She glanced in the mirror. Her facial hair, always a minor problem, had burgeoned overnight. Her chin was a lawn of newly sprouted black grass. She scraped her hand across it, and pulled a razor from the cabinet. It took ages, and much contorting of the muscles, to reduce the skin to a state of acceptable smoothness. The effort exhausted and irritated her so much that she couldn't be bothered washing, much less having a shower.

'Must go to one of those electrolysis places and have my facial hair permanently removed,' she said to Bill, when she returned to the bedroom.

'Good idea,' said Bill. 'Maybe I'll ring one of them tomorrow and make an appointment for you, will I?'

'Mm,' said Catherine. 'But the time, the time, where will I get the time?'

She pulled some grey trousers and a greeny-grey jumper from the chair beside her bed. They looked a bit stained and old and shabby, and she couldn't remember ever having seen them before. But what the hell, it was only Sunday. She dragged them on as quickly as she could and pulled her hand through her hair: after all that shaving she couldn't bear to comb her hair or to spend one more second of her valuable time messing around in front of a mirror.

'You'll have to make time,' said Bill. 'Your personal well-being comes first!'

Personal well-being? This was a hobby horse with him. Time for health, time for children, time for this and time for that. He could not comprehend that time was meant for work, that work took time, almost all the time there was, and that, when the chips were down, when the die was cast, when Judgment Day was come, nothing else would matter. Saint Peter would not ask, Did you take the time to go to the beauty clinic? But he would ask, Did you do your duty at your place of work? Did you develop the talent God gave you and return it tenfold? Did you ask what you could do for your country, and your office, and your institution, or did you spend your time running to the doctor and the dentist and playing with your children? Bill did not understand that a woman had one life only and that she had to make it as productive as possible, or else suffer the consequences.

Ah well. It takes both types, the active and the passive. What a pity, though, the passive spend so much time trying to persuade the active that they, too, should be passive! The reverse is not true, obviously. The active haven't the time to worry about anything except the deadlines waiting to be met.

Catherine pondered these problems as she pattered downstairs in her big flip-flop bedroom slippers, put an egg on the cooker, and poured a cup of coffee from the coffee thing they'd got in Brittany during their camping holiday three years ago – she still hadn't figured out how to use it, and really preferred instant, but Bill had filled the thing, in preparation for his Sunday binge. He sat down with her, drinking what was probably his sixth cup of coffee that morning: he was addicted to the stuff, which tended to make him more jittery than he was by nature. Even now he could not sit still and enjoy cup number six. Instead, he continuously hopped up, like a coffee bean in an advertisement on TV, or a frozen pea, and ran out to the utility room, checking to see if the washing machine had finished its cycle. Couldn't he simply read the timer and re-member what it said? Catherine wanted to ask. But she knew better than to object. Bill did all housework by instinct as a matter of principle, and seemed to have an aversion to timing anything. (At this moment Catherine checked her watch. Her egg had been on for four and a half minutes. Half a minute to go.) Or measuring anything. She considered taking up the egg on a spoon and then hunting frantically for an egg cup. Bill handed her one with a grim expression.

'Thanks!' Catherine said sharply.

But the egg was perfect. Timing did, in fact, work, she thought smugly, spooning white and yellow, albumen and yolk, into her mouth. It really did. And it made life so much more simple.

When she'd finished, Bill had vanished on one of his secret missions to the outer regions of the house. She cleared the table and stacked all the dishes in the dishwasher, except for the fry-ing pan, the pots left over from last night's dinner, when she had also been responsible for the washing-up, the oven dish encrusted with steak-and-kidney pie, many knives and forks, a butter dish containing about one millionth of an ounce of butter, a milk jug, with a sour, creamy coating inside its beak, and several other bits and pieces. She turned on the machine, glanced at the kitchen, failed to see all these objects, and smiled, well-pleased with her morning's work. At least Bill would have nothing to complain about today!

Ginger had eaten only half her food, sated with bird. 'Should I throw this out?' she asked Bill.

'Yes,' said Bill, brusquely.

Catherine looked at him anxiously. What was coming next? 'Poor Pussy isn't hungry,' she said, attempting friendliness.

'She has worms,' said Bill. 'We haven't wormed her for ages.'

'Why don't we do that, then?' Catherine caressed Ginger sympathetically. Ginger scowled and jumped away.

'I can't find the worming pills.'

'Ah!' Catherine decided that saying nothing was the wise option at this juncture.

'She should be neutered, too. She's going to have kittens if we're not careful and then you'll have to drown them.'

'I'm not going to drown them. I didn't want the cat in the first place, did I?'

This was so indisputably true that it took Bill a minute to find a riposte.

'Timmie wanted her. He needs her. The cat does him a world of good. Why should you deprive Timmie of something he needs just to spare yourself some trouble.'

Then let Timmie neuter the goddamned beast, is what Catherine thought. But she said, 'So why don't we get her neutered then? Why don't we bring it to the vet and get it neutered?'

'Fine. Do it!' Bill's voice rose.

'Hm?'

'Bring the cat to the vet. Do it yourself. I do everything around here.'

Catherine sighed deeply and bit back the comment which

rose to her lips. 'OK,' she said quietly. 'OK, I will.'

She left the house before more accusations could be fired at her, walked up to the corner shop and bought three Sunday newspapers. When she returned she could not see Bill anywhere. So she sat in front of the fireplace in the living room and began to read. The grate was full of ashes from last night's fire, but Catherine did not see them, or the bits of black turf dust scattered across the rug, or the empty wine glasses on the mantelpiece. What she did see was an excellent review of a new collection of essays by A.J.P. Taylor, one of her favourite historians. She read it eagerly and determined to get the book at the nearest opportunity. She also saw a good interview with Julian Barnes, a writer she had never heard of but who seemed exceptionally articulate and in command of the English language, which made a change, Catherine thought, a welcome change from the majority of contemporary writers. (Her favourite century was the fourteenth. Indeed, she had liked to proclaim, at parties, that anything written later than fourteen hundred, about the time Chaucer died, was not worth reading. Bill had stopped her declaring this at parties, claiming it was patronising, overbearing and insulting to half the people there, the half that ever read anything. And it was other things as well, which, fortunately, she forgot.)

In the next room Timmie was watching television. Paul, his older brother, came down from bed – he slept very late at weekends, being in a growing spurt – and thumped him, starting the day as he meant it to continue.

'Oh God!' sighed Catherine. But she persisted in reading the paper until the volume reached an intolerably high level. Then she gritted her teeth and waited. Sure enough, Bill arrived on the scene and screamed at the boys. The noises subsided for a short time.

But Catherine's concentration had been disturbed. She went

to the kitchen for a cup of coffee. Bill was there, sweeping the floor. On the table were onions, carrots, garlic, which he had been chopping before taking a break to sweep. He did quite a lot of chopping, and quite a lot of sweeping, both unnecessary activities in Catherine's opinion but who was she to judge? Perhaps they were therapeutic in some way? She never swept, chopped, or cooked herself. She couldn't. She simply couldn't. When Bill went away, as happened (all too often), Catherine and the boys survived on Chinese takeaways and chips and burgers. It was the only time the boys enjoyed their food. Indeed, it was the only time the boys ate their food. But Bill felt cooking was important, and that not eating home-made food was healthier than eating takeaways.

'Anything I can do to help?' asked Catherine. She always asked this. She was nothing if not courteous. Also, she knew there was nothing she could do to help.

'No.' Bill sounded cross.

Catherine wished she had not ventured into this lion's den. But she had, and she was not one to retreat. No coward's soul is mine, she often said, to herself and to others (especially to Timmie, who was young enough to listen politely to parental aphorisms). 'What are we having for lunch?' She asked it to be affable, not because she was interested, not because she cared. But if the truth be admitted, she was a little hungry.

Bill screamed.

Just what she had been trying to avert. 'Oh dear, it's not that time again, is it?' Catherine said.

'No, it is not that time again,' said Bill. 'Stop saying is it that time again every time something goes wrong. It is not that time again, but it is the time again when I realise that I am being trampled alive by you and your damned kids – '

'Och!'

'I'm sick of spending all my free time cleaning up after you lot as if I were some sort of a slave or something I mean it's not fair I don't know how you can simply allow somebody else to do everything for four people it really is preposterous it's un-believable I mean what about my personal well-being? Here I am chopping bloody onions at twelve o'clock on a Sunday morning while they're watching television and you – '

'I try to do my fair share!'

'Your fair share?' He gave her a withering glance.

'I washed the dishes . . .'

'You wouldn't know a fair share if it got up and bit you.'

The black-and-white hound bounded across the lawn. Catherine saw it and lost her temper. 'I spend more time doing housework than you do, if the truth be known!' shouted Catherine, in that stentorian bellow that always alarmed the neighbours. 'I wash the dishes. I carry the plastic bag out to the bin. I put the wine bottles in the bottlebank in the car park. Who takes out the bins every Friday? Who cuts the grass? When did you last cut the grass?'

'Oh fuck off!' said Bill, resorting to foul language, a sure sign that he knew he was vanquished.

'It isn't good for the children to hear language like that.' Catherine spoke primly, pleased to have won the round.

'I don't give a damn. It isn't good for them to live with god-awful parents like us, either.'

Catherine ran a hand through her unkempt hair. 'Why don't you go upstairs and lie down for a while?' she suggested, wearily. 'Maybe you're tired. It's been a hard week.'

Bill stopped in his tracks. He melted, almost to tears, at the hint of sympathy. 'All right,' he whimpered. 'I will.'

Catherine swept away the onion skins and other vegetal debris and threw them into the bin. What a huge proportion of one's time went throwing away rubbish, sweeping it away, washing it away, dusting it away, putting it away! And other equally squalid, mundane tasks. 'As for living, our servants can do that for us!' Yeats had said, in his typical highfalutin way. Well for some, well for some! We do our living for ourselves, we don't even have a wife to do it any more. And it uses up more time and energy and love and friendship than almost anything else we do.

She could hear Bill sobbing upstairs. Sobbing on a Sunday because he had had to sweep one floor too many! Life should have more to offer to Bill, who had read about a million books, written a doctoral thesis, held down three or four not very powerful jobs, parented two children, cared for a cat, driven a family around France one summer and around Italy the next on the right-hand side, cooked many thousand meals. It could, at least, have taught him the wisdom to deal with everyday tasks. It could have taught him to chop onions without weeping!

She sneaked back to the sitting room, intending to seek some solace in the newspapers. En route she spoke to Timmie, who was still spreadeagled in front of the television set. 'Dad's in one of his moods again!' she said. 'Lower it a bit, will you? He's having a little nap.'

'That time is it?' said Timmie, who was streetwise beyond his eight years. 'OK, anything for a quiet life.' He shoved a half-eaten slice of toast under the sofa and reduced the volume on the television.

Many years later it all came to pass.

Catherine got up one morning and Bill had made the breakfast. Catherine got up the next morning and Bill had washed the clothes. Catherine got up next morning and Bill had baked some bread. Catherine got up next morning and Bill had ironed some clothes.

The final bastion was overcome.

Catherine was fifty-nine then, and Bill was sixty-five. He had retired, although she, sadly, had not. On the day Bill ironed the clothes she knew that he had grown at last to be like her, and she had grown to be like him. On the day Bill ironed the clothes, she realised how much she had always loved him.

The battle of the sexes, siege of the kitchen sink, was over.

The best part of life was beginning. But how late it was, how late! How many years had been given over to the conflict! And how long would the best part last, how long, how long?

THE SEARCH FOR THE LOST HUSBAND

Another year passed. And she gave birth to another son. And the little white goat came to her once again and warned her. She was to shed no tears, no matter what happened. Because if she shed one single tear, he would abandon her. And she'd have nobody at all then.

The same thing happened again. The new baby was hardly born when he was taken away from her. And once more she told herself to shed no tears. She tried her best to control herself. But she couldn't. She couldn't prevent herself shedding a tear this time.

The little white goat came to her. And she tried to hide her tears from him. She put a little handkerchief up to her eyes so he wouldn't see they were wet.

That's how it was.

'Now', he said. 'I won't stay with you for one more day.

You can't keep your eyes dry,' he said, 'so you can't have me. I warned you,' he said. 'You can cry away as much as you like now, but I won't be here to comfort you. I'm leaving you now, and you will never see me again.'

'If you leave, I'm going to follow you,' she said.

'There's no point at all in you doing that,' he replied. 'Because you haven't got a chance of getting me back. So don't bother your head following me. I'm going now, and you go back home to your father and your mother and forget you ever saw me.'

LILI MARLENE

IT COMES AS A BIT OF A SURPRISE that the end of love can make me happy. Maybe I'm flawed in some deep terrible way? Perverted, like a serial killer, or like a masochist? Maybe when you dig inside my heart what you'd find is a block of white, hard ice which never thaws, instead of what should be there: gunge, hot and squelching. I don't know. But what I know is that I am elated, not miserable, to be shot of that man, the man I was in love with for longer than the most avid reader of romances would want to believe.

Once a colleague of mine, in the bookshop where I work, asked me, 'Do you hate men?' He asked me this because he has categorised me as a feminist, much in the way that we decide to put a book on the shelf marked Women's Studies, or Life and Health, or Philosophy or Modern Literature, even though we know it belongs to all of these categories at once: we have to plump for one of them. Everything has its overriding, its most marketable, feature. And he thought hating men might be mine. Well, he was drunk. I was so taken aback at the question that I laughed my shy little laugh and mumbled an inaudible response. Do I hate men? It seemed too unlikely and also too dangerous to contemplate.

Still, I have to admit to being happy at this moment – more

than that, I am glittering and sparkling with a crystal delight, a brilliant optimism which drenches the ordinary details of my life with a silvery light, very much as the early stages of love did. What I feel is very like what I felt at first, but it is not the same. I know it is not the same, and I wonder if it is better.

It's not that I have had no regrets and no heartbreak. Indeed I have, long wringing ages of them, months of impatience, jealousy, anger. Weeping. I have had months of weeping, silent and interior, raging and noisy. But that passed, as it usually passes in such cases. And now I have arrived at a stage where love is a word that is distant from me and cold. I glance at it as I might glance at a cream bun behind a confectioner's window and for that cream bun I no longer have the slightest appetite. Perhaps it's made of plastic or papier-mâché. It neither repels nor draws me. More significantly, I am not afraid of it, as for months I was. I can cast a cold eye on it now, and observe it with the dispassion I feel for lovers on the street or in the park, people who, for years, aroused in me the strongest sensations of envy and anguish.

There are times when I even believe I could see him, the man in this story, and pass him by without a blush or a twinge of longing. But here I am less sure of my ground, and perhaps indulging in illusion. I am, however, certain that if I did see him, as is most unlikely, I would have the strength to pass him by. I would pass him by no matter what I felt. My head would rule my heart, where he is concerned, at long long last. It is that certainty, the knowledge that I have given myself my freedom papers, which brightens my days and sends my heart soaring.

I am cultivating my own garden, literally. It is a pleasure to do so. For ages it has been left to its own devices and the brambles and nettles and thistles have overwhelmed it. And now I am there again, in my boots and rubber gloves, rake and secateurs in hand, cleaning and scraping and pruning, full of plans and hopes. Soon I will plant. Soon I will take a bucket of a thousand bulbs, and soon my garden will be crowded with golden daffodils. And later I will have gillyflowers and delphiniums, jasmine and clematis and honeysuckle. Parsley, mint and thyme. Lemon verbena, rosemary, rue. I will have built a red curved Japanese bridge and I will dig a pond for frogs and lilies and I will raise an arbour or an arch or a folly or some damned thing. Because I have been idle for a long long time, idling in the haystack, idling in the featherbed, idling in the sauna, idling in my heart. My body and my mind, and, I think, my soul, were limp and vapid. But now they are muscular and powerful, primed for action. I am full of power.

Elizabeth is clearing nettles and brambles from the garden at Barn Lodge. She plans to grow potatoes, cabbage and onions. The patch she has selected for these vegetables is at the end of the garden which catches the sun almost until nightfall. The late morning sun shines now, a lemon water sun, warming the back of Elizabeth's neck as she works. Under her feet the ground is soft from the rain but still cold. Also stony and difficult to prepare for planting. Elizabeth has no gloves. She works with a long spade, too long for her. Its edge is not as sharp or effective as it should be.

She has been working for two hours. I see her sitting at the edge of the clay patch, on the grass. And I take this as a signal. She asked me to make tea and bring it out to her in the garden at one o'clock. It is not even twelve yet but I assume I have made a mistake, as I often do. Adults are always right, children usually wrong, in my experience of life so far. Why does Elizabeth want tea in the garden, in the mud of the vegetable patch, when it is only a short step to the kitchen? I don't question her motives, watching her as she sits with her head bowed, the spade across her knees. That a tableau had been arranged for dramatic effect has not crossed my mind, as it certainly does not cross hers.

When I reach her she is crying. Her face is creased and ugly like a dark cabbage, and her hair, usually neatly pulled into a bun, straggles wantonly across her cheek and shoulders. I feel like crying myself. She looks so terrible.

'What's wrong, Mammy?'

Have I made her cry? I am responsible for so much sadness in her life, it seems to me. If it were not for me, for me and all the rest of us, Elizabeth would be leading a different life. She's fond of us – that's her word, 'fond', it's as far as she can go with words – but we know we are a burden. Should I have been out with her in the garden, digging? There is only one spade though, and I haven't any shoes.

'Look at me hands.' She holds them out, palms up, as we do when the teacher wants to give us a slap of the ruler. Or as Jesus Christ does on the crucifix over Elizabeth's bed. The palms are red with white spots – blisters. Some of the blisters have broken and are beginning to ooze. Elizabeth is crying. 'Look at me poor hands!'

I am sad, I am embarrassed, I am ashamed, I am puzzled. I look at her hands. I pour out some tea. What am I supposed to say? What am I supposed to do?

I am fourteen, the eldest of us all, and a very mature fourteen. But still fourteen.

This was just after the Emergency, the Second World War. For us, Elizabeth and the ten of us, the Emergency was that Tom, our father, had died of cancer in January. He had worked as a groundsman for Lord Mainpatrick, the landlord who owned all the land in our area. Our cottage had belonged to Lord Mainpatrick originally but he had given it to Tom in lieu of wages, or from pity. That meant that we were very lucky, Elizabeth said. Luckier than some ('some' – a sad category of humanity she often referred to. 'Some', or 'some people' or 'some poor cratures'. We were always luckier than them, poor things!). It meant we had a roof over our heads. A roof, but no money, no money at all. There were no pensions, no support for women like Elizabeth. What were they supposed to do? Maybe there was a workhouse somewhere. Maybe there was an orphanage. But she would not put us there. She would not dream of dumping us in one of 'them places'. That is what she told me, and Peter, many, many times. Peter was thirteen, one year younger than me, and we were immensely grateful to Elizabeth for not doing what some would have done and handing us over to the tender mercies of the nuns. Our gratitude did not stop us from holding the orphanage as a threat over the heads of all the little ones, when it suited us. 'If ye don't stop it, ye'll be for the Orphanage.' And Elizabeth's vow did not prevent her from using the same threat. She would never, she would never – and yet she would. One way or the other, we knew the decision was hers. She was our mother and she had the power of life and death over us, of that she and all were quite convinced.

John, the man, came to the bookshop where I work. I was at the cash register when he came in, and my first sight of him was on the security monitor – even through the fuzzy medium of in-store television, I recognised him, limping about near the philosophy stand. He had changed: he was thin where he had been stocky, his black curly hair was grey and surprisingly straight. His appearance was smooth, suave, milky, whereas in the past all surfaces were sandpapery, rugged. But his stance had not changed, or the way he picked up objects and held them at a distance from his eyes, using his exceptionally long arm as a sort of crane.

I watched him, dispassionately. My main shock was at

seeing him in a bookshop. No doubt he would have been shocked to see me in such a setting, too. When we had last known one another, I had never read one single book in my life, nor had had access to one.

I observed him, coldly, surprised, even disappointed, that my sensations were so neutral. Had the passage of time hardened me to this extent? He might have been some neighbour or casual acquaintance encountered after an absence of some years, a harmless bygone resurfacing in a garden, not a buried landmine, primed to destroy.

How wrong I was!

He came to the counter after a while, with a copy of a novel by Margaret Drabble, *A Summer Bird-cage*. So much for the philosophy.

'It's a great book,' I commented, as I took his cheque.

'Oh? It's for my daughter.'

'What age is she?'

'She's sixteen. Almost.'

'That's about right. She'll love it.'

He sniffed, thanked me in an offhand way, and left.

Had I aged so badly?

But a few days later he was back.

'She had it already,' he said. 'Can I exchange it for a token?'

'Certainly' – I took the slim volume from him – 'would you like to pick a card?'

He selected one and I pasted on the tokens.

'There you are!' I smiled. 'You never know with books, do you?'

'Will you have a cup of coffee?' He smiled, for the first time. But I wasn't sure.

'Sorry?'

'Don't you know me?'

'I knew you the minute you walked in the door.'

★

Elizabeth worked for the Mainpatricks as well, when she was a girl. She worked as a dairymaid on their estate in Cabra, Dublin. Cabra was still the country then, a valley of lush fields and spreading sycamores, filled with herds of Jersey cows, beige and creamy. She herded and milked the cows, filled blue-rimmed basins with the milk and left it to settle. She skimmed the cream from the surface with a special bowl and churned once a week.

> Come butter come butter come butter come!
> Every lump as big as my bum!

She sang stooped over the churn, turning the crank as fast as she could to the rhythms of her song. She patted the butter into pound pieces, embossing each piece with the Mainpatrick crest, a fleur-de-lys. Around the edges she made a swastika pattern.

Her complexion was dewy and fresh: peaches and cream, or, to be more exact, strawberries and cream. All the girls who worked in the dairy had perfect skin. But that had nothing to do with the cream or the milk, Elizabeth explained. Girls who worked in the pork butcher's had the same complexion. It came from the coldness of the surroundings, and the constant exercise.

Elizabeth was like Tess of the d'Urbervilles, but she did not meet an Angel Clare. Instead she met my father, Tom, a labourer on the farm. They married and she stopped working. Those were the days! Even the wives of farm labourers felt it was correct to give up their jobs and stay at home. It must have been fun, at least for the first few months – she moved from an attic room, which she had shared with four other girls, to Barn Lodge, and that must have seemed like a very good move to her. Barn Lodge looked like its name: it was custard-pie cottage, with cut stone walls, little mullioned windows, all that Snow

White stuff. In front it boasted a pocket handkerchief garden, not a chocolate box fountain of flora but including geraniums and wallflowers, and, in spring, daffodils. Behind was the large garden, boasting nothing. At first they grew vegetables. Then there was a hiatus, when Tom was ill and Elizabeth busy with him and babies. And then she started the vegetables again.

Elizabeth was beautiful. I did not know it at the time, but I realise it now, remembering. Strawberries and cream. Good thick chestnut hair. Her eyes were wide grey pools. By the time I began to pay attention to her she was well on the way to losing her looks. Her body had thickened and sagged from the constant pregnancies. (And why was she always pregnant? People got pregnant because of their religion, is what we say. Catholics. But can this be so? There was more to it than that. Every Catholic did not have a child every nine months, even then. Some kept their families small enough. How? Abstinence, I'd say, was the birth control. Not doing it. And the couples who were in love or passionate or greedy were the ones who got the big crowds of children.)

Elizabeth's face was lovely, but it was also lined and sad, with a deep hopelessness in it, like a landscape on a dreary November day. Many women wore that expression then, in Ireland. It was not caused by babies but by poverty. She had to think about money constantly. Even when Tom was alive they had a pittance. His job was one of the very worst you could have in Dublin at that time. (But 'some' had no work at all. 'Some' were starving.) His conditions were feudal. He had the cottage and two pounds a week, when labourers on building sites had six or seven. He got old clothes, though, from the Mainpatricks, and other odds and ends – scraps from the kitchen, a chair they were throwing out. Elizabeth spent a lot of time mending their castoffs, for us, although she had no talent for sewing and hated it. As a matter of fact, she hated most things she did – that was the impression she conveyed. There was too much work, and she was always stemming the tide with a little finger.

But she retained her lovely eyes. They don't go away, no matter what happens to the rest of your face. And her hair was not bad either – it remained thick, and its chestnut colour did not fade badly for a long time. I can see why Tom had fallen in love with her. And he stayed in love with her. We all knew that, I think, unconsciously, even when we were very small. We knew our parents had been beautiful and we knew they loved one another. I think that was the lucky aspect of our lives, and the thing that stood to us for ever.

My connection with John progressed rapidly, friendship escalating into love in a matter of weeks. We met twice a week – once after my late night at the bookshop, and once on my day off, Monday, usually in the morning. On the nights we went for a drink or, more often, a drive. We drove out of the city and along the coast, stopping at some quiet spot to hold hands and talk. At first we made love in the car but that was so uncomfortable that we gave it up after a month or two. By then we made love in my bed, on Monday mornings. He'd come at about eleven, we'd go to bed and then have lunch. He never seemed to have trouble getting away from work – he was his own boss, as head buyer for a large department store in London.

I loved him a lot. I loved him completely. Do you know why? Well, there are always many reasons for love: he was good-looking, of course, and warm, and all the things that make a man attractive. But he loved me, deeply and crazily, then as before. He phoned me several times a day to hear the sound of my voice. He buried his head in my hair. 'Don't ever go away from me!' he said. 'I don't want to lose you now that I've found you again. I couldn't bear that.'

I used to laugh and my eyes filled with sentimental tears, tears of joy and tears of love. He sounded childish when he said these things, as men can sound when they are expressing emotions. I knew what he said seemed true to him, at the time, but I laughed at it privately, aware that in the context of history it would ring hollow and naive. Still, I listened and patted his thick hair and kissed his forehead. And it is surprising how much of what he said sank in. All those phrases which I was condescending to when I heard them sneaked into dark crevices in my head or my heart, and I stored them there, along with the tone of his voice, the expression in his eye, when he said them. They were there to be pulled out later and analysed, questioned, yearned for, despised. At the time I enjoyed it all, with qualifications. Why was I so wise? Why did I introduce qualifications?

There was no question of marriage. I would have considered it. It seemed to me the right thing, in this day and age. The hole-and-corner affair is outmoded, in my opinion, and more dishonourable than ever. But John did not seem to agree. When I hinted, once or twice, that we should tackle the implications of our relationship in some practical way, he bristled, stiffened his nose and his back, and coughed drily a few times: he always behaved in this way when he was not prepared to countenance a suggestion made by me. His reaction, all this stiffening and sniffing and withdrawing, terrified me physically. I felt squashed underfoot by the sheer force of his disapproval. He is a quiet man but one with a forceful character. That, I think, is what being a forceful character means: having the ability to force people to cringe, shut up, drop everything, go away, with a single twitch of your body.

He never discussed his wife and I never asked about her, although we talked about Cyril, my better half, all the time. We were, after all, in Cyril's house, surrounded by his things.

We were, for heaven's sake, in Cyril's bed! And perhaps it was hardly possible for me not to talk about Cyril, anyway, no matter who I was with. He was such a huge part of my life, no matter what else was going on.

I did not talk about John's wife, but I did think about her. First I thought of her with pity, although it was not a pity that moved me to help her in any way, by, for instance, giving up her husband. Then I thought of her jealously. And finally, recently, I began to think of her with interest, as somebody I would have plenty in common with, as a sister sufferer. I thought I'd like to meet her and get to know her.

When Tom died I became the breadwinner. That is how Elizabeth referred to me. 'Lily is our breadwinner now!' I had liked that word when I'd heard it applied to men. I could see them, reaping in cornfields, their scythes swinging. But I hated being called 'breadwinner' myself. The word was a burden. I saw myself as a girl in Africa or Asia, or some far-off place, walking along a dry path, with a heavy load of parcels balanced on my head, forcing me to restrain every movement, and move with a steady rhythmical sway, more like a plant than an animal. What I longed for first was money, or the dignity money confers, and then freedom. My mother's words warned that I would not have both.

My job was in a big hotel in the centre of Dublin, and I was known there as a chambermaid. What I had to do was clean the bedrooms. I started work at eight, except when I had to do early morning teas, and I finished at three. Then at six I had to go back to turn down the beds – that meant folding back the tops of the quilts so the guests would not have to perform this onerous task themselves before they slipped between the covers. It seemed like a very pointless exercise to me. What possible difference could it make to anyone whether the quilt was pulled down or not? But I had to do it, for about an hour every evening, walking through the rooms in my clean clothes.

I loved that. I loved opening the doors of the clean, neat rooms, gentle in the evening light. I loved walking across the carpet and folding back the swathe of silk, or satin, and then walking slowly out again and on to the next room. For this job, myself and the other girls always dressed up, and made sure our hair was combed. It was easy and ceremonious. And it allowed us to review our morning's work before it was all destroyed again by untidy, messy guests.

I loved all the work, actually. I just loved working, and feeling that I was making something – in this case, making beds, and making rooms shipshape, rooms that looked like the wreck of the Hesperus more often than you'd ever suspect. Also, I liked feeling that I was making money. Every minute I spent working in that hotel was different from the time I spent working at home, because every minute was money in my pocket. That gave my time a new meaning, and it made me feel valuable, precious. All the money I earned I handed over to Elizabeth. I would have liked to have kept some for myself but it wasn't possible. And Elizabeth seemed to believe that the money I earned was hers. She believed that everything and everyone in Barn Lodge belonged to her. I didn't mind too much. It was almost a privilege to be in the hotel, anyway. It was much warmer than Barn Lodge, and I was well fed.

After six months I got a new, extra job. Still-room waitress, this job was called. So now I was two things, chambermaid-cum-still-room-waitress. Still-room waitressing meant washing up mainly. It meant standing at a big porcelain sink with my arms up to the elbows in hot greasy water for two or three hours. I enjoyed that, too: the hot water, the feeling of being immersed in it, the steam that comforted my face and softened my complexion. It was like a sauna; so much of what is called work is like something else that is called play. Or maybe it was, that after Barn Lodge, the sheer misery of that place, almost everything was play.

I even had a helper. He was a man aged about sixty, called Bertie. I'm not sure why he worked there; maybe he was a distant relative of the owner, something like that. He had one of those walrus moustaches men used to have before the First World War, and white stubble on his chin. And he was fat, with a big belly, so that his whole shape was conical, with the small end of the cone at the bottom, like a man in the *Beano*.

The delph was lined up on a steel rack, dripping sudsy water. He dried and the delph was stacked on shelves, gleaming.

When he'd finished drying he danced. 'Here ye are me ould segotia!' he'd say. 'Grab a mop and join the party!'

We'd waltz around the slippery floor. When he'd finished dancing he sang.

The Charladies' Ball.

Biddy Mulligan the Pride of the Coombe.

In Glendalough Lived an Ould Saint.

His favourite was 'Lili Marlene', and that became my favourite, too.

I got him to sing it every night, when the last diners had gone home, and we were finished at last. The delph was on the shelves, the cutlery shone in its tray, the floor was washed and the sink empty, with rags dripping on the brass taps. The kitchen would look perfect then, as perfect as the bedrooms in the early evening. It glowed in the orange light. He'd stand under the lamp and sing. When he came to the last lines, he'd turn his big, very pale blue eyes on me, and act being soppy and heartbroken,

> My Lili of the lamplight!
> My own Lili Marlene!

Soon the song was over. We'd stand there, under the lamp, for a little longer. And then he'd stop being sentimental and soft. He'd turn and say briskly, 'Tomorrow is another day!'

I'd yawn. I'd be so wrecked, up since six, that I hardly knew if I was on my head or my feet.

Tomorrow is another day.

John lost his job. Rather, he resigned, in umbrage, because he had been subjected to a sideways demotion. This was about a year and a half after we had met, and all through that time he had been complaining: his boss was sneaky and unreliable, nice as pie to people's faces but seriously given to backbiting. At any one time in that job half the staff were violently unhappy and half were thrilled with themselves: the boss always managed to retain a proportion of courtiers, people in favour who were promoted and cosseted, and who were intensely loyal to him in return. The others sulked and fretted and cursed. So John said. He had never belonged to the happy camp, always to the outcasts. On the day the boss told him to manage the food warehouse he walked out.

'I didn't think you had it in you!' I said admiringly. At that moment he seemed to me as brave as Hercules. I loved a dramatic gesture, proof that there were people in the world who could take a risk and did not cling so desperately to security as I myself did.

'The mouse roared!' he said, pleased that I condoned his action. His wife did not, not completely, for obvious reasons. He was forty-five, they had children, she had no job herself. But John was not worried. I could hardly believe that anyone could be so sanguine and optimistic.

'I've lots of contacts,' he spoke firmly. 'Friends who can help me while I find my feet. It will be easy for me to get a loan from the bank.'

'Will it?'

'Certainly. The economy is good.'

It was 1980. I thought we were in a recession. Actually, I thought we were always in recession, and when I was told we were not I knew we soon would be. I would never in a million years resign from a job because I didn't like it. I would never assume I could rescue myself and make a success of something new. But I believed John would. I could see it in his eyes, I could see it in the set of his shoulders.

He was going to open a restaurant.

'It's a good time to open something like that?'

'As good as any.' His shoulder stiffened and he drew back from me. 'I'll get backers.'

I wondered, fleetingly, if I should offer him money. Should I say, 'Look, take this! I'll look on it as an investment.' It would be proof of my true friendship, my true love. Or maybe not. Maybe it would humiliate him? Maybe it would make him despise me?

I thought about it for some weeks. But I did not get around to making an offer. My money was Cyril's money, after all. I felt it was all right to offer him love that was Cyril's love, but Cyril's money seemed different and much more valuable than my love for Cyril, something which I could never have considered as any kind of asset.

I worked in the hotel for three years. Then two things happened. Mary and Paul, my sister and brother, contracted TB. Paul died soon, and Mary lingered in Peamount Hospital, hoping for a remission. (She did get a remission, some years later, and during that remission she married another patient whom she'd met in the sanatorium. Four months after the wedding she died. I don't know what happened to her husband. I don't even remember his name.)

The second thing that happened was that Peter, the brother

next in line to me, lost his job on the buildings in Dublin and had to go to England. He decided to go, not to Liverpool or Birmingham, but to Portsmouth. The reason for this decision was that a friend of his lived in Portsmouth, and he recommended it. Portsmouth had been bombed during the war, and there was plenty of construction work going on.

I said I'd go, too.

'We'll all go,' Elizabeth declared, surprisingly. 'I want to get out of this terrible country!'

It seemed to me like the wildest thing she had ever said, and the most courageous and the best.

She sold Barn Lodge and with the proceeds Peter bought us a house in Portsmouth – a small, terrible house, but we did not know what it was like before we left Dublin. We travelled so hopefully that nothing would have stoppered our joy, anyway. Elizabeth was ecstatic. Moving away was what she had always wanted. From the moment she said 'We're going!' her face became radiant, and she glowed with energy. Moving on, moving away: the excitement electrified her. We were far from being the heartbroken emigrants of the traditional songs. Infected by Elizabeth's enthusiasm, we were convinced that a golden future awaited us on the other side of the sea, and we prepared to say goodbye to Ireland with the lightest of hearts.

But we looked like the shabbiest and poorest of migrants, as indeed we were. Everything in Barn Lodge had to be packed and transported by our own steam to the new house in Portsmouth: pots and pans, knives and forks, cups and plates were packed in newspaper and stacked in boxes. Our sheets and blankets, our towels, our mattresses, our pillows, had to be rolled up and hauled across the Irish Sea and across England. We could not afford help, and so the old furniture was sold to the pawn shop, but everything else we took with us, in bundles and rolls and parcels.

A man on the estate who owned an old van drove us to Dunleary. When we arrived at Euston Station we hailed a taxi to take us to St Pancras, where we were to get the train for Portsmouth.

'Bloody Irish!' the taximan said, when he saw the stuff. It took him at least a quarter of an hour to pack it all in. 'Brought the kitchen sink an' all, did you?'

'We had no choice, sir,' said Elizabeth. She was not taken aback by his remarks. It was the reaction she expected, from everyone. We all knew that being poor was generally regarded as a crime, like being a thief or being a drunkard – indeed, people clearly assumed these things usually went together. We believed, ourselves, that we were to blame for our poverty and we were ashamed of it, deeply ashamed.

'That's the way,' he said more kindly.

Elizabeth was as white as a ghost, after the night on the boat and the train. But she had on her good navy suit with a white blouse, and a pair of shoes I'd got at the hotel. She wore a small red hat. She looked lovely, in a drawn sort of way. And, separated from her mattresses and shabby bundles, she did not look downtrodden or even poor, but hopeful and brave.

'Where are you off to, then, madam?'

'St Pancras station.'

'And after that?'

'We're going to Portsmouth. We're going to live in Portsmouth.'

He drove Elizabeth and me and the youngest child the whole way to Portsmouth with all our belongings. The rest of the family went by train. It was a black London taxi, and we rode in style along the neat country roads, through the villages which seemed to have been unaffected by the war. He drove us to the door of our new house and he charged us nothing.

An omen.

'Nobody in Ireland lifted a finger!' Elizabeth said, not quite truthfully. 'And on our first day in England that happened!'

On our first day that happened. That taximan drove us sixty miles, for nothing, and we felt welcome to England. We felt grateful, blessed. We felt lucky. And so we prospered.

Of course we continued to be poor but it was not like Barn Lodge, ever again. The younger children had shoes and free dinners in school, and free books and free school. The older ones had jobs. Even Elizabeth had a job, in a hotel, for the season, which lasted in Portsmouth from May to October. There was no more kindling. We had coal on the fire. We had chips and spam, chips and sausages, chips and eggs, to eat. After a few years we took a holiday. A holiday! Three days on the Isle of Wight, staying in a boarding house overlooking Sandown beach, a long golden beach with striped beach huts, red and white, all along it, proclaiming its gaiety.

I can remember Elizabeth, watching Jimmy and Sally paddling in a red paddle boat around and around a blue pond on the seafront. The bunting fluttered in the breeze, a brass band in the fairground played 'It's a Long Way to Tipperary'. Elizabeth did not cry for joy, watching them. She smiled, she beamed with pleasure. She had become a little fatter. Her dress was a flowery summer print with a small waist and a flared skirt, and a rose nodded on the brim of her straw hat. That year she was forty-two, the best age for a woman to be, I have read somewhere – probably in a Sunday newspaper, where you read most things like that.

John worked from home for a while, with that wife of his whom I had never seen. 'You won't be able to phone me,' he said with a sigh. 'Not until I get fixed up. It'll only be a few weeks.'

'You can phone me.' I was exasperated. 'I hope you will.'

'Yeah,' he sighed again. And I knew what was going through his head. That it was time to stop, that he was going through a difficult patch, that I was becoming an extra burden, an unnecessary complication. I knew he was thinking that if I could not phone him, I could not expect him to phone me. I could no longer expect him to work at this old, tired, wrong relationship. It had reached the stage where it was all dependent on me. If I wanted it badly enough, and was prepared to take the responsibility for continuing it, it would continue. But if I flagged at all, it would end. I am sure that it is at this stage that mistresses pick up the phone and reveal all to wives, or otherwise arrange for a confrontation which would resolve the affair one way or another.

I was John's mistress. Like a lot of mistresses, he gave me carte blanche to do what I liked. Continue the affair or end the affair or tell his wife or don't tell his wife. I had the responsibility of the mistress to organise this thing as I wished, as long as I did not expect John to take the initiative in any way.

I loved him and I had all this power.

Also, I had Cyril.

I married Cyril when I was twenty-six and he was forty-four. I met him in the hotel where I worked at that time, in the bar. He drank fairly regularly and I became friendly with him. One evening I left work early and he followed me to the foyer of the hotel, which was in Southsea. We walked along the marina. It was June, warm and summery. Cyril wore tweed – even in June – and smoked that tobacco with a rose-leaf smell. Mixed with the smell of the sea, it is an intoxicating perfume.

He owned a big house, which he called a cottage, outside the city. When we married I stopped working in the hotel and spent my days in the house. I became a housewife. This was the first rest I had ever had in my life. Of course there had been short holidays. But now I was a married woman, a lady of leisure. I could get up more or less when I felt like it. My days were my own to fill as I pleased: the housework, the cooking, were harmless, easily achieved tasks for someone who had worked for as long as I had in one hotel after another, cooking or cleaning for dozens of people every day. I could not believe my good fortune.

I had not married Cyril for his money, but because I loved him. I had not realised what being his wife would mean. That just by marrying someone you could have all this freedom and leisure and beauty in your life came as a huge surprise. I felt like Cinderella. All my life I had had to work so hard for everything, and now I received so much more simply by virtue of being myself. And I was not even beautiful, not particularly, certainly not in the Cinderella sense.

Cyril thought so, though, or said so. 'God you are beautiful!' he would say, when I stepped out of my nightgown in the morning.

When he said that I believed him.

We hoped to have children, but we did not. After five years I took classes at a night school in Portsmouth, and then I took the part-time job in the bookshop. I did not need the job for economic reasons, and I was not bored at home. But I felt guilty, not going out to work. Cyril was in good health, but I fretted about him. I worried that he would die. He wanted me to take a course at the university, to develop and to enjoy my life. But I could not go too far along the road of personal pleasure. I had started working when I was fourteen. Somehow I could not permit myself to stop.

But I did not work hard. The bookshop was not like the hotels, and I loved to read. I spent many days at home, anyway, with Cyril, or with Elizabeth. She, too, had worked all her life after she came to Portsmouth. When I had been married for ten years she retired, however, and bought a small flat on the Isle of Wight. Sometimes I crossed the Solent to visit her, and walk with her along the hilly streets of Ryde, where the flat was. More often she visited me. We liked to sit in my garden, a dream of a garden, rich with fruit trees, with brilliant flowers, with butterflies and insects. We had hedgehogs sleeping under the fence, a fox crossed the terrace sometimes in the early morning. Elizabeth liked to sit on that same terrace and simply gaze around her. But she did not gaze for long. Two years after her retirement she died. Two years. Better than nothing.

In the hotel in Dublin there was a boy who did odd jobs around the place. He cut the grass on the patch in front, fixed the gutters when they leaked, took care of minor plumbing problems. He came from Kildare and walked with a slight limp.

'What happened to your foot?' I asked, when I'd become acquainted with him. He ate with me and Bertie in a room behind the kitchen.

'Nothing,' he bristled. He was a bristly, hedgehog sort of boy. He had scrubbing-brush hair and a big toothy mouth, which could sneer as well as beam.

'Excuse me!' I said. 'Have some queenapuddin'?' I was eating a big dishful. I loved queenapuddin' in those days.

'No thanks,' he bristled again, and rose to leave the table. 'I think it's digusting.'

'Don't mind him' – Bertie winked at me when he had gone – 'come here to me.'

I didn't want to, but I sat on Bertie's knee, as I had been doing for some time. He rubbed my breasts and other parts of me, under my clothes, and scratched my neck with his walrus whiskers. And what did it matter? What did it matter, I thought? It was just skin. It was just a body, my body, my body that I washed dishes with and scrubbed floors and wore out from dawn to dusk. Bertie caressed me, and nobody had caressed me before. Not for a long time, anyway.

But the boy with the limp changed my attitude to Bertie.

He was handsome, chunky. You could tell he'd always had enough to eat. And you could tell, I thought, that his mother had been kind to him. You could tell he was a pet from the way he behaved, as if he were someone to be reckoned with. Even though he was just the odd job boy, the lowest of the low, with no uniform and grubby clothes, he carried himself as if he owned the hotel.

I fell for him in a big way. He became my boy, and after that I did not want to be with Bertie. I did not want him to sing 'Lili Marlene', or anything, any more. Bertie saw what was happening and let me alone. Sometimes his eyes looked angry when he dried the dishes, but he did not annoy me about it.

I used to meet the boy from Kildare – he was John, he was the John I met later in the bookshop in Portsmouth – when I'd finished the evening's washing up. The light would be on, and sometimes Bertie stood under it, and sang 'Lili Marlene', slowly and ironically, with his arms extended like an opera singer.

John and I would leave and walk in the dark streets, lit by the eerie yellow light of the streetlamps. There were puddles of that light on the pavement, glittering through veils of rain. We huddled in doorways, down back lanes, kissing and cuddling. We'd stand for ages, but the time flew away very fast. That's what I remember most about those times, how there never was enough time, how he was always glancing up and saying, 'It's late, you've missed the last tram!', when I felt I had been with him for a few minutes.

After a while he said we should use a room. What he meant was a room in the hotel. The rooms were pretty. They were big, with wide, frilled beds, dressing tables with gilt mirrors.

It was not a poky commercial hotel but a good classy one. There were three lamps in every room, and red Turkish carpets on the floors.

The best rooms were often vacant and it was one of these we borrowed. I had a master key, as a chambermaid. It was so easy to slip up to the room after we'd left the kitchen that I was surprised I had not thought of it before – even when I was alone, it would have been convenient for me to sleep at the hotel, and who would ever find out? But I hadn't thought of it, because I had not John's adventurousness, or his confidence.

At first we did not stay all night. We'd stay for an hour or two and then sneak off at two or three in the morning. But as time went on we got bolder. We brought food to the room – biscuits and cakes. Bread rolls and butter. Bottles of stout.

'Room service for madam!' he'd say, bringing a tray to me, as I sat up in the wide bed.

'Thank you, Boots. That'll be all for now!'

I got caught. I was cleaning up after us, as I did, alone, every morning. It was five o'clock. The housekeeper, a rip from Rathmines, came in, and found me sweeping crumbs from the counterpane. She'd had her suspicions.

Of course I was kicked out. But John was not, even though the housekeeper must have known he was the man involved. Everyone did. But for some reason he was allowed to stay on, while I got the boot.

And that was when we went to Portsmouth, me and Elizabeth and all of us.

And in Portsmouth, I forgot all about John. Somerset Maugham says, in *Liza of Lambeth*, the first book I ever borrowed from the library in Portsmouth and read – one of my favourite books to this day – that nothing cures love like a journey across water. He might have added that good books help, too. In Portsmouth I forgot about John. Even when he wrote, which he did, once, I did not bother to reply.

When John left me the second time, I missed him a great deal initially. Later I learned that he had, indeed, opened a restaurant, out in Southsea. I could have called on him there but, of course, I had enough pride not to. After a while I didn't want to see him, anyway.

I missed him when I heard sad songs, or watched films with a love theme. Once, when I'd watched *Doctor Zhivago* on television, I telephoned him, but somebody else answered the phone so I said, 'Wrong number.' And after that I did not call him again. I was angry at him for not being like Doctor Zhivago. For not keeping me, his great love. But life is not like that, for people like me, people who ... what do I mean? Compromisers?

What I think is that life is like *Doctor Zhivago* up to a point – more like it than some would admit. People can have a great, passionate love. I have. Probably you have. But it doesn't seem to survive. One way or another it gets done in, either because you stay together or you don't.

That's what I think. If I were more loyal, or brave, or generous, perhaps it would be different. But how do you know if you are brave or just an eejit?

I am so much happier with Cyril. I have never told him about John, but I think he must know. I think he knows and I think he forgives me. And I love him for that. I love him for being there, for being kind, for giving himself to me. For marrying me and for trying to make me a lady of leisure, a princess in a garden. He asked me to spend my life planting bulbs, and walking along avenues overhung with the golden blossoms of easy living, the silver stars of a quiet conscience. Even if I can't accept that role, it is good to have been offered it.

THE SEARCH FOR THE LOST HUSBAND

The little white goat left her and went away.

But she got up out of her bed and went after him.

He moved far ahead of her. And she was worn and torn by briars and brambles as she followed him. But she crossed every kind of terrain, keeping him in view all the time in case she'd lose him.

And then the dew fell and evening came upon her and the little white goat was seeking the shade of the dockleaf and the dockleaf was eluding him, and the fox was going into his own small den.

Darkness fell on them. And the little white goat sat down on a tussock and waited for her.

'Why are you chasing me like this?' he asked.

'I can't help it,' she said. 'I'd follow you through fire and water.'

'You must stop following me,' he said. 'You must know that you'd be far better off going back home to your father.'

'Ah, I've no business at all going home to my father. It's you I should be with, because you are my man. And I will follow you anyway, no matter what you say.'

'You are tired out,' he answered. 'And what good does it do you to be chasing after me like this? You'd be far better off at home.'

HOT EARTH

BERNADETTE CLIMBS THE SHADY ROAD which links the modern outskirts of Perugia to the ancient hilltop town. In one hand she carries a brown briefcase containing photocopied handouts of a passage from *Dubliners*, and in the other, a large handbag made from undyed, yellowing leather, one of those handbags that looks like an old school satchel. Both are heavy and she has to keep moving them from one hand to the other – the traditional method of dealing with a double burden – and it works, temporarily at least. Her coat is uncomfortable as well: long thick black wool, much too hot for this part of the walk but right for the winds that whip smartly around the corners of the high, narrow streets up above.

Pale sunlight shakes through the trees, dappling the road with shivering silver, carefree-looking as the students who pour now from the Law Faculty building in a thick river, forming cliques on the path which impede Bernadette's progress. It is thin sun, faint and airy – thin, not because it is young, but because it is old. It is November. Even in Perugia, you know it.

Bernadette has lived here for four months. Quite often she feels like a young girl starting out on a big adventure – she feels as she did when she was twenty, overtly conservative and calm, but secretly fizzing furiously, a Bunsen burner of expectation and ambition. She had been certain that her future would be as dazzling as a jeweller's window. Her life spread before her, year after year, tray upon tray of luminous sapphires, rubies, emeralds. Clumps of lambent amber, rich with secluded life.

Now many of the years are behind her, and for her, years that are gone no longer glow, even the ones that had, in their time, a brilliant lustre. Sometimes, lately, Bernadette feels profoundly tired. She has begun to understand what being old will mean, to body and soul. What she seldom feels, however, is despair. The great troughs of youth, as well as its peaks, are past, apparently. On the whole, this is a welcome development.

Volterra was the site of her last youthful stand. For that is where she decided to take one final dramatic step, to smash the window and grab – something. And what was it? A bloodstone set in lava? A pearl in pewter?

A terrible mistake?

Volterra is another Italian town, another hilltop town, another Etruscan town, fifty miles away in Tuscany, more trim and menacing than Perugia, more viciously windswept, more violently coloured, more dangerous and combative in design. Bernadette visited it while on holiday a few years ago with James, her husband at that time – beloved, beloved, the word slips into her head – a shadow, treacherous, mocking and blaming.

They came from their coastal hotel to Volterra, to see the Etruscan museum. They parked their rented car on the ramparts of the town, and then wandered about until they found the surprisingly small building which housed the relics of the earliest inhabitants of the surreal place – those sly and compulsively defensive people who chose to build a city on the top of a fiery hill that looks as if it belongs on the far side of the moon.

The entrance lobby to the museum was grey and startlingly cool. It was cluttered with visitors, wearing bright tourist clothes and dark anxious expressions. Confusion peppered the dusty air, as in so many Italian museums. The hall recalled post offices and was redolent of dull pedestrian affairs. Far from evoking grand and ancient richness, it managed, contrarily, perhaps charmingly, to convey a discouraging impression of pettifogging seediness – shabby notes stuck on grills, narrow holes through which voices must channel their requests, slits for hands to steal through, delivering lire, receiving tickets. And not enough signs, not enough attendants, not enough information to cater to the tourist's need for spoon-feeding at every turn. Where and when and how much? the puzzled frowns asked. Why? responded the smooth Italian foreheads.

The place would close in half an hour for a board meeting, of all things, and wouldn't open until three o'clock. A coach party from Germany was up in arms. They'd driven from Florence and had booked a lunch in Sienna. The whole building seemed to shrug, Italians and Etruscans and pictures and artefacts and walls.

'Let's go in now anyway,' Bernadette said. Her face feigned disappointment. In fact she was glad. Half an hour would be more than sufficient, she was thinking. She didn't like museums. This was something she had never admitted to herself, never mind James, who was a curator in one in Dublin. Once, Bernadette had shared all his enthusiasm for bygones, but that time was past.

'Of course we must go in!' beamed James. He began to fiddle in his wallet for the twenty thousand lire admission, and then to count it out in notes and coins of tiny denominations while the woman behind the grill and the party of Germans looked on, willing to be entertained by a display of even the mildest eccentricity. Bernadette, who had seen James counting out coins before, turned her back on him, and examined a glass case full of reproductions of the little green emaciated figures the Etruscans liked to twist from bronze. The figures reminded her of toasting forks, and other things.

Everything tended to remind her of something else. She was – and is – a compulsive comparativist. Occasionally she tries to cure herself of the habit. She looks at a thing and says, 'It is itself. Just itself.' She urges her senses towards a realisation of the fact of the thing. With some it is easier than with others. Some items have more *Ichtikeit*, as the Germans, who have good words for obscure abstractions, put it: haystacks, for instance, or forks. Things with Germanic names. It is the things with borrowed names which tend to be like something else.

Bernadette had considered discussing this theory with James but had never got around to it. He tended to dislike speculation based on fanciful notions and limited information. Such an attitude was natural in someone of his profession. After all, the museum in Dublin was overrun with flamboyant speculators, high as kites on theories about Saint Bridget and Newgrange and the fairies, insistent on the latent spiritual magic lurking in every Bronze Age necklace and Celtic cross – certain that magic lurked not far under their own aura-blessed skin, an ancient powder waiting to be ignited by an expert the like of James. These people always had plenty of theories, but their knowledge, although also frequently plentiful, tended towards the chaotically selective. And so, in its own way, did Bernadette's. 'There are terrible gaps in your education,' James had often told her. 'Sometimes you'd be well advised to keep your mouth shut.' This remark was kindly meant. But after the first year or so of marriage she seldom received it in the right spirit.

The museum was deliciously cold, like William Carlos Williams's plums (oops, there I go again, thought Bernadette).

Its walls were alabaster, its floors paved with marble mosaic, criss-crossed with bridges made of raw wooden planks. You were not supposed to walk on the mosaics, which were museum items in their own right, not belonging to this old house but having been transported there from other, even older, places. People did walk on them, nevertheless, sidestepping the planks naughtily, or slipping off them by accident. The attendants turned a blind and weary eye.

The majority of the rooms were full to the ceilings with Etruscan tombs, chock-a-block with them. In one or two there were cases displaying the skinny sculptures, and in another an array of black vases, engraved with orange figures, as in Keats. James agreed with Bernadette on this. 'Yes. There would have been Greek influences. Greek, African, even Roman. Aren't they magnificent!'

He stooped lovingly over a case of the sculptures, a slender, classically handsome man, dressed in subdued shades of khaki. James was happier with this kind of art than with the fleshpots of Florence. He'd enjoyed reading about Michelangelo and Leonardo in Vasari's book, but he had been genuinely, if discreetly, unimpressed by the great works themselves. The statues had seemed too reproductive to him, plastic, a bit too obvious to be aesthetically interesting – those large, white, naked bodies, so realistic you could imagine they might step off their pedestals at any moment and shake your hand, or, preferably, thought Bernadette, do more than that. But since most of them were gay, that wasn't likely, as far as she was concerned.

James favoured stylised art: the rock drawings at Lascaux, slender Aztec carvings, Byzantine lozenges. In Italy, it was the Etruscans who attracted him, and not the Romans or the Italians. The Etruscan sculptures looked, faintly, like something a child of Greenland might have fashioned from a scrap of driftwood or walrus tooth. The Etruscan language was interesting because it is unintelligible. James was fond of difficult languages, minority languages, endangered languages. What could be better than a language that has been dead so long that its every meaning has been lost? If he had a dream it was that a Rosetta stone of Etruscan be found. And he would not have minded finding it himself, although he was too genuinely pure in spirit to nurture personal ambitions in connection with any matter of serious scholarly importance. 'It doesn't matter who finds it!' he said with a laugh, when Bernadette hinted that he would like to. 'Do you remember the name of the man who found the Rosetta stone?'

Bernadette didn't, although James did, and had told her the name often enough. She didn't remember, and yet she would have been glad if James's name became linked, for ever, to some great discovery. Even for him, she yearned, secretly, vulgarly, for fame and fortune and recognition, all things he would much rather do without. James was modest, exceptional, precisely brilliant, wearing his knowledge lightly as a feather. Bernadette was made of common, denser stuff, delph to his eggshell porcelain, farmyard duck to his ... snowy owl, arctic tern.

One of the commonplace characteristics of Italy that appealed to her was the reliable shining of the sun. She worshipped it and lapped it, like the sun-starved Irish peasant office girl who fried greasily in the pages of the agents' brochures, like the sun-starved Irish peasant office girl she was. Thus at midday she could usually be found stretched by the pool of the hotel where she and James were staying, letting the lovely beams beat relentlessly against her skin. In Ireland people worried constantly about ultraviolet rays and skin cancer, but this anxiety had not yet reached Italy. Everywhere on the beaches or by the pools bodies sizzled and roasted. Was it, pondered Bernadette, turning from her back to her stomach, that their skins were less vulnerable? Or was it that in a hot country like this some kind of censorship, imposed or organic, militated against the spread of anti-solar propaganda? What could they do about it anyway? They lived in the sun. If scientists decided that rain was carcinogenic, would Irish people be informed, or pay attention if they were?

Thus meandered Bernadette, in her meandering idle way, letting her thoughts straggle meaninglessly across worn old terrain, rubbing lotion into her skin, burning in the seductive rays, watching the swimmers glint under the pink acacia blossom.

Sometimes she speculated about Italy and the Italians, or about what she had seen and what she would like to see. She considered James, and his passionate love for artefacts from the Neolithic age, and his gentle, unthinking indifference to contemporary humanity. It seemed to her, basking in the heat, that they were now two different planets, Bernadette and James. Once they had been linked by irresistible gravitational pulls, now they spun helplessly farther and farther apart, powerless to stop the separation.

James did not lie in the sun. He was the other kind of person, one of those refined creatures who favour cloudy days, who like November, the kind of person who says 'the weather doesn't matter!', meaning it's tasteless to grumble about rain, sensible (rather than brave) to walk for miles with the mist skinning your face and steeping your bones in gloom and arthritis. While Bernadette burned in the midday sun, James sat at the dressing-table-cum-desk in their slender room, reading, planning expeditions to museums, marking maps. Sometimes he snoozed on the bed, and no doubt dreamed, but he revealed neither the snoozes or the dreams to her.

And Bernadette dreamed, too, not the drifting, spontaneous, disjointed dreams of the subconscious, but strategically planned daydreams, plotted entirely by her wide-awake and subversive mind. Even as she sealed her freckled body into a silver swimming suit, draped a white towel gracefully, toga-ishly, over her shoulder, she plotted. An hour by the pool, eyes closed, to let the other man of her life loose in her head. Give him the run of her. Anything could happen there, the red light a backdrop in her eyelids, the sun hot on her stomach, breasts, speckled, frazzled thighs. She talked to the man, told traveller's tales, cracked brilliant jokes. She stared at his face, fingered his bones, felt his skin hot against her cheek, the soft hairiness of his chin on her neck. She kissed him, sang to him, drove him through woods and forests, to shell-encrusted beaches. She made passionate and fulfilling love, wrestling with him on sand and grass, stone and feather, their bodies and the earth, represented by scraps of flora, blissfully at one. Karma, mandorla, paradise. Daydreams.

To an observer she was another reddening woman in a white swimsuit, sleeping like a lazy cat in the sunshine. Who would have guessed what was really happening during her mornings at the pool?

There was a slender reality at the root of the fantasy – his name was Kevin – but it was easy to forget the grubby nature of that reality in the unbelievable heat of the sun. She was able to forget the shabbiness, the subterfuge, the anxiety which had become the main features of her connection with him. She forgot its uncomfortable locations: crowded cafeterias, offices thorny with suspicion, street corners. She forgot the incredible, shameful, laughable lack of glamour that characterised the relationship – she could hardly call it an affair, since an affair conjures up an image of something much more exciting than egg sandwiches and coffee – the endless agonising about how it should be ended, which had been the main topic of conversation almost from day one. Even his wife, she forgot: his unfortunate, put-upon, betrayed wife (betrayed in Bernadette's view, though not in Kevin's, who agonised about that as well, but never reached a decision even about this abstract question, as he seldom reached a decision about anything). The wife. At first the thought of that woman's existence had filled Bernadette with dismayed resentment, with cold, not hot, jealousy. Even though she had a husband, even though she was – she believed – betraying a husband, she did not want Kevin to have a wife, or to talk about her.

But he did. Talk. She was mentioned slightingly, disparagingly, in the early days of the affair, later mentioned guiltily, latterly mentioned proudly, in tones of grave propietorship. My wife. My loyal and faithful wife. What had been faults, what had seemed dull and shameful and unsuccessful, had been transformed to virtues, alchemised by Bernadette the unfaithful. His wife gained in wifehood as Bernadette shrank to non-wife status, diminished and became nobody's wife. There is a scale in the affairs of men. At first you are worth your weight in gold, the balance is tipped entirely in your favour. But as time progresses you lose ballast, little by little by little, until finally you are swinging, high and dry, worthless as a bubble. And the other side gains proportionately.

She pushed all that aside. At the pool she was alone with her imaginings, in sovereign possession of the image unadulterated by the reality. She could enjoy the illusion without torturing herself with the hope that it would materialise. Sexual fantasies are always tinged with gloom. But the torturer's knives are much more active when the object of the fantasy is nearby. The purer the image, the pleasanter the dream.

The pleasanter, but the more vapid and transient, because the imagination, however wild and powerful, feeds on reality. The holiday wore on and Kevin became blotted out of Bernadette's mind. She tried to retrieve him but his image paled more every day, in the strong light of the sun, until by the end of the first week there was nothing left, apart from a white foggy spot on her mind. Her eyes stopped seeing red, her skin peeled, she soaked in the heat and the light and Kevin melted away.

At Perugia the Etruscan coffins are shaped like dormer bungalows, but in Volterra they are abstract, and look more like microwave ovens. They are carved from alabaster, the local stone, and decorated with friezes of fruit, leaves, slaves and dancers – usually an abundance, a host, of these things. On top of each box is a statue, representing the person whose ashes are deposited within. These statue figures recline like quadrupeds: their heads and shoulders are upright, while the rest of them flows along behind. This is an easy way to place a whole human figure on top of a box and still show the face clearly, Bernadette surmises – she is crafty, always vigilant for the tricks of any trade. But according to decent-hearted James, it is not just a convenient trick of the sculptors. The Etruscans did, in fact, spend a lot of time dossing around. They reclined while they ate, just like the Romans. They reclined while they were relaxing with friends. They reclined while they were conferring and plotting invasions and wars.

'Such a civilised habit!' says James.

'I suppose it would relax you,' agrees Bernadette.

But the faces on the supine bodies look anything but relaxed. They are stern and authoritarian, as uptight as any face attached to any body perched on a hard upright chair.

When Bernadette and Kevin first fell in love, they were perched on such chairs, in the office where they worked. He was in the same department of the civil service as she, in the same room. They had worked together for a year or so before they ackowledged, touching hands one morning, what their tender feelings were. Their eyes had often met before that morning, in understanding or friendship, sometimes in flirtation. Now they met in love. Such things happen, now and then, in offices and colleges and neighbourhoods and conferences, and nothing more transpires (except, perhaps, at the conferences). But fate ordained that this brushing of fingers would progress inexorably to its natural conclusion: two days later the annual office party took place.

In the next phase of the affair, the couple reclined a few times, in Kevin's car – an eight-year-old Toyota Starlet. On six occasions during that phase, which lasted a year, James went abroad to guard precious objects loaned to other museums, leaving Bernadette unguarded in their house, and once Kevin stormed the bastille, telling some story to his wife. (What? Alas, he refused to divulge the fascinating details to prurient Bernadette, schooled as he was in keeping officially secret practically every detail of his life.) They reclined for about half a voluptuous hour on the sofa in the living room. Kevin was too shy to go upstairs and so was she.

That visit marked the end of Phase Two.

Phase Three involved a reversal to perching – this time on bar stools. Kevin had been promoted and transferred to another office, coincidentally, naturally. He had not, of course, applied for the transfer. So why had he been moved? He did not know. Nobody knew – it was one of those official secrets.

They missed one another badly as office companions, because they had been good ones – cheering one another with jokes and with warm encouragement of their own efforts in every area of life, and with bizarre and exaggerated denigration of their worthless superiors, like all the best office mates – before the mischief started. There seemed to be no point in going to work in the morning any more, as far as Bernadette was concerned, and Kevin insisted that he felt just the same (although she knew differently, from the thin high tone his voice took when he made such protestations).

They continued to meet for a quick drink after work, or for lunch. But gradually the meetings became less frequent. Situations allowing intimacy, infrequent at the best or worst of times, never occurred at all now. They had not kissed one another even in the most perfunctory way in at least a year. Bernadette checked for bad breath about twenty times a day, and sometimes blamed that; sometimes the Christian Brothers who had educated Kevin. The wife, she thought, would have proved little deterrent to him if he'd really been interested.

Why he refused to make a complete break, Bernadette did not know. She knew it would probably be easier, and certainly more attractive to her moral conscience, limited as it was, not to see him at all. But some neediness, and some curiosity, kept her dangling, apart from her passion for his body, which she acknowledged as a simple fact of her being, but accepted as a cross she would have to bear. Usually it was not very heavy, and the less she saw of him, the lighter that particular burden became. By now she knew there were pieces in the jigsaw of the relationship which she was lacking. She could see what was in it for her: hope and despair, a diverting, if destructive, seesaw of excitement. But why would he want to keep the connection going?

'The most important one is in this room,' said James. Tall, laughing, light-hearted: the sight of him stooping under a transom filled her with guilt. Who could not love such an innocent genius of a man? She still loved him, and once she had been deeply in love with him as well. Bear it in mind, she said to herself sternly, feeling tears pricking the back of her eyes. Eternal love indeed!

The man she had vowed eternal love to, *one* of the men, unique, irrepressible, like nobody at all but himself, padded across a plank in the small room at the top of the house to find the main object of their visit.

The famous tomb, the David of the little museum, was one which contained the ashes not of one but of two people: an old married couple. Everyone came to the museum to admire this rare Etruscan monument to enduring marital love. But when they came to the sacred spot, the niche was empty. The tomb was not in its place. Instead there was a small photograph, showing the statue of the elderly pair (you could buy this photo, as a postcard, in the shop in the hall – if it ever opened). A note, handwritten in Italian on a scrap of lined paper, explained that it had been removed for a travelling exhibition.

'Gosh!' said Bernadette. 'They've gone on holiday. Imagine still having to go two thousand years after you've kicked the bucket!'

'Travelling exhibitions are a bad idea for more reasons than one,' muttered James, not listening to her. 'In the first place, they're bad for the material, and in the second, people who come to see a certain thing never see it at all . . .'

All the faces on the boxes looked the same. They all looked stern and haughty, perhaps because that's the way aristocrats felt they ought to look, as models on the catwalk look today. But the wife's face on the photograph was even more disapproving, disdainful, than the others. Disappointment was etched into its many tight lines, disappointment or suppressed anger. It was carved into her bones. She'd remained married until death and for two thousand years after, but what was hidden in the ashes that were touring the world? He'd probably been unfaithful all the time, with those dancing girls that flutter around all the tombs. Or dancing boys. They all did, didn't they? The Greeks, and the Etruscans, and the Romans.

And the Irish.

All after their own fashion.

★

Kevin was a successful and fairly powerful man – otherwise Bernadette would not have been attracted to him. But he was not the kind of man who worked too hard. He liked to describe himself as a 'people person'. 'What's life about, if it's not about friends?' he said, and Bernadette agreed wholeheartedly. What is life about, if it is not about talking, laughing, enjoying the here and the now? The companionship of one's warm-blooded, merry fellow human beings?

The friendship of women: Mary and Aoife and Orla and Cassandra and Lydia and Julianna. Lunch with the married ones and coffee with the busy ones and cosy nights in the pub with the single ones.

'Friendship, my arse!' swore Bernadette, aloud, breast-stroking through the pool. Nobody heard her. She said it into the lukewarm, chemically scented water.

There was a woman in the new office called Jacqueline. He mentioned her just once, in an offhand way, shyly. His voice was high and thin, as close to quaking as that voice would ever get. The missing piece, a girl called Jacqueline (he'd say woman, but Bernadette knew she was a girl). Bernadette burned with suspicion for a while, then stopped burning. Jacqueline was the unlucky one. She would be wet-blanketed too, in time, her fire put out by the milky watery mistiness which had enchanted her to begin with. Kevin was an Irish lover. He was a magic mist. He was a clump of emerald moss on a dark seashore rock, he was a soft day on the bog, he was a feminist, he was a friend, he was a mirage.

Bernadette drove in Italy, not James. James didn't care for the right-hand side. She was pleased enough – always happier driving than being a passenger – and she loved motoring along the country roads, across the low hills and the groves and the vineyards, as well as speeding along the autostrada being honked at by irate Italians (because she never speeded enough for their high standards).

Corn was the crop in the Volterra district, not grapes or olives. The landscape there was dry and burnished, the predominant colours reddish–gold and terracotta. It reminded her of Egypt, Carthage, or Africa, rather than of Europe. Volterra had flame red walls like the edge of a volcano. Spiralling up the baking road, round and round, round and round, with the hell-toned walls looming, Bernadette felt her head grow dizzy and her stomach turn. Turreted, flaming, it looked like an illustration to Dante's *Inferno*.

Bernadette held James's finely boned hand as they stepped from the chilly museum onto the grey street, which was cool and breezy. The milky face of Kevin was in her mind, brought there by her irritation at the tomb of the married couple. He glared at her from a street corner, a remonstrating Saint Paul, a disappointed Moses. A snow cloud, thick and white and deadly. Let me go, his icy stare says. Let me off the hook.

She could let him go. If she did, she would not have his Irish ghost shivering in her head. She wouldn't get a cold shiver in her heart when her husband grasped her hand, a shiver caused by guilt and sorrow in equal portions.

Suddenly she longed to be at the equator. Next year she would go to Africa. She would feel the sun at its strongest, she would feel what it could do. They came to the ramparts of Volterra and looked over the cooked red slopes, the fields of burnt corn. It was like Africa but it was not Africa. Imagine the Sahara. Imagine plains of parched gold grass. Imagine the golden lion, the dark skin. Bernadette wanted to be black. She wanted to be black in Africa at midday on Midsummer's Day. She wanted to be the Sahara.

★

But she was an Irish office girl. The land of compromise was where she thrived. So she did not go where she longed to go, to Africa. Instead, some months after her return to Dublin she ran back to Italy, which was familiar, and closer to Africa than Dublin was. To Perugia she came, softly grey, seated in the hills of Umbria, green and gold and red and ochre. Milk and honey, mist and sun.

It still stuns her that she was able to do such a thing. It stuns her that once she decided to do it, it was so easy. Running away. Disappearing. It seems so daunting, but all you have to do is pick up your bag and walk, and still people put it off for whole lifetimes. They believe they cannot do it.

She lives alone in a small apartment out on the highway to Rome, and teaches English for twelve hours a week. She earns just enough money to pay the rent and buy food, and lives the life of a governess of slender means in a novel by Henry James, the circumscribed life of a poor female expatriate.

She is not twenty. She is not even a Henry James style governess, in a shabby hat, with youth and beauty, canniness and high hopes and a clean record on her side. And even in this lovely place life is not a window in a jewellery shop. But the town is perfect, and is surrounded by other perfect towns, a perfect landscape. It is a landscape which she remembers from her childhood, because it formed the backdrop of so many of the religious oleographs which hung on her parents' walls. The virgin with upturned eyes against the green hills of Umbria. The Sacred Heart of Jesus plonked on the terracotta walls of Assisi. Or somewhere similar.

James, honest, decent James, visits her from time to time, and does not remonstrate. He laughs, rather kindly, at her change of direction. He considers it typical of her, and believes she will one day, soon, change her mind again and return with him to Dublin. To her surprise, he was able to forgive her, rather easily. His love was loyal and enduring, if not very passionate. Probably it is loyal and enduring for that reason.

Kevin left her mind on that day in Volterra. That was the last she'd see of him, she thought. But a few times he has returned on flying visits. She sees him flitting across an archway, glancing over his shoulder, surprised that she should have finally broken free. She sees him grinning from the belly of a gargoyle that coils into a ruby window in a church. She sees him and his wife on a bed in Dublin, reclining, arm in arm, stern and serious, smiling – accusing, disdainful, proud, immutable, stone, marble.

Married.

THE SEARCH FOR THE LOST
HUSBAND

'Since you insist on staying with me,' the little white goat said,
'I'll give you some advice. Do you see that small house down
there in the valley?' He pointed to a house. 'You go down
there and ask for a bed until the morning. And I'll wait up here
for you until you return. And if they don't welcome you and
won't give you the night's lodging, tell them you are a friend
of the little white goat, and then you'll be welcome.'

She went down to them and asked for shelter until morning. But the woman of the house did not want to give it to her.

'Wisha,' said the girl, 'I am a friend of the little white goat.
He told me I would be welcome here.'

'You should have told me that at first,' said the woman of
the house. 'Any friend of his is a friend of mine. You are more
than welcome to stay here for the night.'

The girl sat down. And she was given food and drink and a

bed to sleep in. And when morning came she was given a good breakfast.

And when she was about to leave the woman of the house gave her a comb. And when she combed her hair with this comb, she got the most beautiful golden hair that ever a young girl had.

She thanked the woman for the comb and went back to the little white goat.

'You should give up now,' he said, 'while you still have a chance.'

'I will not give up,' she said. 'I will follow you for ever.'

He set off again and she followed him. He took the hardest route, going through every bit of bramble and thorn and briar that he could find, in order to force her to give up.

And she was torn and worn by briars until the dewfall and night came upon her, and the little white goat was seeking the shade of the dockleaf and the dockleaf was eluding him, and the fox went into his own small den, small blame on the gentle fox.

And he sat down on a tussock and waited for her.

'There is a house down there in the glen,' he said. 'And you go down there and look for a night's lodging. If they don't welcome you, tell them you know the little white goat.'

She went down to the house and asked for the night's lodging. And they didn't give her much of a welcome.

'Oh, if you please,' she said. 'The little white goat told me to come here. I am a friend of his.'

'Any friend of his is a friend of ours,' said the woman of the house. 'You are welcome, for the sake of the little white goat.'

She got food and drink and a bed to sleep in. And when she got up in the morning they gave her her breakfast. And when she was leaving the woman of the house gave her a pair of golden scissors.

'Here's a nice little pair of scissors for you,' she said. 'And when you cut those old rags you have on you now with these scissors, you will have the finest dress a young girl ever wore.'

The girl thanked her and went back to the little white goat. And he was waiting for her. That was the second day.

'Ah, go on home,' he said. 'Go on home to your father and your mother. Do me a favour and leave me alone.'

'I have no intention of going near my father or my mother,' she replied. 'I've decided to follow you and that's what I'm going to do. It doesn't matter what you say or where you go, I'll stay with you.'

'It's a fool's errand,' he said. 'Nothing will come of it. I'd far rather you left me in peace.'

SPOOL OF THREAD

FIFTY PER CENT OF FEMALES PRACTISE ENDOGAMY. That leaves fifty per cent who are adventurous, liberated and verging on the foolhardy in their socio-sexual explorations. That fifty per cent is for me.

I do not mean to imply that half the women of Ireland mate with their third cousins. Clearly this is not the case. But half of them go out with the boy next door, or their friend's older brother. Their husbands – or 'partners', as they are nowadays called – are somebody they met at a tutorial in first honours English, or who played squash with their gay friend in media studies. When these women have affairs – and they do, a shocking number of them do – it is with some colleague whom they have courted with exceeding caution for two years behind the filing cabinet, or with an old flame from school or their next door neighbour's husband.

They do not know what they are doing. They do not know that they, while seeming to make a string of tough, liberated, individualistic choices, are conforming to the tradition of a hundred conformist centuries. They do not know that every time they kiss a man they are obeying, not an irresistible personal impulse, but an atavistic law which was written in the cells of their blood ten thousand years ago.

And what are the others, the other fifty per cent, up to? Going to discos. Attending nightclubs and designer bars. Trying out single's safaris to Greenland. These are the women for the brief encounter and the ship passing in the night. It is among their number that you will find the few who yearn for – to paraphrase the immortal and vulgar phrase of a contemporary sexual connoisseur – the zipless fornication. (*Porn* and *forn*, are they related? Is this another example of the linguistic phenomenon known as Grimm's law, or is it a coincidence?) Within this group you find the girls who are pregnant at fifteen and grandmothers at thirty, the dizzy, bubbly ones who marry men they have known for two weeks, the crazy beauties who love at first sight. This is the fifty per cent who may end up living in a garret or a palace, who give it what they've got and do it their way, who *regrettent rien*, except perhaps their latest man. (The earlier men are always blurred by rosy mists, their dastardliness blunted by the swift progress of frenetic years.)

These women are not uglier or more desperate than the others. In fact they are usually much more attractive than the cunning Lindas. Not always but often. Beauty confers upon them confidence and courage; it renders them cheeky and assertive. Most exogamists are beautiful.

Well, that's my theory of the moment. A thought for today. You may not like to speculate and generalise about social and sexual mores. You may, sensibly, consider all speculation to be worthless and a waste of time. But I have always enjoyed my own thoughts and loved to linger, when I have moments of tranquillity, in the shady groves of my personally evolved philosophies. And of my unique sociologies, and psychologies, and criminologies. It is a harmless form of entertainment. A great deal more harmless than some of my other habits.

Have you ever wondered where disappearing women disappear to?

You know who I am talking about.

Monica Frawley left home at eight p.m. last Wednesday. She caught the eighty-four bus from Cabinteely to Dublin. When last seen she was wearing a black sweater and black skirt and a dark blue jacket. Anyone with information, please phone the *gardaí* at Cabinteely Garda Station.

Guards at stations like that don't investigate serious crimes. Nowadays that is up to detectives. Specialisation affects everything. If variety is the spice of life, a policeman's life is not as happy as it once was. But the local *gardaí* are still permitted to take telephone calls about disappearances, or rapes or murders, and pass the data on to the experts. It is better, perhaps, than nothing.

I digress. A bad habit, but one of a number to which I am, I should confess before you listen to me any longer, addicted.

What happened to Monica?

You might see her, in your mind's eye, catching the bus, stepping on and handing over her fare to the bus driver, who doesn't grant her the favour of a single glance. His eyes are focused on the coins she gives him and on the little stacks of coins in his coin machine. He, for one, will have no information to give the *gardaí* at Cabinteely Station.

There she is, stepping off the bus, her face taut with terror, a man close behind her with the point of a knife pressed into her blue jacket. The rest of the knife is, you know not how, concealed up his sleeve. What sort of a face has this man? Oily black hair, dark shadows on his chin. A grim pugnacious pout (are you perhaps recalling a poster of Elvis Presley?). He is probably dressed in black, too, possibly an old black leather jacket and shabby blue jeans. Trainers. A shabby, sulky, resentful type.

Or you see Monica, long descended from the bus, strolling down a dark Dublin street, alone, with her head carelessly carried aloft. It could be Pearse Street, at the Westland Row end. It could be Grand Canal Street or Parnell Street or North Great Georges Street, or any of those hundred dark, ill-lit, shadowy ways with which Dublin is bountifully blessed. Upper Mount Street. The black leather arms emerge, rapidly, from behind a hoarding (there is always hoarding in these places), or from the door of a dilapidated lodging house. The thuggish hands clamp themselves over Monica's wretched mouth. She is pulled roughly into a deep dark place.

Or perhaps the best you can rise to is a dubious-looking creature attempting to lift a huge sofa into a Hi-Ace van. (This image you have taken from a movie. The sources of your other imaginings are not so obvious but they are probably equally unoriginal. The imagination is the world's most respected thief.) Monica, kind and considerate Irishwoman that she is, offers to help this dangerous-looking stranger. He says, 'Get into the truck, it'll be easier.' Monica has never entered a Hi-Ace van before in her life, but on this occasion she conveniently and meekly obeys.

The rest is Hollywood.

Will anyone with information please . . . ?

It is dark where the Monicas have gone. They go to a place deep in the earth. A cellar. A dried-out well. A cavern far under the city's surface. Down through the trap door they have been dragged, to a place as deeply mysterious as the gloomy interior of your sleeping head. To a place as wickedly secret as the nearest Disney fairy tale.

It is easier than that. And less clichéd.

I just go to a club.

I don't have a favourite haunt. Favourite haunts are not a good idea if you are a professional stranger. But it is not difficult to frequent a varied circuit of night spots in Dublin nowadays, and, in truth, my visits need not number more than, say, half a dozen annually. Often they are much less numerous, much much less. The quantity of my visits is so low because their quality is so high. I have a sixty per cent success rate. I am drawn, like W.B. Yeats, by the fascination of what is difficult. But not too difficult. Note the discrepancy between my earlier statistics on exogamy and endogamy and my personal success rating. Let me remind you that it is ten per cent. Deduce what you will.

My own theory is that the ten per cent could be accounted for by my body. I am no ghoul to look at. Indeed, the opposite is the case, and, of course, my task would be very much more difficult if I did not present a perfectly attractive appearance to the world. That is not to say that I am Robert de Niro or ... well, is there anyone else? Hugh Grant, perhaps. I am not like them. Looking like them is as disadvantageous as looking like the hunchback of Notre Dame. If you met me in the supermarket – and you might. I shop in Dunne's Stores. Not Superquinn. I have Superquinn tastes but I am not a snob. I am happy to indulge those tastes at Dunne's Stores prices. As you undoubtedly are, too – if you met me at the ice-cream freezer, searching for my favourite lemon sorbet, or browsing among the New World wines, examining all the lovely labels, Jacob's Creek and Oxford Landing, Pearl District and Malpo Valley, you would think, he is just ordinary. An ordinary nice guy, convinced, like so many others, that if he browses long enough among the seductive green bottles, he will discover a good one that is cheap.

And you would be right. The fact is, ordinary nice guys are not so ordinary. Just look at the others in the store – seedy, or old, or scruffy, or sulky. Too thin or too greasy-haired or too angry or too smooth. I am almost the only ordinary nice guy you will find. Not too tall and not too short. Not too untidy and not too neat. Clean as a pin, but not ostentatiously so.

I am not going to give you a closer description, for obvious reasons. Believe me, you may meet me, but you will not know who I am. I will smile at you, swiftly and kindly. I will make a very brief tasteful joke about the wine or the ice cream. If you drop a tin of cat food, I will lift it up for you and refer humorously to kitty, and you will think, what a charming, kind man. You will not recognise me, even after this.

I have blue eyes. That is all I will tell you. The best kind. Also, by far the most common.

Last time I went to a place called Pinkie's, a club which is attractive to older women. Older women are the women for me. They are, of course, more flabby. But I prefer flab to anorexia with its invariable accompaniments – frigidity and a large gang of friends. With flab comes sexual maturity, lust, and, not more but certainly equally important, vulnerability.

Veronica (not her real name) was alone. This is vital. If the woman is not alone, or if you find out, too late, that she is not alone, you must capitulate immediately, no matter how tempting it is to complete your assignment. Friends are your enemy. I mean, of course, female friends; you will not usually make the mistake of initial moves with a woman who has a male friend on the premises. The woman has to be entirely unaccompanied.

Veronica was sitting at a table for two in the bar. She was looking like a woman whose friend has just gone for a moment to the toilet, or who is dancing, but, luckily, there was no friend. (This is an area in which you can err. Check the table for signs of a second glass, and the seat for a garment or a handbag, before you make your move. But there is no foolproof way to detect solitariness with the naked eye exclusively. Forbearance is necessary. If I make a mistake, I simply escape from the situation politely and quickly, and start from scratch.)

ca was drinking a pint of lager – how I wish I could

say a Daiquiri, but this is Dublin. She was on her third pint. I could tell from the bulge of her stomach under her black lycra dress. It was unsightly but it would disappear, more or less, overnight.

Veronica was what I would describe as *jolie laide*, and that is by far the best type. She had a good figure, beer bulge apart, and a good head of chestnut hair (achieved with the help of a friendly dye called Conkers). Her dress, as I have mentioned, was black and hugely flattering to her pale complexion. She relieved its plainness with goodish silver jewellery. What gave her away and let her down were her bad legs, lumpy and thick-ankled, revealed by her too-short dress, and her red shoes. Mutton. Mutton.

Her face was made up in the too-careful way of the not quite pretty. She had lovely eyes, large and grey, soft, limpid. But her mouth was thin and her nose left plenty to be desired. Why don't women with salaries get those noses changed? Tradition, I suppose. They are so frightfully traditional in all their habits.

I sat beside her, saying as I took my seat, 'May I?'

'All right.'

Of course she said that. They always do. They are there, in the nightclub, waiting to be joined by complete strangers. By anyone. That is what nightclubs are for. It is extraordinary, when you think about it, but there you are. I did not invent nightclubs.

'Can I get you something?'

'No. Not yet please.'

Not yet.

I ordered a drink from one of the perky little girls in red dresses that serve in Pinkie's.

'I'm Ciarán,' I said. Not my real name. Never use your real name. It's bad for your style, apart from anything else. And let me give you one good tip. Always use an Irish name. I mean a name *in* Irish, a Gaelic name. Almost anyone will trust you then. They may be exogamous, your little friends, but even they will have certain endogamous prejudices. Try calling yourself Hans or Jacques and you'll soon see what I mean. But a Colm or a Cathal will get away with murder.

'I'm Veronica,' she said, smiling broadly. Half-shot already. Oh God, how easy this one was.

'Nice club' – I waved at the floor – 'I don't go to clubs much myself as a rule. But it is almost Christmas.'

'I'm the same myself.'

'Are you married?'

They like this, even though they very seldom are. Married men go to nightclubs but not married women. I have many theories as to why this is so, but I will not digress further at this gripping plot point.

'Separated. Divorced, maybe, soon.'

'That's a coincidence. I am, too. I've been separated for six years.'

'It's a long time.'

'Yes. The marriage was very short lived, I'm afraid. One of those things.'

'Everyone can make a mistake.'

'Even in Ireland. If it weren't for the anti-divorce lobby.'

We were away. The wife-swapping sodomites, the Family Values brigade. It is an ideal topic, an ideal type of topic for Stage One of the conversation. Political and sexual at the same time. Impersonal and intimate. Ostensibly pure as the driven snow but full of opportunites for innuendo and teasing sugges-tiveness. Few topics are so ideal, but of course the referendum will not last for ever. You must exercise your discretion and imagination. Princess Di is a good standby if nothing more original is available. Overt sexual scandals in Ireland are not, however, tactful, and neither is anything to do with abortion. Paedophile priests are all right at the moment but I believe that it is a fad which will fade.

It isn't always easy to initiate Stage One but if you are intelligent you will manage. It can also be borne in mind that females are less critical than you might think. Princess Di, so boringly unoriginal, is fine with them. So many of the women you meet will have little familiarity with any other current topic, anyway, and I have seldom met one who does not have a hundred opinions on the good princess's face, nose, hair, morals, bulimia and role as an ambassador for the British Empire. This interest is shared by women right across the social spectrum, from hairdressers to senior civil servants and university lecturers. I have been using the Princess of Wales for ten years and have every faith in her longevity as a topic of conversation. She has good bones and self-discipline. She will certainly outlast my need for her.

After twenty minutes on divorce and Di I bought her a drink – yet another pint. That stomach! She was utterly reckless, poor Veronica. An outward sign of an inward lack of self-esteem. Their bodies theirselves.

When you have bought them a drink you can progress to Stage Two.

I brushed a fleck (of spat-out beer) from her shoulder and asked: 'What kind of house do you live in?' And I added, to clarify my question and to encourage her, 'Is it an old house or a new house?'

She glanced at me very briefly with a tiny, tantalising, suspiciousness, and then launched forth. 'Well, it's about thirty years old. It was built in the sixties . . .'

The house is one of the very best Stage Two topics for women over the age of thirty, always providing, of course, that they have a house. Or a flat. If they have not, you may find it easier to talk about their job at Stage Two, but that is very much less satisfactory, and is actually halfway between a Stage One and a Stage Two topic type.

Veronica chatted for about half an hour, telling me about her house, her sofa, her wallpapers, her Iranian rug and her Turkish rug, her plans for a conservatory. Her cat.

A dance. Sometimes I almost forget to dance, so engrossed are we in conversation.

One close, long dance. Her body was warm and pudgy and feminine, its every secret revealed by the thin fabric of her dress. I held her tight.

And so to the second drink.

Then it is time to talk about clothes and body. Stage Three and Stage Final. Not the dress she is wearing. Women are un-critical but not moronic. Clumsy compliments will distance rather than attract them, at this as at all stages.

'Do you wear black often?'

As if they didn't all wear black all the time! I'd love to be able to ask, 'Do you wear yellow often?', but your females, my females, will not wear yellow at all, ever. They will wear black. With, possibly, a blue coat, but only if you are lucky. Mostly the coat when you finally see it is black, too.

'Well. I don't know. Quite a lot, I suppose.'

They usually say something like that. Something which im-plies they fling on whatever they find at the end of their bed, and which does not imply that they have spent a small fortune and a sinful amount of time choosing yet another boring black dress.

'It suits you well.' That's much better than 'very well'. 'Suits you well' sounds Irish and of the earth. It goes with the Ciarán. Please remind yourself from time to time that you are a Ciarán. If you do not remind yourself, you will certainly forget, and behave like a Jacques or a Hans, which, of course, you are at heart, no matter what your real name. But do not make this mistake if you mean business. 'But they say it is worn by women who are mourning for something. Who are . . . sad . . .'

'I just think it's easy to wear. It's handy. And . . .'

The big eyes open.

'I feel safe in it.'

'What sort of clothes do you wear normally?'

Jeans at home, suits at work, dresses for parties. Yes, yes. Ask anyway. You are merely paving the way.

'What sort of nightgown do you have?'

I said this to Veronica. But I would not try it with everyone. You must judge the specific situation, sum up the character of your victim. I was almost sure that Veronica would accept this final stage of Stage Three – and by accept, I mean, not tolerate but enjoy. Love. Veronica, I guessed, was the kind of woman who would get wet between the legs talking to a man – a man who looks like me – about nightgowns, pyjamas, bras and panties (once you slip in the nightgown, you are on your way – she is yours). She was the kind of woman who is turned on by language, especially the language of lingerie. There are plenty of them out there.

But there are also plenty of the other type. One mention of personal linen and they will vanish like Cinderella and her uncomfortable slippers. All your work will have been in vain.

We left Pinkie's at five past one.

Veronica didn't have a car. She had planned . . . well, what do they plan?

I have a car.

I stole it two years ago from a driveway in Shankill. A five-year-old grey Toyota. Five years old is good; Toyota is good. Remember, Ciarán, you are not a young blood fired by a desire for one-upmanship. The latest BMW is not for you. Your taste and aims are complex.

She demurred about the lift. This is always a moment of acute suspense. And there is absolutely nothing you can do to render it less dramatic. When she goes into that cloakroom you are in the lap of the gods. She may emerge as trusting and trapped as when she went in. Or she may not emerge at all, at least as far as you are concerned. She may, crouched over the bowl, or prinking at her vanquished visage in the glass, change her mind and embrace self-preservation.

Veronica came back, smiling. 'I think I'll take a taxi,' she said.

I hid my disappointment as best I could.

'After all –'

You win some, you lose some.

' – I don't want to take you out of your way.'

'Whatever you think best, Veronica,' I said.

Never try too hard.

A week to Christmas. A quarter past one a.m. White frost. The sky was velvet, a glorious, darkly Prussian blue. Electric blue stars twinkled all across it like a thousand diamond bracelets, and closer to our nudging heads Christmas baubles sparkled. Graceful people with smiling faces glided up and down the street like dancers on ice. Droves of taxis flashed past, festive and merry as taxis appear late at night a week before Christmas.

Festive, merry and full.

Poor poor Veronica.

Last seen wearing a black skirt and a blue jacket.

Wrong.

Veronica had a coat. Blue wool and cashmere, bought at the BT sale in January. A year ago now. Before they moved across the street and disembowelled themselves.

I should know.

You might ask, why? I could have slept with her and let her

go. It happens sometimes.

If they fall in love with me, I let them go. They stay with me for a week or two, or longer. They cook my meals and pleasure my beautiful body, and then I give them their walking papers.

The *gardaí* at Cabinteely are told that Monica went on holiday. They shrug and there are a few days of embarrassment. That is all.

And if I fall in love with them, they don't reappear. They become a xeroxed picture on a railway ticket office. They become a prick in the conscience of the city, a moment of anxious pity in the helter-skelter of the working day. They become a statistic in a newspaper.

You would like me to pause on the threshold, hand on the knob, and turn to you. You would like me to profer the explanation. When I was eight my kitten was crucified by my father. When I was ten the parish priest raped me. My long black soutane swung, the censer swung and the Gothic chapel filled with the smell of incense. And I felt his powerful eyes upon me and I dropped the golden boat of oil. My mother beat me black-and-blue and then she died when I was eleven and I lived in a cold grey orphanage in the middle of a bog.

But I am not going to pause on the threshold and explain all. I do not feel like explaining. I do not know how to explain, with words, why I do it. My life is spent thinking and listening, and, only very occasionally, doing. But I have no words to explain what I do, although I have often sought after such words. Perhaps there is a place in my head where words cannot reach?

Stand there yourself, with your hand on the door knob. Imagine what I am. Imagine why I do it.

Stand on the threshold to the dark labyrinth of human nature and use your own imagination.

(And don't forget your spool of thread.)

THE SEARCH FOR THE LOST HUSBAND

But she persevered. She followed him that day, too.

And he made it very difficult for her. He went through every bit of bramble and briar and thorny glen. And she was worn and torn. And the dew fell and night came down upon her, and the little white goat sought the shade of the dockleaf and the dockleaf eluded him and the red fox went into his own little den, small blame on the gentle fox.

And the little white goat sat down on a tussock and waited for her.

'You're not going home?' he asked.

'You should know that by now,' she replied.

'You've no sense,' he said. 'There is a house down there. And you go down there and ask for shelter. And I'll wait for you until morning. But this is the last time I'll do that for you.'

'Thanks very much,' she said.

She went down, and she told the woman of the house that the little white goat had sent her. So she was made very welcome, and given food and drink and a bed for the night.

And when she got up she noticed three little boys playing about the house. She couldn't take her eyes off them, they were so lovely.

'What are you gawking at?' asked the woman of the house. 'Why are you staring at my children like that?'

'Ah, I don't know,' she said. 'I've no special reason to look at them. No. But I think they're very nice. They are very nice children.' She looked at them again. 'I don't think I've ever seen three such beautiful children.'

'Well stop looking at them now,' said the woman. 'Good day to you.'

Before she went the woman gave her a tablecloth. And when this cloth was spread out all kinds of food and drink appeared on it, plenty to eat and drink.

And she went back to him.

'Very good,' he said. 'But this is the end. I won't wait for you any more. It's over. And you accept that now and go home to your father and your mother, and forget all about me.'

'I will not,' she said. 'I will follow you, through fire, through water, through ups and downs, through thorns and brambles and briars and ditches. I know we will be able to settle down together somewhere, somehow. I will not give up.'

That's how it was.

SWISS CHEESE

The most potent weapon the colonisers of America had was disease. They wiped out more native Americans – Red Indians is what Clíona actually calls them – with the smallpox than with gunpowder, which is saying quite a lot. The Innuit suffered a similar fate, though not intentionally, when the Danes landed in on them: one tubercular Dane sneezed and down they dropped in their thousands. No immunity.

No immunity.

Why is Clíona thinking about diseased Red Indians? She doesn't know. For the past year her mind has been visited irregularly by stray pieces of information, by ideas which pop from her memory or subconscious for no apparent reason, other than that she has been on daydream drive for much of that time. She is losing touch with what happens outside the confines of her own head; her mind is unfocused. This is not the same thing as being unhinged, but it comes close enough.

The door creaks as she swings into the pub, and she winces, suspecting some malicious motivation – on the part of the door, yes, or even the hinge. To confirm her paranoia, everyone looks up and stares at her as she walks inside and lopes around the room, glancing as discreetly as she can at all the tables and bar stools and snugs and niches, her eyes trying to look nonchalant as they search, search, search. Women take a good long look, examining the cut of her pink jacket and the length of her short skirt. Men gaze brazenly at her face, then her legs. Clíona knows that they subject every single woman who walks into the pub to the same treatment, but in her present mood she takes it as an affront and a punishment.

It is a pity Paddy can never come on time, but never. It would be so much easier if she could simply walk into a place like this, catch sight of him drinking a pint at the bar, and simply join him. Men do not stare for long at a woman who is with a man, a woman who is part of a public heterosexual unit. A woman alone is quite a different story, mysterious and provoking, at least if she is young or halfway attractive.

To pass some time Clíona goes to the cloakroom to check over her face and hair. She is tall, very slim, graceful. Her face is oval with intensely regular features: it is the kind of face you see on the cover of women's magazines, and indeed, Clíona has, in her past, done a bit of modelling. Her skin is smooth and unwrinkled, except at the corners of the eyes, so that she doesn't need to wear make-up. And as a rule she doesn't, except when she is meeting Paddy. Then she puts on some eyeliner and mascara, to enlarge her blue eyes, and softens her lips with a lipstick called Plum Blush. It wears off soon after it has been applied, although it is supposed to last 'All Day', so she puts on a bit more now, enjoying the sticky slither of it across her lips. Its taste appeals to her, too, that special lipstick flavour, sweet and mildly poisonous. It makes her feel tougher and more female than before: there is truth in the war paint sobriquet. Maybe that is why she uses cosmetics for Paddy – not only to enhance her appearance, but to aid her in battle. She needs all the help she can get.

She knows, anyway, that it is her hair rather than her face that attracts him. So he told her, in the early days of the relationship. 'Your hair is so incredible!' he said. 'I have never seen anyone with hair like that. I mean, I never never want not to be able to see it!' Her hair is white, completely white, and has been like that since she was nineteen. (At first she used to dye it back to its original blond, her mother forced her to. But when she got married she stopped doing that.) It is thick hair, and she wears it in a simple, fluffy bob, with a thick soft fringe flopping down to her eyebrows. In combination with her neat features, this white hair suggests that Clíona has lived a wholesome and serene life. Her looks are those which could be associated with rare, beautiful nuns, or statues of the Virgin.

These looks have served Clíona well, not only in matters of love, where good looks are less important than people sometimes believe, but in her career, where they can matter. She has had her modelling job, and several well-paid, rather exciting positions in public relations. Three years ago she was appointed as special assistant to a government minister, one of the women who won Dáil seats in the spate of feministic good will which followed the election of Mary Robinson as president of Ireland. Many envy Clíona her good fortune, and her good job. She loved it herself at first.

She spends five minutes in the cloakroom but when she returns to the pub Paddy still has not arrived. She gives it one more encompassing glance but hasn't the courage to do the full tour again. Then, abruptly, with a lack of deliberation which is totally alien to her true character, she sits down at the first empty table she can see. It is plonked right under the television set. The six o'clock news is on and a few dozen eyes are directed at the newsreader and by extension at Clíona.

To block them out she opens her *Irish Times*, which she has already looked at many times today, since reading newspapers is part of her job. 'Clinton Says No To Peace Talks' is the headline. It is 1992. Gerry Adams, president of Sinn Féin, cannot be interviewed on either Irish or British television. He is *persona non grata* (to put it politely) to Clíona's minister, to her party, to most of the members of Dáil Éireann. The idea of a ceasefire by the IRA would be greeted with derisive disbelief by them, as by most people in Ireland, England, even, apparently, the United States. Clíona belongs to the class of Dubliner who despises violence and terrorism as a matter of principle, and loses no opportunity to say so. She also belongs to the class who find the Troubles in the North an embarrassment and a bore, more like bad breath than won't go away than anything more painful, such as toothache. It is a silly inconvenience. She wishes they would stop, but she has forgotten why they started and hardly cares.

She turns the page and reads an article which interests her much more than academic discussions of a peace which will probably never happen. The article is about a film star, a man who has married for the fifth time. His fourth wife learned about the fifth marriage in the *New York Times*. His third wife, interviewed on the networks, said that he had ended the relationship with her by sending her a fax. (What did he say in the fax? She didn't say, or at least it wasn't mentioned in the *Irish Times*. Maybe she'd forgotten, although it was only two years ago and you'd probably remember the contents of a fax like that. 'Sorry it didn't work out. I love you. Be in touch.') The report, which was headed 'Genius or Rat', universalised the experience of these wives and women (there were girlfriends on the trail as well, ones who hadn't made it to the altar or whatever before he sent them the fax). What motivated men like this film star, asked the reporter? Their mothers, was the answer. Their mothers had been emotionally distant so they learned to be sensitive around women. Well, that explained why women fell for them, not why they ran off. Their mothers had nagged their fathers and persecuted them, so they were afraid and spent their lives running away from women. Men like this should carry a government health warning, the reporter wrote. Women who get involved with them will end up with two things: a large library of books called *Women Who Love Too Much*, *Smart Love*, *Get Rid of Him*, plus one small broken heart.

Twenty minutes past six. The news is over. The barman switches off the television set. Clíona feels totally exposed, stripped of the blanket of electric sound which muffled her nerves a little. She orders a small whiskey, a drink she dislikes but the only one she could bear to drink now, in the state she is in. Her stomach is chilled and cramped, she is shivering. Waiting for Paddy gives her diarrhoea. She hardly admits this to herself and would never, of course, say it to him. I mean, what sort of word is that to enhance a romantic relationship? 'Your hair is so incredible. I want to know I'll always be able to see that hair, always, do you hear?' 'Yes, darling. And did I ever tell you, you give me the runs every time I have to meet you?'

Clíona is married to Martin. He is an engineer, specialising in hydraulics, who works on behalf of clients in Africa and the Middle East. His work takes him abroad, often, to advise people on how best to extract water from places where there is little or none. A lot of his time is spent in various deserts, while Clíona and their eight-year-old daughter, Afric, fend for themselves in Terenure.

When she was first married Clíona hated this. She knew very few people in Dublin at that stage, and she missed Martin dreadfully when he went away. She had never lived alone, hardly ever spent a night in a house where no other adult slept. The house without him seemed alien.

But after a few years that changed. Clíona found she loved

to be home alone. She loves the sense of space opening around her, which she gets as soon as he walks out the door. Martin is too big for this place: he is six foot four. Such a man, and even much smaller men, do not fit into suburban houses, which are designed for small people, for women and children. Martin wants to move. He is uncomfortable in the narrow hall, the low-ceilinged rooms, and by now they can afford something much older and bigger and more stylish. But Clíona loves the flatness of the house, its open plan, its picture windows. She loves what other people hate: stucco walls, too much glass, big flat radiators. She loves the lawn with its suburban shrubs – forsythia and broom, escallonia and redcurrant blossom. Its cherry blossom, its almond blossom, its weeping willow. She loves the iron gate and the low-slung garage and the crowds of children that play on the road all summer long.

For the past four years she has had Afric, as well. Their relationship changed, for the better, as soon as Martin left for the airport. Clíona stopped resenting the time she spent with her child, as she often did when Martin was around, and enjoyed her company instead. Afric responded by becoming calm instead of nervous, helpful instead of contrary.

All this Clíona loves. Or used to love, before Paddy came along, and all her energy became concentrated on him.

Paddy is a politician, a TD. Clíona knew she would bump into him sooner or later once she took up the job with Angela, the minister. In fact, it took quite a while – a whole year. This is because Clíona works in Angela's office, in a government department which is situated quite far from Leinster House, and never attends sessions in the Dáil. Paddy doesn't even have an office in Dublin. His party is in opposition and he is a back-bencher. He comes up only when the Dáil is in session, and not always then. The rest of the time he is back in his constituency, in the south, two hundred miles away.

Clíona finally encountered him not in Kildare Street or Leinster House, but at a reception in an embassy. She remembers it well – a long, elegant room, pale blue or pale green, with high windows opening on gardens full of busky old trees. A large black cat slept in front of a turf fire, and Paddy was standing close to the cat and the fire, and to a woman, a chic woman, who worked at the embassy. He was warming himself, patting the cat, and listening with close attention to whatever this woman was saying when Clíona caught sight of him.

Immediately she moved away to the back of the room and stood by the window, sipping her drink and pretending to admire the garden. Almond blossom, forsythia and lilac dissolved before her eyes. In whirling maelstrom of white and mauve and yellow stars her certainties disintegrated; the present was ambushed by the past. That a single sighting of a simple human being could cause such havoc is astonishing. But it could. And Clíona's carapace of sophistication, experience, her career success and her domestic happiness, even her true loves, were not proof against that onslaught.

She knew, standing by the long pale window, that the correct and sensible course of action in the circumstances was to run for her life. Even a leap from the window to the green grass below might have been advisable.

But she turned and looked at the man on the hearthrug.

He saw her. He came over.

That was that.

Great waves of sexual pull, deep abysses of ancient emotion, starry high roads of future promise. Either of them could have said no, presumably. They were adults, not teenagers. They were not swept along by an utterly uncontrollable force. Nobody ever is. Not really. Not *uncontrollable*. Still, once his eyes – brown, witty, seeming full of insight – looked into hers, once his hand touched her skin, it would have been very difficult indeed not to meet him again. The cliché of being swept off on a tidal wave of passion did not absolve them of responsibility, and what could? But the cliché was not too far from the truth.

At twenty to seven he has still not arrived. The pub is filling up. People keep asking if the seat next to her is free. She feels a right eejit, saying no, no, I'm expecting a friend.

She gives up. She leaves, searching one more desperate time as she passes through the crowded room, its smoky cheerfulness an affirmation of normal human friendliness, a reminder to her of the great distance she has placed between herself and all everyday warmth, everyday comfort and civilisation.

She even examines the street, when she gets outside, looking first one way and then the other, in case he is rushing towards her even now, his beige cashmere coat clutched to his tall, overweight body. Of course he isn't. Of course he isn't. Numbed rather than sad, she collects her car from the car park and sets off home.

Her house is on the western edge of the city, in the foothills of the Dublin mountains. By now the clotted rush-hour streets have diluted, the traffic is a sluggish but mobile stream, and the journey will not take more than half an hour – twenty minutes from Kildare Street to Rathmines and ten minutes the rest of the way. Sitting in a minor jam on the Green, she stares at the numberplate of the car ahead of her. He simply didn't show up. (He sent a fax. I read it in the *New York Times*.) It is so paltry and petty, the lowest cliché of sexual bungling, the most ridiculous, the most risible. Also, when you experience it yourself, the most humiliating and sordid. Clíona had imagined herself protected from this kind of behaviour by her smart suit, her good job – even by her husband, by Afric, who right now is waiting impatiently with Evelyn, her minder, for Clíona to come home. But she is not protected. She is not a smart professional married woman as far as Paddy is concerned. She is just another woman he has had enough of. A whiny, clingy, irritating woman who loves too much, who loves illicitly too much. She's a bore. She's dumb.

She is filled with loathing for herself, as she edges along in the thick murky file, around the Green, along Adelaide Road, slowly to the lights at Kelly's corner, the ugliest, messiest corner in the whole of Dublin, it seems to her at this moment. What would Martin think? What would Martin do? And Afric?

But by the time she has passed Rathmines – the bulging cauliflower church, the Dürer town hall, coppery red, Grimmsily gorgeous – and is zipping up the Rathgar Road, self-hatred gives way to hatred of him. Fucking bastard. Fucking rat. She'd like to ring up his wife and tell her. She'd like to spill the beans to the tabloids, or tabloid, the office of which she passes on her way home. Isn't he going a bit too far? Isn't he trusting her a bit too much?

A meeting. A vote. Maybe he'd been called in suddenly, couldn't possibly get away? Maybe his wife is ill, his children are ill? Maybe he had an accident? A heart attack? But. She'd been in her own office until ten to six. He could have phoned the pub, even – unless it was a heart attack. Also, it is not the first time. Not the first, not the second time, he has done this to her, on account of the greater importance of his job, his career, his family. On account of the greater importance of himself.

She'd like to kill him.

She will wait outside his office, vengeful as Medea, bent on retribution, and when he emerges late at night, she'll say, Step this way, please, sir. And he'll smile his bland and wily politician's smile. And she'll smile back and show him the chilly muzzle of a pistol. This way, she'll say, letting him feel the coldness of it on the nape of his neck. Down this lane here. Yes. That's right. Don't try anything. Stand against that wall over there, beside the bicycle. Yes. With your back to me. Yes. That's it.

Bang.

Where would she get a pistol?

Somewhere. She's been in public relations all her life. She works for a government minister. If she can't get hold of a gun, who can?

By now she is passing the Yellow House. The sun is shining on its hopeful walls, the mountains behind glow, duskily amethyst, a rich, dark-textured colour that sucks you in. She feels steady, driving towards that colour, solid and calm as a slab of slate. Her stomach has stopped its collywobbling, her hands grasp the wheel with authority, her mascara has not run down her face, the fine pink woollen skirt of her suit is unwrinkled.

Nothing has happened, actually.

She allows her mind to flit over other murder scenes, but half-heartedly. Poison. Plant food is deadly, and, unlike pistols, can be bought over the counter. A drop in his coffee every so often, every time she sees him. And in her new rationality she knows she can see him as often as she wants, if she still wants to. A drop today, two drops tomorrow. His insides will slowly rot away. And who would ever suspect her, Clíona Brosnan? Nobody knows she even knows him, least of all the people who would be questioned in connection with a slow murder by plant poison: his tweedy, brown-bread-baking wife, his undisciplined, confused children, all tucked away in a little village in Cork, miles from the scene of the crime.

Nobody would ever suspect. Anyway, there are probably about twenty people, men, women and children, who have felt like murdering Paddy at some stage. There are probably

dozens who feel like murdering him at this minute. He is one
of those delightful men that attract that sort of passionate wish
among others.

Afric is not at the door when Clíona arrives home. She is in the
conservatory, surrounded by Swiss cheese plants, sewing.

'Hi!' Clíona gives her a hug.

Afric looks up but continues working.

'She's busy.' Evelyn winks at Clíona. 'Refurbishing Teddy
Dropear's wardrobe.'

'Yes! So I see. I didn't even know you could sew so well,
Afric!'

Afric gives her a disappointed look.

'See you tomorrow!' Clíona smiles at Evelyn, who is standing by the door putting on her jacket, looking disapproving.
She is a great child minder but she often makes Clíona feel
guilty for existing. How much does Evelyn know? She has
the kind of knowing eyes, twinkling and intelligent, that convey the impression that she knows absolutely everything. But,
of course, she can't, not always.

'What time?' This is her way of reminding Clíona that she's
late.

'Nine will do, OK?'

Evelyn takes her bag and goes.

'What are you making, Afric?' Clíona says.

'Making a suit.'

'It's lovely. Did Evelyn show you how?'

'No.'

'Did you have anything to eat?'

'Yeah.'

'What?'

'Chips and sausages and rashers and yoghurt and tea.'

'Great! So you're probably not hungry now?'

Afric shakes her head.

Clíona doesn't believe a word of it. Afric doesn't eat, not much. Sometimes Clíona wonders if she has some childish form of anorexia. She is very thin: her dark brown eyes are enormous in her tiny face, her ribs protrude like the ribs of a ship through her golden skin. Clíona is afraid that the lack of appetite is a symptom of something dangerous – loneliness and insecurity – because of Martin's absences and Clíona's strangeness, or, more likely, some deep homesickness.

Afric is not from Ireland or even from Africa. She is a Romanian orphan, adopted by Clíona and Martin four years ago. Bought her, is closer to the truth. They spent five days in Romania and visited twelve orphanages, staring at hundreds of brown-eyed, golden-skinned, wistful-looking children. The worst cases had been kept from them by the orphanage authorities, men and mostly women who seemed as charming and winsome as the lovely children, but whom Clíona had come to hate, seeing beside every smiling face callousness, cruelty, apathy.

They were told to take their pick, but in the end that had not been at all possible. The year-old baby boy they had selected had not been given to them – red tape, complications. She cannot bear to think of it any more, although sometimes she awakes weeping at four o'clock in the morning, wondering what had become of that baby, whom she had held in her arms and kissed. They had got Afric instead, then named Yana, already four years old and tall for her age, considering where she had been brought up. She had been unable to talk, not a single word.

Now her English is perfect. Clíona hopes to get lessons in Romanian for her later, when she is about twelve and really settled. She wants Afric to have a real connection, a linguistic connection, with her home. But not yet. Just now she doesn't

want to burden her with unnecessary baggage. Already she has
had to carry so much.

Clíona loves Afric more than she loves anyone in the world,
more than she has ever loved anyone, and more than she ever
will. She knows this perfectly well. She knows she would die
for the sake of Afric, if that were necessary. She knows that the
love she feels for Afric is of a nature utterly different from what
she has felt for Martin, although closer to that than what she
feels for Paddy. Also, she knows that all these feelings are love,
although it would be easier to dismiss one of them as something else.

'When is Martin coming home?' Afric says.

'He's not coming home tonight, pet. He is in Riyadh,
remember?'

'Oh yeah! I forgot.'

'Do you miss him?'

'Naw. Not really. Do you?'

'A bit.'

That is true also. She used to love Martin a lot and miss him
a lot, and now she misses him a bit. This does not seem to make
any difference to him. In fact, he seems not to have noticed.

Clíona had fallen in love with Paddy – in those days, Pádraig –
when she was fourteen years old. He had always been her
neighbour in the Cork village where he still lives. They had
sat in the same classroom in the national school. When they
were twelve, Paddy had gone away to boarding school and
she had stayed behind, at the local Convent of Mercy. The
summer when she was fourteen, they danced one night at a
youth club hop. He had grown about a foot since she had last
seen him, at Easter; his childish features had transformed into a
bonily beautiful face, aloof and assured in a way which she
knew was the essence of masculinity – although she had never

given any thought to this subject before. At the same time his
skin was light, with a pinkish tinge, achingly translucent – she
longed to touch it. He dived, that night, into her dreams. And
there he stayed, all that lovesick summer, and for several years
afterwards, a secret hidden in the darkest depths of her imagination, while she studied and played, danced, even dated other
boys. She did not think of him constantly, but as the shadowy
king of her imagination, he held his sway.

When she was eighteen she went to the city, to the university. Pádraig – this was when he became Paddy – was there
too, at the college of art. She encountered him at a party the
first weekend, at the flat of some older people from their village. Clíona had herself changed, over the last months. From
being a clumsy, thick-ankled schoolgirl, she had become
something nebulous and willowy. She was not yet beautiful,
but her pale slenderness, her air of frail vulnerability, attracted
many young men. She had allowed her fair hair to grow past
her waist, in the fashion of the time. It was a thick blond plank,
and seemed much too heavy for her delicate head. She wore it
like a burdensome veil. Men longed to snatch it off and reveal
whatever lay sleeping beneath it.

Paddy lifted the mane to the candlelight. 'You are like a
medieval Madonna,' he said, very seriously. Later he showed
her the one he meant – Fra Filippo Lippi's, a sad, pale gold pro-
file, sweet, subdued by dark indigoes, shadowy ambers. Paddy
was like Samson, Clíona thought, amazed that she could joke
about him, even to herself. He too had let his hair grow, and
sported a wiry black mane, tangled, electric with energy. His
clothes were a purple shirt and filthy paint-bespattered jeans.
On principle he seldom washed or shaved. His once translucent chin looked like a patch of burnt parsley; he smelt not of
Old Spice, as he had at that dance long ago, but of sweat and
turpentine.

Clíona loved to be scratched by the black hairs, which were not as rough as they looked. She loved to bury her Madonna head in his acrid, sweating arms, to draw his cherished body into hers. That her dream had become reality she could hardly believe. For so long he had been a figment of her imagination, and now here he was, solid, stinking, lovely – the most real fact of her life. Patience paid off apparently. You trimmed your lamp, you bided your time. Your prince came.

She was blissfully happy.

They spent every waking minute in each other's company for about six months, never bothering about lectures or work. Clíona's friends took her aside, advised her to proceed cautiously. But she didn't care. She couldn't. Any time spent away from him was time wasted. It was as if she had moved onto a new level of existence with him, a level where the ordinary rules were as irrelevant as clocks in paradise.

What they did not do was move in together. That never occurred to them, although they were both paying money for rented accommodation. In those days, young men and young women lived apart until they married. Flouting all other sensible conventions, this one they never even considered breaking, although if they had, their lives might have been considerably less chaotic.

'Let's go away. Let's go to London.'

Paddy was urgent in his love. Also, he disliked the college of art, where he was in trouble because of his abysmal attendance.

'Mm,' said Clíona.

She knew she would never do it. Breaking out, breaking away from her parents, buying a ticket and setting off to an unknown place: that seemed all but impossible to her. She did not believe that people, young college people like them, ever did such wild, senseless things (there she was wrong). She believed she was a liberal free spirit, who read Herman Hesse and wore a long flowery smock, and skipped lectures recklessly. She believed she was wild. But she was not wild enough to take a drink. She seldom had proper sex. She was not wild enough to make a run for it.

The idea of not finishing her degree was unimaginable. Although it was clear that her destiny now would be poor results, she clung to that ambition, not realising that at every stage of her life she would find there was a degree to finish, another stage to go before you could rationally break away and change your course, until, finally, as you waited and dreamed, your course is changed for you, irredeemably changed.

London might as well have been the moon, as far as she was concerned. How could they get the money, get the tickets, get the boat, get the train – get there? And why? She and Paddy were together anyway. Why did he want to run away?

To get married, he said. That seemed impossible to her as well, although she knew there was no other man she would ever want to marry. Now she thinks that he just wanted to show off, to show how big and macho and wild he was. Or maybe he wanted to make some meaningful gesture against the terrible conventionality that would grip him if he remained at home? Maybe he saw what was ahead?

They did not run away. And then they split up. Paddy met someone else at a party one weekend when she was at home, visiting her parents. The new woman was buxom, red-haired, freckled. She drank pints of Beamish and told Paddy a story about a surprise birthday party: a naked couple walks into their dark kitchen, the light goes on and all their relations and friends sing 'Happy birthday to you!' To Paddy this woman, whose name was, incongruously, Maud, seemed vulgar and loud. But she made him laugh and when he left her, the image of her flaming hair remained in his head. She caught his

imagination, as he had caught Clíona's. There was nothing he
could do about it. One night she was telling him a silly story,
the next he was in love with her. She was a Titian. She was
Profane Love. She was the Mona Lisa, she was Jeanne Samary,
she was Rubenesque and Goyaesque and Renoiresque, electric, giddy, laughing with energy. And Clíona was still a
Madonna, a Madonna with angels.

He fell in love headlong, helplessly. Nobody could blame
him for that.

Except Clíona.

After the parting they never talked – she couldn't bear to see
him. Jealousy devoured her, and she felt like a field which had
been trampled over by a rampaging army. Their iron nailed
boots ground into her skin, ripping her to ribbons. Paddy
was kind, and stayed out of her way, but she saw him all too
often, his beloved purple arm cradling the Titian, his dark head
whispering in her big, beringed ear. The city was small, and to
Clíona it was a minefield. Turn any corner and they might be
there, charmed, beautiful, in love, while she was a cold, be-
draggled, skinless animal, trying her best to survive in a world
which was utterly hostile.

After a while the situation improved. She met Martin, and
dated him for entirely selfish reasons: her pride was salvaged.
Not much else. She grew fond of him, although the feeling she
had for Paddy was never repeated. Besides, she had something
new to worry about. She was pregnant.

This she did not discover until she was already involved
with Martin. She was almost nineteen, but her knowledge of
the physical facts of life, as of so many other facts, was sketchy.
She discovered the pregnancy when she miscarried, one night
at home in bed. She did not know what was happening – 'a
haemorrhage,' her landlady said, tactfully, alarmed and disbe-
lieving, calling the family doctor. It was he who told Clíona,

patting her on the head and asking her to come and see him again, in a week, when she was feeling better.

She felt better much sooner than that, and she did not return to that doctor, in a week or ever again. Nor did she mention the event to Martin. It was not his business, and she did not know how he would react: he was kind, but conservative. His hair was long but it looked as neat as a short back and sides. At that time everyone was still deeply ashamed of sexual matters, in Cork and perhaps elsewhere as well.

Martin courted Clíona for six years. Such courtships were not exceptional then, but the norm. Most young people seemed to be blessed with more patience than Griselda. Girls found men and handcuffed them, tight as oysters, until they had a job and a car and a down payment on a house. Then they married them. It was the seventies, swinging and hippy, if you felt like it. Or safe as a job in the civil service, if that is what you preferred.

Afric makes a terrible botched job of the suit for her teddy, but she is immensely proud of it. 'It's nice, isn't it, Clíona?'

They pull it over his fat teddy head, and he sits, with thread stretched across his bulging stomach, and scraps of coloured cloth hanging on his arms. A teddy bear in ten pieces of cloth hanging together on thick black thread: he doesn't look like anything else except that. His button eyes gaze, shining, with that sad wistful look teddy bears have. You can imagine that he is suffering humiliation and indignity for the sake of all children, but bearing it well.

'It's lovely, darling!'

'Tomorrow I'll make him something else. What will I make him?'

'An overcoat, maybe?'

'A tracksuit. He needs a tracksuit for basketball and gym.'

'Yeah. He plays a lot of basketball.'

'Teddy Dropears loves basketball.'

Afric takes him from the locker and tucks him in bed beside her. 'Will he be too hot in his suit?'

'Ah no,' says Clíona. 'I don't think it'll bother him too much. It's very light, really, isn't it?'

'It's a summer suit. I think he likes it.'

'I think he does, too. And so he should. Goodnight love.'

'Goodnight!'

Paddy's politics are left wing, not conservative, but Clíona believes that right now being on the mild, right-veering left wing of Irish politics is the most conservative place to be, especially for someone who entered politics in the seventies. She probably believes this because she spends such a lot of time thinking discrediting thoughts about Paddy, but there is some truth in it. He has always been a captive of his immediate history.

Before entering politics, in which he'd had no interest whatsoever while in college (like most art students), he moved to West Cork and started organic farming, that being a fashionable thing to do at that particular time. While he was there, he got married, not to the Titian or to any of his Cork girlfriends, but to a German, who ran one of those hippy potteries. Now she runs a restaurant, which started off being vegetarian but specialises at this stage in seafood, since tourists prefer fish to vegetables. Paddy still favours the latter, and eats couscous and baked parsnips whenever he can. He has stopped wearing striped jumpers, though, and instead has a selection of tweed jackets, with contrasting ties. His wife does the ties. She weaves on the side, during the winter, making scarves and ties and little, cheapish things that can be sold in the reception area of the restaurant during the summer. He buys the jackets in the

Donegal tweed place in Dublin.

He is his party's spokesman on Women's Affairs. He is a loud, vociferous feminist. So is Clíona, so she should be glad. But she isn't. She finds it unbelievably irritating. It makes her want to scream when she thinks of him blathering on about equality and sexual harrassment.

'It's ironic, your being a feminist,' she once suggested, unable to suppress herself.

He stiffened, not understanding. Maybe that's what it takes to be a successful politician? Maybe you need to lack self-irony, and perhaps lacking self-knowledge helps a bit as well.

Afric falls asleep at nine o'clock. As usual, Clíona checks from time to time to see that she is all right, and as usual stands and gazes at her sleeping face for five minutes or so. Afric is clutching Teddy Dropears, like a child in a storybook. Her face is angelically beautiful. This is perfect human beauty, Clíona thinks, not for the first time. This is it, the calm small features, the skin as smooth as fresh snow, the even little breath. We all start off like this.

The phone.

'Hello, darling.'

Martin. Her heart, which had been thudding violently on the way downstairs, wilts.

'Hi! How are you?'

'Great. The usual. You know, hard work.'

'What time is it?'

'Middle of the night.'

'Is it hot?'

'Incredible. OK indoors.'

'Martin?'

'Yes?'

'Could you get me something?'

'Sure. Anything you want!'

'A gun.'

'What?'

'You know, a small personal one.'

'Has something happened?'

'No, no.'

'Are you really so frightened?'

'Yes. I am.'

'Listen. I'll be home in five days. We'll talk about it then.'

'So you can't?'

'No, of course not ... Love? Don't worry. Put on the alarm.'

'Yeah, yeah.'

'How is Afric?'

'She's fine ...'

She told him about the suit for the bear, and then said goodnight.

She has a photo of Paddy, which she cut out of a newspaper – several, in fact, since his photo appears frequently in the papers, not because he is one of the most important politicians but because he is one of the most good-looking. The one she is looking at shows Paddy, his wife, and their three children in the sitting room of their cottage. Paddy is smiling, and has one arm thrown over his wife's shoulder and one over his daughter's. The wife is small, with a mop of frizzy blond hair, what used to be called an Afro. She has on some sort of floppy West Cork artistic skirt and a thick chunky jumper. The girl is slender with doe eyes, a beauty. The boys are background, unimportant in Paddy's life. There is a bowl of daffodils to the right of the picture and a glimpse of landscape through a window to the left. It is all contrived, posed, folksy. Paddy the family man. Paddy the organic farmer. Paddy the feminist.

'Newman' is his surname, in fact, and the paper makes some stupid play on that.

Clíona doesn't tear up the photo, or throw it in the fire. Not yet. She just looks at it and feels miserable, eaten up with a mixture of self-pity and hatred. She thinks of those words the self-help books use, words like 'rat' and 'Don Juan', but they don't help her much. She knows nobody in the world is a rat, so what's the point in pretending they are?

The phone.

'Hi!' Paddy. 'How are you?'

She feels her treacherous stomach lighten just on hearing his voice, his warm, ordinary, kind voice. He sounds so normal and human, like a father and a husband and a brother and an uncle all rolled into one. He doesn't sound like a rat, or some troll from the dark caverns in the mountains. He sounds like a friend.

'Where were you?'

'What do you mean? Was I supposed to . . . oh no!'

Clíona laughs. She actually laughs. 'Six o'clock. The Bailey.'

'Oh God, I'm really sorry. Were you there long?'

'Not so long.'

'I completely forgot. I am so stupid, how can I keep doing these things?'

'You are so busy, I suppose.'

'Can I see you tomorrow?'

'Mm.'

'Same place? Same time?'

'OK.'

'I'm sorry. I'll see you tomorrow . . . I love you.'

She puts down the phone and waters the plants, sprinkling the shining broken leaves, leaves that spread and flourish just to break into sharp-edged, airy holes. Now you see them, now you don't. Her heart is light and her head is clear. A calm serenity spreads along her nerves, it spreads through the flat, light house.

'This makes no sense,' she says aloud, pouring a stream of silver water from her green can to the terracotta pot, watching the clay soak it in. She is thinking of the crazy swing from hatred to love, from despair to happiness, rather than of the other dangerous, cruel aspects of what is going on, rather than the madness of the addiction which has her in its grip.

She knows she will break out of that madness, and unless she does, her life is useless, finished. She thinks that somewhere, probably not far away, there is a calm, peaceful, loving, civilised life beyond the startling volcanic landscape, full of deep treacherous pits and gleaming glass mountains, which she is now inhabiting. There was a verdant valley before, with Afric and Martin and the house and the job, before she let this monster invade her. She is naive enough, optimistic enough, sheltered enough, to believe it is there at the other side of the desert. She believes she has a return ticket, and that what is done can be undone, and will be.

But for some reason she can't begin the journey back as yet. Not quite yet.

THE SEARCH FOR THE LOST HUSBAND

The little white goat started off again, and she went after him. But on this day he did not stop at all to take a rest as he had on the previous days. Dew fell and night fell and still he did not stop, but went on and on, through bramble and briar and bracken, through hill and dale. And she became exhausted. But she didn't give up, because she knew that in the end he would be forced to stop. She was almost dead with tiredness. He went on and on and on and on, and she kept her eyes on him. Finally he stopped on top of a cliff. And the ground opened up and swallowed him.

She kept her eyes glued to that patch of ground. She walked over to the patch. But there was nothing there. Nothing but a patch of green grass. There was no way up or down or east or west.

She sat down and she began to scream.

'What am I to do now?' she cried. 'Or where am I to go?'

An old man came to her. And he asked her why she was crying.

'It's a long, sad story,' she said. 'I'd hate to bore you with it.'

But she did anyway. She told him everything.

When she had finished he said: 'You wait here. I'm going to fetch a spade. I'll bring back a spade and we'll see if there is any way of getting down there after him!'

'Oh, thank you,' she said.

The old man went off, and back he came with a big sharp spade. And he started digging. He dug and dug. And after a lot of digging he hit a big slab of stone. And he levered up the slab and beneath it was a flight of stone steps, going down as far as the eye could see.

'Well,' he said, 'here's a flight of stairs, and they seem to be going somewhere. Maybe you could try them.'

'Wisha, with the help of God,' she said, 'I'll get down them.'

'Oh you'll get down them all right,' he said. 'Never you fear. But what will you find at the bottom, that's the question?'

'God knows,' said she. 'Nothing would surprise me now. But I'm certain I'll find something. There must be some sort of a land down there, a place, or a country.'

'Right you are,' he said. 'And good luck to you!'

MY PET

IT IS TWELVE TWENTY-FIVE, a Friday in November, close to Armistice Day – a few people display red poppies bobbing on their lapels. Karl has been standing in front of Patsy's Pantry, in a south-side shopping centre, for half an hour. He is waiting for a woman named Alison, a well-known novelist who is hardly known to Karl at all, to pick him up and give him a lift to Enniskillen, where they will both give a creative-writing workshop to prisoners on some sort of experimental day-release from Long Kesh. Karl, who teaches English in a Dublin detention centre, was asked to attend this a few days ago, when somebody else dropped out with flu. He accepted the invitation as he tends to accept all invitations, and also because he would have felt guilty about not contributing to such a worthy project: creativity, prison and the north of Ireland, all packed together like a health-food sandwich for the soul. (Add some cross-border co-operation for seasoning.)

The message from Alison about the time and place of the pick-up came last night, when Karl was out in the local pub watching a Man United v. Barcelona match and drinking the three pints he allows himself when he's feeling below par. The Red Devils lost, and then he'd had a fourth pint, like practically everybody else in the bar. Alison's message was relayed to him after midnight by his sleepy housemate, Jim. Rushing out this morning, Karl forgot the piece of paper on which he'd written the name of the damn place he was supposed to meet her. Maybe it wasn't Patsy's Pantry? Maybe it was some other café in this shopping centre? There are two others that he knows of, and probably several that he hasn't noticed.

He walks around the corner and has a look at Bewley's, sniffing the knock-you-out smell of roasting coffee on the freezing air. Then he peers into the eye-blowing brightness of McDonald's. No sign of somebody who looks like block-buster Alison in either. He comes back to Patsy's Pantry and stands outside it for five minutes. Hundreds of people walk past him, and cars roll in and out of the car park ceaselessly, as if they were on rails, in and out, in and out. It's a day, and it seems an hour, when half the neighbourhood comes shopping.

By now the time is half past twelve. He should have phoned the damned romancer this morning. Maybe that is what he was supposed to do – Jim got it arsewise, not for the first time. Alison is probably standing by her phone cursing him for a rude bastard. Or, more likely, halfway to Enniskillen, muttering under her pink bestselling breath as she speeds along in whatever sort of goddam rich woman's jalopy she's got for herself. Why should she hang around doing a favour for him, somebody she's met at most once in her life before when she floated into his prison to do a workshop, dressed in black and orange and wearing Chanel Number 5, by the tubful, upsetting half of the boys for weeks afterwards?

Christ!

Karl started out this morning in an optimistic mood, considering. The sun was shining as he drank his coffee. There were oranges in a bowl on the blue gingham tablecloth and Jim had left a croissant on a yellow plate. He'd savoured it in the warm kitchen with the radio playing, and then packed his bag quickly, pleased enough to be buoyant, to be efficient. He didn't know what the weekend would bring, but the woman who'd phoned him said the hotel where the workshop was taking place was good; there was a pool and a sauna. Like the popular concept of a prison, he'd joked. Well, yes, actually, she'd said, in her low-key, west Ulster accent, which sounds ironic even when it isn't. He looked forward to the pool, and the sauna. The latter would ease the pain he'd had in his back for two weeks, and the pool would help ease the pain in his heart. Exercise helps. It releases endorphins into the bloodstream and lifts the spirits. He's read this in one of the women's magazines Jim's teenage daughter, Sarah, leaves lying around the house.

But by now he's back to square one. The weather's taken a nose dive, and the trip to the shopping centre had been a trial. Karl and Jim live miles from anywhere, courtesy of Jim's taste for salt water and mountain air (and knackers and burglaries and cider parties every night of the summer to enliven your dreams, and bonfires all the time). Karl doesn't even have a car any more. He lost his licence a year ago, just before Christmas. That's how unlucky he is. He is the one person in Dublin he knows who has been breathalysed and convicted after drinking two and a half glasses of wine – in the prison, actually, at a party they had on December twentieth. He'd forgotten he had the car (he doesn't usually bring it to work, the prison is down the road from where they live, handy for him, but yet another aspect of the location's great undesirability).

By the time he'd reached Patsy's Pantry he was down in the dumps. And now he is further down, down as far as you can get, nearly, wherever that is. Pretty far down, actually. He's feeling so rotten it's like there's a black curtain just behind his eyes, and his stomach is doing its level best to get into his boots.

He spots a kiosk on the side of the dual carriageway out

front and tries to phone Alison from there. But although the telephone is inside the box, this being a decent suburb for all its ugliness, Alison's number is not. She wouldn't be listed, a famous novelist like her. A novelist, so damned feminist she won't list her own name in the telephone directory in case some rapist lets his fingers do the walking. I mean, if these people could think straight, they'd cop that that's not the way the average rapist or even house-breaker operates.

There is no way of contacting Alison. And there is no way of getting to Enniskillen by public transport in time for the start of the event – that is, if he could bear the thought of getting there by public transport, which he can't. He will have to let them down.

That's when he gets his next shock. Tears begin to flow from his eyes and his nose bleeds slightly. These effusions of liquid seem to be involuntary, like the feeling of depression that has taken over his body. His mind has no control any more. He feels so rotten that for a minute he considers telephoning Jim and blurting it out. But he resists the temptation. He's going to have to tell him sometime, but not over the phone from the side of the dual carriageway. He'll find a better place, a good time. Maybe. Maybe not.

He decides to go home. He is not going to get to Enniskillen, so goodbye prisoners of the North and the swimming pool and the sauna. Somehow getting to Enniskillen has assumed some outlandish proportion in his head. He hadn't even heard of this damned conference until three days ago and now he feels as if he were letting down a life-long friend. Another life-long friend. He feels as abandoned as a baby on a dungheap out on the edge of the dual carriageway, with its sad banks of straggling trees and high concrete walls, its hissing traffic, its forty shades of grey. Grey car after grey car churns along, belching out grey exhaust fumes, chugging along the grey dual carriageway, towards a huge dark grey empty horizon. Bullets of grey rain beat against the windscreens, the wipers swipe viciously at them, bashing the hell out of them: he can almost hear the hiss of wipers, the cross crankiness of too many people driving in Dublin on a grey Friday afternoon.

And here stands Karl, here on this Calvary, stretched against a breeze block wall, at the mercy of pink-lipped, flouncy-dressed Alison (is she flouncy? he forgets) and the public transport system and his own sloppiness. Karl the Messer, the Big Bad Effer. Karl who can't even cope with the complication of propelling himself from Dublin to Enniskillen, a journey of one hundred miles, approximately. How can Karl survive the complications of reality? Might as well do himself in, go home and do himself in.

This is a sort of game with Karl, thinking of ways to give the old bucket a kick before it kicks him, and Jim, and the rest of the human race in the teeth – forty, fifty years and everyone he knows will be gone, anyway, so what's the point in sticking around to rot? Thinking of methods, though, has the curious effect of getting him out of it – he can think himself in and out of the grave. Two bottles of whiskey. Razor to the wrists. Cliffing. Hanging is the way they do it in prison – not in his, which is not that sort of place, but the real one on the north side. It always fascinates him that they can do it with a grey prison blanket – I mean, you really have to have skill and drive, willpower. He'd probably borrow or steal a car, now that he doesn't have one himself, and drive up the woods behind the house. It's relatively painless (nothing is painless) and also sure. Also dignified. Probably a guard would find you, not your nearest and dearest. Hopefully the one who breathalysed him. Serve him right, little motherfucker.

See? By the time Karl's picturing that pink-faced gobshite poking around the door of a Ford Fiesta holding his perky little nose, he is not cheerful, but ... calmer. Something has changed and then, of course, the bus comes, rescuing him from the roadway, at least. Maybe he could've got the bus down in the centre, anyway? Too late.

This is happening four years after Karl moved in with Jim and Sarah, and six months after he fell in love with Andrew. He'd never got around to telling Jim about Andrew, not only because he knew it would hurt him, although, of course, that was part of the reason. But he was never quite sure about Andrew, anyway. Not about being in love with him – he adored him. He had never loved anyone the way he loved Andrew, of that he was certain. His desire for him was like a hunger monster, it was like a famine stalking the land, it was like a whale. He was the whale and Andrew was Jonah. But Andrew was younger, sexier, not too serious about anything in life, least of all a lover like Karl, of whom he'd had about twenty, it seemed, at the last and most conservative count.

And now Andrew was going.

Not going to die. He didn't have AIDS – he wasn't as predictable as that, if he had been, Karl probably wouldn't have fallen for him in the first place. He was just going away to a place. New York.

'I've got to give it a go, love,' he'd said to Karl yesterday.

They were in a dark corner of a pub having lunch. They risked holding hands there, regularly, and the barman hadn't caught them yet, although, of course, he knew. Barmen are canny souls.

'Why?'

'You know, time and tide and all that.'

'You're doing fine here. And New York ... come on!'

'You'd go yourself.'

But he wasn't asked, not by Andrew, and he knew that was not the intention.

'You can come and visit. It'll be a gas.'

Andrew's voice was smooth as treacle. He was fair, smooth all over as an iced bun. Inside Karl there was a hollow full of stones and pins and dustballs, but inside Andrew there was marshmallow, or whipped cream, sweet and certain, luscious.

'Oh sure!'

'Soon as I get settled in.'

Karl clasped Andrew's hand in desperation. Andrew stroked Karl's foot with his.

'Come on. You've never even mentioned New York before . . . what is this?'

'I hadn't thought about it, much. But the offer came up . . . I've got to take it. It's a good one. Here you know how limited it all is.'

Andrew was in films, like half the population of Ireland. Karl hadn't taken it very seriously before. Andrew had been doing a bit of scriptwriting, he'd got development money from the Film Board for two outlines over the past few years. But so had heaps of others, it didn't mean a thing. Now some Irish guy with a company based in New York was offering him a real job, as a scriptreader and editor. Sixty thousand a year, which was money for Andrew.

'It's not so much.' Karl earned twenty-two thousand a year, half of which went in tax.

'It's just for starters. I'm sorry, love, I love you. But . . . why are you looking at me like that?'

'I love you, too. I love you so fucking much I could eat you.'

Karl stopped looking and ripped a bite from his ham-and-cheese sandwich.

He isn't sure how he'd have handled the creative-writing

course in Enniskillen, anyway. Down home – in the detention centre – he doesn't teach writing, just English, which is more about reading, very basic reading. He'd gone to a workshop on a Greek island once, given by an American novelist, and the American novelist had got them to do this imaginary walk exercise psychiatrists do with you. You describe exactly what you see on this walk and then come to a door in a wall and open the door. Who is inside? What is inside?

A topic suggested by the American novelist had been 'My Pet'. That had worked better than the psychic walk in the woods. He'd written about a goldfish and the novelist had liked his piece and said it showed promise. Other members of the class had been imaginative. Some had pet mermaids; one, a wolf. Some had used the opportunity to describe their children, although that was cheating, the novelist had wanted an animal.

The walk might be a bit tactless, given the prisoners aren't allowed to leave the room they're assigned to in the hotel. (Why hold it in the hotel then? For a change. To boost the morale. Boost it and lower it at the same time, so what's new? It's a lesson, another lesson, about the human condition.) On the other hand, 'My Pet' sounds stupid to Karl. The only one he can think of himself, as a topic that interests him and everybody and is of some relevance to life and literature and creative writing is 'Love'. But maybe that's the kind of topic you have to avoid in workshops. Too embarrassing. Too revealing. Too general. He'd have to think of something else.

He'll have to go, Karl decides, as the bus, full of ordinary, kind people carries him homeward. Someone talks to him and does not seem to notice that he is distraught, has been crying. Better to go to Enniskillen, by taxi if needs be, than stick around at home, thinking of ways to kill himself. If Jim's car is still there, he'll take that. Jim will be annoyed, he needs the car to drive Sarah to ballet and things on Saturday, but he'll get over it.

I never had a pet, Karl remembers, walking down the road from the bus to his house. It's raining seriously now, hard, spitting rain bouncing off his jacket, flattening his curly brown hair to the crown of his head, revealing how thin it's getting. We didn't have pets at home.

But then he realises that this is not strictly speaking true. They had a few, but for short periods – a cat named Snowy, and a Labrador called Belle. Before Belle they'd had Buster, after Fatty's dog in *The Five Find-Outers* – a big black short-haired collie which they'd brought back as a puppy from a holiday in Mayo one year and put in a kennel in the yard. It had lived there, locked up as often as not with a chain round its neck, and became increasingly wild and vicious as it grew big and strong and unable to bear the restraints of its miserable life. His father beat the dog mercilessly with a stick in order to tame it – that was how things were done in Mayo when he was growing up, Karl reckons. Sticks were the answer to most problems. In the end Buster had escaped and run away, probably to be run over at the next bend, but who knows, maybe the poor thing made it into the countryside? Became the wolf he'd always resembled? It was comforting to think of him even now, prowling the Dublin mountains, chasing hares and sheep, like the great strong untamed creature he was by nature.

Belle came when his parents were older and calmer, and she was calm and old herself, or acted like it. She'd slept under the fireside chair in the kitchen and grew fat on scraps – potatoes, apple tart, roast beef. Cornflakes. She ate anything and had become too fat to walk in the end. But she had walked away, somehow, and also vanished from their lives. The history of Snowy the cat, he could not recall. She had made little impact on him one way or the other.

Little grey bollards separate the path from a sort of waste-land-cum-football-pitch that stretches from the road to an estate of white houses. Big bindwood leaves, frog prince leaves, twine around the bollards, and there are trees, oaks with ivy covering them here and there, not enough to hide the rows of houses, regular and repetitive as the chorus of a bad cheap lyric. Corporation, dragging down property values more and more by the year, as it stuffed more houses in. Who knows when the pitch will be submerged by a few hundred terraced two-up-two-downs, nests of drug-peddling, child-mugging fledglings destined for the detention centre? Karl has nagged Jim to move, in the past, when he didn't feel too guilty and two-faced to nag. Jim was for egalitarianism and no ghettos, unlike Karl, whose work made him cynical. Jim didn't care that the value of his house was constantly dropping behind values all over Dublin, so that eventually there'd be no hope of moving. He didn't want the trouble of moving under any circumstance, being lazy about practical matters and having moved many times in his life before. He's a Cancer, Jim, and has worked in the county council for about thirty years. Budging him was never going to be easy.

Karl's halfway down the road when he gets the smell. Bramble. The rain sucks it out of the ditch, that punchy, acid, sweet, blackberry smell, still there, mid-November nearly, still there in with the crisp wrappers and cider cans and condoms and whatever. It's a shot to his bloodstream, a shock to the system. Stunning, beautiful, are the words his nose thinks and at the same time what it does is fill him with a huge new impersonal sadness. Also, it gives him the beginnings of an erection. He grimaces and shakes himself, walks quickly on.

Andrew is overweight. 'Comfy!' he laughed, a few weeks back. One of the girls in the office called him that. Gee, time to get skids on, said Andrew. He doesn't like being overweight but it suits him. He's creamy, blondie, plump, an ice-cream pudding.

Jim is skinny. Jim the Beanpole. Old to Andrew's young, wise to his wild, nervy to his blasé, quick-moving to his slow, steady, inexorable steamrolling. Jim talked fast and hesitated often – um, eh, ah, oh – while Andrew talked in a steady stream, like a bolt of thick soft velvet being slowly unrolled in front of your feet. Velvet that could caress you, or trip you up, or choke you. He was so bloody invulnerable. Sure, you can come and visit. Down the Village, Karl can just imagine, New York, where there are more gay men than any other kind. Well, maybe, maybe ... But there was Jim. Life pointed a way, as it does, and in this case it pointed back where he came from. Home is where your heart is going to stay. It's better and it's the only way, which doesn't mean it's easy.

Last night he'd dreamed about a dog. He was in a car with his sister, driving along by the sea somewhere near the city. There was a small white puppy on his sister's lap. Even though Karl was driving, he could see this puppy clearly – it was soft and tender like all new animals.

It was not well.

Karl insisted that the puppy was going to be all right. It was going to get better. Everything in him insisted that this must happen, that the puppy must get well.

'He's all right, isn't he?' he kept saying to his sister, in a cheerful positive voice. 'He is all right?'

His sister answered at first in doubtful tones. Then she stopped answering.

When the car stopped Karl jumped out onto the footpath. He opened the back door to let his sister and the white puppy out. He smiled hopefully as he opened it and said, 'He's fine now, isn't he?'

The puppy was lying on his sister's lap, small, white, its little body looking warm and vibrant. His sister stroked its little plump side. 'Cold,' she said. And Karl, not touching it, could nevertheless feel it stiff and cold. His sister took the small white body and laid it in the gutter.

After the dream Karl recalled that he had had one other pet, a dog called Buster, another dog called Buster, the first Buster. Also Karl's very first pet. This Buster was a puppy he'd got from Santy when he was eight, a black and white, some sort of mongrel, maybe three weeks old, a very cute age for a dog. Karl's father had made a kennel – that was when he'd made it, the same kennel – for the puppy out at the back of the house.

On Christmas Day Karl was allowed to play with his new dog in the kitchen, which was as warm as an oven, heated by a great big range full of burning coke at all times of the day and night. Buster scuttled about on the polished red and blue tiles, sliding, running under the chairs, his big eyes shining, his face happy and mournful at the same time, his ears pricked up, tail wagging. It was heaven.

But he wasn't allowed to stay inside, even at three weeks old. Karl's father said, and believed, that it would be bad for him, bad training, unhealthy. He had a slight cold, but he still wasn't allowed to stay inside. Some funny country idea – country people are, used to be, mean to animals. Or maybe not, maybe some funny city idea, maybe even Karl's mother's idea. 'I'll get him a dog on condition that he does not piddle in my house . . .' 'The fresh air is good for him,' they both said, several times, because Karl put up a fight.

Karl kept going out to the back to see Buster. The kennel was in a grubby bit of the garden, under the toilet window, near a coal bunker and the place where they left the dustbins, a drab bit of the garden where nobody went if they didn't have to. Buster lay on a blanket in his kennel. It was very, very cold, the afternoon of Stephen's Day, there was frost already at four o'clock. Buster shivered and coughed and Karl kept picking him up to comfort him. He didn't seem to get comfortable. Karl's father told him to stop picking up the pup, he'd make him worse, picking him up. But Karl couldn't stop. He'd never loved anything as much as he loved this dog.

When he went to the kennel next morning Buster was dead. Little cold lump on the blanket, curled up like a slug, trying to warm himself, his eyes shut for good.

He checks the garage before letting himself into the house. Jim's car is there – he took the train to work. With any luck, the keys are in the kitchen. He'll go in, telephone Jim, and head.

The keys are on their hook. He rings Jim, who is not at his desk, but he leaves a message, and promises to ring later. Then he calls the woman in Enniskillen. He says he'll be late, but will arrive. The warm, rather girlish voice of the woman is so sane, so normal, that it is a comfort in itself. 'Och, don't worry at all about that!' she says. 'It's great that you can come at all, at such short notice, and save this workshop!'

Save this workshop. Jesus. Karl feels much better after the call, though. He makes himself a cup of coffee in the kitchen. The oranges are still there, the blue tablecloth, and the sun begins to shine, weakly, while he's drinking the coffee. Sunshine to cheer him up. This is the sort of thing that happens often when he's close to the end of his tether. Life plays a little party piece, pats him on the head, pulls him back from the brink. Sometimes he wishes it would not, but there you are. A ray of sunshine, a lightening of his belly. Snakes slide back into their spiral circles, panthers slink off, snarling, into the undergrowth.

He goes to the bathroom, pats his eyes with a damp

facecloth, scratches his face with a disposable razor. His eyes are bloodshot but by the time he reaches Enniskillen they'll be back to normal. While he is spraying on a bit of aftershave to cover up the pong he got doing all that walking, the phone rings. Jim, he thinks. But no, it's the lady novelist.

'What the hell are you doing?' she yells, angrily. 'You fucking eejit.'

'Sorry. I waited for an hour . . . or so. Actually, I thought I'd got the message wrong or something . . .' All his excuses sound like that. Phoney.

'I've been all over the place looking for you. I told whoever it was last night to tell you to wait at Patsy's Pantry so you could have a cup of tea, keep warm, if I was late. I've been trying you for ages. We're hours late.'

'Um.'

'You get into a taxi and come right over here this minute, do you hear?'

Alison has a warm, bossy, yeasty voice. She told him to wait in Patsy's Pantry so he could get a cup of tea and keep warm. She hasn't gone to Enniskillen without him, even though she hardly knows him. She's late for the workshop but she hasn't abandoned him. Alison is a lady, apparently, a kind good lady, as well as a writer of novels-cum-feminist-cum-carowner-cum-wearer-of-flounces.

'All right,' Karl responds meekly, keeping the gratitude under control. 'I'll be there as fast as I can.'

And every single thing inside him rises.

THE SEARCH FOR THE LOST HUSBAND

She went down the stone stairs – down and down, down and down. She began to fear that she'd never hit land. But in the heel of the hunt she came to the bottom. And there was another country there that looked very much like the country she had left behind at the top of the stairs.

She walked through this country. And after a while she came to a cottage and she went inside. And there was an old couple who greeted her and asked her where she had come from.

'I hardly know myself,' said the girl. 'It's a long, sad and complicated tale. I don't want to bore you with it.'

But she did.

'God love you, you poor child,' said the old man. 'You're to be pitied, there's no doubt about it. But you're welcome to stay with us, dear child. We'll share our bit of food and drink with you!'

'Thank you kindly,' said the girl. 'But as to food and drink, I've plenty of it. I've enough food and drink to feed an army.' And she spread her magic tablecloth on their table.

Every imaginable kind of food appeared on the tablecloth, more than they had ever seen in their lives. And they sat down and they ate their fill. And if they had been eating from that day to this, they wouldn't have finished what was on that table.

'You've got a good thing there,' said the old man. 'A very good thing, indeed. And it will stand to you all your life, I'd say.'

'Wisha, it's all the same to me,' she said. 'I'd rather have my little white goat than all the food and drink on that tablecloth.'

'You're in a bad way,' said the old man. 'But I'll tell you what. There is an old woman living in the castle over beyond, and that old woman's name is the Scabby Crow. She has three daughters and a son. Her son is the little white goat. And you've met her daughters as well. They are the women you stayed with, the ones who gave you the comb and the scissors and the tablecloth. And if you find that Scabby Crow, she might be able to help you.'

So the girl went out the next day. And she met an old woman. And the girl started cutting her clothes with the magic scissors. And her rags turned into the most beautiful dress you've ever seen.

'Will you give me those?' asked the old woman.

'Who are you?' asked the girl.

'I am the Scabby Crow.'

'I will give you this pair of scissors if I can spend one night with your son, the little white goat.'

'That won't be easy,' said the Scabby Crow. 'We are all under a spell from a wicked old witch who lives in that grey castle on the hill. But I'll see what I can do.'

ESTONIA

LUNCH TIME, THE BEST TIME OF THE DAY, IS OVER. Emily has spent it as she often does, walking the streets, not altogether aimlessly but permitting herself to digress every step of the way. First she window-shopped in Grafton Street, going into one shop and examining three racks of evening dresses: still black velvet; stiff noisy taffeta. She is not going to a ball, she does not require a frock, but as she stroked the cloth she remembered dances she had attended and dresses she had worn. Life can be measured in skirts of satin, as well as in years of work, as well as in examinations passed and books read, or husbands married or children offered to the world. (Emily tends to philosophise while she shops. Maybe that's why she likes lunch time so much.) After the dresses, she bought an egg mayonnaise sandwich at a takeaway and ate it in Stephen's Green, sitting on the grass on the bank of the olive duck pond, surrounded by hundreds of other lunchers. It is still possible to sit out in late September. The temperature is nineteen degrees. Low yellow sun bathes everything that is not golden already in syrupy light. When Emily was a child and still believed in heaven her picture of it – a high, pinnacled golden gate, shut – was coloured in this precise tone of sunlight.

★

'Wasn't it terrible, the disaster in Sweden?' Her colleague, Frances, meets her at the door of the office where they both work.

Emily is a librarian. She spends her day cataloguing books, sitting at a computer from nine to five with a box of fragrant volumes at her feet.

'What disaster?'

'I just heard it on the news at one. A ferry sank last night in the Baltic.'

'Oh!'

'They don't know how many people are lost. Hundreds, though. It's the biggest disaster since the war, in Sweden.'

Frances speaks urgently, with the mixture of excitement and thrilled incomprehension which people cushioned in safety feel for distant calamities. But she has a special reason for telling Emily this news, news which will cause only the faintest ripple of interest among Irish people in general. Emily's husband is Swedish, or half Swedish, and he is in Sweden at the moment at a football match.

The news does not cause Emily any personal alarm. She knows he could not be on any ferry, since he is fully occupied with the match. It is being played in Stockholm and when it is over he will fly to Umeå to visit his mother for two days, killing two birds with one stone. Emily glances at her watch. Tuesday. Today is his last day in Stockholm. Tonight he'll take the plane and fly north. She knows he has not drowned. Neither has his mother. It is too bad about the others, whoever they are, but Emily is not going to feel more than a vague, intangible, ineffective dismay on their behalf – more of a disappointment in being reminded that this is a world where accidents can happen than a grief for the suffering or destruction of people who are, dead or alive, strangers.

Much more real to her, in fact, is her own irritation – that lunch time is over. Altruism is not one of her gifts.

She sits down at her computer and pulls a book from the box at her feet: the one unpredictable factor in her working life is what the box will contain. She enhances this small pleasure by treating the selection as a lucky dip. Closing her eyes, she feels covers and weights, surfaces, thicknesses. It's not entirely a game of chance: you can tell, with your fingertips, the difference between a literary novel and a blockbuster, a collection of poems and a scientific treatise, a children's book and an official report. She is, after all, mildly depressed today, so she chooses what she likes best – a volume hard and solid, with a gloss that caresses the skin, smart sharp corners. As she hoists it aloft its scent assails her: the seductive perfume of a smart new novel. And here it is, seduction, *The Seduction of Morality* by Thomas Murphy: shining as a sixpence, adorned by a tenderly brushed portrait of a little girl in a flowing white dress, with sheaves of promising auburn hair braided over her shoulder. The novel, Emily notices, glancing inside, is set in the 1940s. Did girls look like that then? Did they ever look like that? She'd love to read the book and find out what's inside. But that is not what she's paid to do. Her task is cataloguing. In this case, all she needs to do is key in the cataloguing data, which some other librarian, in some other library (the British) has decided already.

The *Estonia* was making the crossing from Tallinn to Stockholm. A storm blew up when she had been at sea for a few hours, but nobody felt concerned. At midnight a loud rumbling sound was heard by those in the cabins above the car deck, and people in the cabins below the car deck noticed water dripping through the ceiling. Twenty minutes later the *Estonia* was at the bottom of the sea. More than eight hundred passengers were still in it. Others floated on the surface of the water, in life jackets or on rafts. Many of them were dead, too.

By five o'clock Emily has catalogued twenty-five books, an acceptable rather than a remarkable number: she can do fifty if she rises to the challenge of her task and puts her mind to it, and one of her colleagues can achieve that every day. But Emily's mind wanders; she spends time thumbing through the pages, or talking. A larger part of her time than she would care to admit is devoted to day-dreaming.

When she started working here books were catalogued on slips of paper, which were passed on to typists. The work could not have been described as exciting, but in those days it did demand a certain, limited, intellectual effort: cataloguers made decisions as they went along. They examined the contents of the books, they discussed subject headings with colleagues. Now most of that is done for them when the book is being published. All they have to do is copy information from the back of the title page and co-ordinate it with the computer system in operation in their library. Occasionally problems occur: old books; books published by tiny publishers who do not know the rules; pamphlets. If it were not for these items which escape the technological net, Emily's job could be done by a robot.

In the old days staff working with books had other privileges. They were allowed to borrow the books and read them, for instance. Now that is not permitted: it would breach security regulations seriously. This loss bothers a few people, like Emily and her friend Frances. But most of them don't seem to mind very much – the most efficient librarians, Emily has long suspected, seldom read books.

Lars is not a librarian but a sports journalist. You see him on television, on the sidelines of a football stadium or on the bank of a swimming pool, interviewing managers, footballers, swimmers who have just won or just lost the eight-hundred-metre freestyle. Often he simply sits in the studio reporting on the events of the day. On television he adopts the anxious, urgent voice of most reporters. His face, however, as befits a sports reporter, remains good-humoured and benign, belying the desperation of his tone.

'You always sound as if you'd run a race yourself,' Emily nagged, in the early days of his career. 'Does it have to be so unrelaxed?'

She'd tried to make him change his style completely, in more ways than one – to stop wearing a jacket and tie, for instance, and have a jumper instead. Is there some rule which says that no man on television can ever wear a jumper? Or, say, a colourful, checked shirt? He laughed, but he hadn't changed his outfit or his voice and at this stage she didn't care. She had stopped watching television. Even news programmes, which had been her favourite, she had dropped from her schedule. It was as if her interest in what is going on in the world, the disasters of the world, had changed from being minor to being non-existent. The news seemed to seldom intersect with her life. And it seemed more and more like one of those games people play at parties, where one starts some story and others tack bits on to it. The inspiration is arbitrary, the plot is seldom strong. The ending, in particular, invariably fails dismally.

Emily met Lars when they were students together, studying third year English and Latin. Instead of concentrating on work for their finals, they concentrated on one another, for a whole year of green, sublime, fraught passion. At the end of the year Emily graduated with mediocre results. Lars failed altogether. He didn't care – his real love was running, or hurdling, to be specific. He managed to get a part-time job in a leisure centre, and hurdled competitively for a few years. When he was twenty-two three things happened: he ran for Ireland in the

European Games (coming third in his event); he got a job as a sports reporter with a newspaper. And he married Emily.

Or, it would be truer to say, she married him.

She had already got the job in the library then. It wasn't anything she had planned, but simply an opportunity that had arisen. 'You might as well do it,' her parents had said. 'You might as well take it,' Lars had also said. It was not as if there was a great deal of choice. There was then, as ever, it seemed to Emily, a jobs crisis. The attitude in the air around Emily, in her home, in college among her friends, was that jobs were so scarce as to be like gold dust. Any job at all, no matter how unsuitable, was better than none.

Emily felt lucky. She was without career ambition. A job she considered to be simply an adjunct to reality, not a major component thereof. Many girls she knew then worked in department stores, in restaurants. They became secretaries. These were girls with good degrees, some with postgraduate degrees. They were a carefree lot, mostly beautiful, mostly convinced that their destiny was to be taken care of by a husband. This was in the 1970s, a time when you might have expected more ambition in young women. Emily had one ambition: to marry Lars.

She felt if she were married, all the other problems of her life would fade into insignificance. Being married to Lars would compensate for its shortcomings. It would liberate her. Roads, green and juicy with promise, rainbow ended, would open before her.

But after they married it seemed that whatever choices she had had earlier began to vanish altogether. Lars's job was on temporary contract, from the beginning and always. Emily's cheque was needed to pay the bills, to make sure the roof would be over their heads, to secure the children's education. Lars became successful, but never successful enough to bolster up Emily's need for security, which perhaps could not seem to be bolstered up. Perhaps she did have a deep famine-fear inside her, which nothing could appease.

So she worked, she raised the children as best she could. She stayed in the same job, doing the same things, year after year: the cheque was regular, and swollen by increments until it became significant, almost an end in itself. For many years dreaming of alternatives and complaining about the reality were her hobbies. Eventually she realised she couldn't change and no longer wanted to: she clung to her secure, familiar work as a drowning man clings to a straw.

And she became, in her spare time, a poet. Whatever qualities she repressed as she worked during the day found an outlet in the words she wrote at home, late at night. 'Found an outlet' is not the right phrase. The poems erupted, like volcanic dreams, full of strange, exotic images, narratives whose relation to her days was as tenuous and slender as the link between the black and silver world of fairy tales and the grey world of farm labourers, as the link between the haunting notes of southern spirituals and the bleak monotony of days on the plantation. Her poems were so strange that at first they were unpublishable. But, schooled to perseverence, she continued. Anyway, she had no choice. She wrote as she dreamed, relentlessly, spontaneously.

There were practical advantages to this habit. As a hobby, poetry was flexible and versatile. She could write on scraps of paper as she travelled to work, or during lunch break, or even at her desk when nobody was looking. She could write in her head, in her blood, in her heart. In her sleep. And she did – it was as necessary as breathing to her, if not as easy.

Her luck turned. She found publishers; she won attention. By now, her children at college, she is established as a minor Irish woman poet – that is how she would place herself, being

as sensitive as anyone else to the literary hierarchies and fash-
ions, if asked to make a public pronouncement. Secretly she
knows, like every poet, that there is no hierarchy in literature
as far as the writer is concerned. Writing is art; writing is work.
The artist simply does the work – simply, with total concentration, makes the thing itself, the thing in hand. And then it is
finished, for better or worse, and goes away to find its own
place and context, its own judges, in another world, the world
of the reader. The writer goes back to the empty page and stays
there. The work is its own highest reward. Of course, Emily,
like everyone, hopes there will be others, and usually there are.

There is a price to pay. She has made no progress in other
aspects of her life. She is still at the lowest level in her job,
where she is likely to remain – in any case, there have been no
promotions in fifteen years. Once married women began to
stay on at work, all promotions stopped. It has nothing to do
with discrimination against women, it's just a coincidence. If
anyone suggests otherwise, the management laughs and says
they are prejudiced and hysterical.

Estonia became independent a few years ago, around the time
of *glasnost* and *perestroika*. Before that, if you were a person like
Emily in Estonia, you would have slaved all day in a paper factory. You would have shared a one-room flat with another family, and a toilet on a landing with fifty people. You would
have spent your spare time queuing for bread and soap.

In those days if you offended the regime in the slightest way,
you would be punished. Lars had heard of a woman, a university professor, who had had an illegitimate child. She had the
baby smuggled out of the country to Sweden. When the
authorities discovered this, many years after the baby had
grown up, this woman was dismissed from her job at the
university. She was stripped of her degrees and removed from

her apartment. She was sent to work at a jam factory. Somebody in Sweden had told Lars about this woman, or he had read it in a newspaper. In fact, hardly anyone visited Estonia in those days: you needed a visa to get in; you needed a visa to get out.

All has changed. Estonia, and the other Baltic nations, Latvia and Lithuania, have become the darlings of Scandinavia. So Lars says. There is always a bunch of Estonians and Latvians at any event, at any inter-Nordic gathering. They are eager to discover the way of life of their Baltic brethren. They are busy trying to get their countries off the ground again, after many years of suffering and stagnation. The Estonians Lars meets are always very friendly and very poor. They are a mixture of naivety and cunning, as they try to learn the ways of European life.

Scandinavians love to visit Estonia. Tallinn, the capital, is old and picturesque, and the way of life still impoverished enough to be fascinating to well-off Swedes and Danes. Besides, many commodities are cheap – alcohol, caviare, handcrafted goods. Swedes go to Tallinn on shopping trips, and bring back food and drink. The *Estonia* was one of the huge ferries which plied the Baltic, from Tallinn to Stockholm, Stockholm to Tallinn, carrying a dual cargo of container trucks and tourist shoppers. It offered an attractive package: a round trip, one night in a hotel, breakfast and dinner on board the ferry, for eleven hundred Swedish krónur, or about a hundred pounds, all in. There was a disco, a cinema, and three bars on the ship. When it began to list many people were dancing or drinking. Many more were asleep.

Emily could now survive without her job. She could give it up and concentrate on being herself, on being a poet. The children are almost grown-up. Lars is still on contracts, but he is so successful that the chances of his ever being without work are practically nil. Emily could write a novel. She could do even nothing. Just nothing. That is the idea that attracts her most of all, after twenty-five years of trucking in and out of town on the bus, day in day out, after twenty-five years of being what history decided she should be: a working mother.

But something prevents her. The older she becomes the more reluctant she is to give up anything. The library has changed in many respects since she started to work in it, many of them for the better. It is warmer, it is more comfortable, it is more humane than in the old days. And it has become so familiar to her that she needs it. It has become so familiar that she, who had once hated the place, loves it.

So she stays put.

She is doing well at her poetry, anyway. She has published four volumes. It's not enough to make her a household name. It's not enough to earn her much money. But as a quiet writer, she enjoys quiet success, and participates in the literary life of Ireland, at one of its levels – not the most exalted, but not the lowest, either. She is invited to give readings and workshops. She is asked to book launches and parties, to which she goes, and to conferences, residencies, seminars abroad, to which she often cannot go, because of the job. Still, her life feels active and full. As compensation for career mistakes, her choice of pastime was good – better, probably, than golf or drink. Poetry consoles her in more ways than one, as it has consoled people in hospitals and in labour camps and in death camps. And she is in none of these things, but in a large, rich, gracious library.

She was in Oslo six weeks ago at a gathering of writers. She had given a reading and a talk on Irish women poets, and listened to other people, from all over Europe, doing the same kind of thing. In the evenings there were receptions and parties, and dinners at restaurants in the centre of town.

There were no other Irish people at the conference, so Emily attached herself to the Scandinavians, with whom she felt an affinity, because of Lars, and whose language she could speak, also because of Lars.

Olaf she met on the second night at a reception in the city hall. A woman from Helsinki introduced her to him just before the speeches began. He had laughing eyes and looked as if he were permanently on the verge of a fit of the giggles. He giggled all the time, as the Lord Mayor, who was hosting the event, spoke. Well, the Lord Mayor would make anyone laugh. He was a huge rotund man, with a round face, a red beard, little glasses. He looked like a troll. He looked like Santa Claus.

The Lord Mayor joked about the traditional enemy, the Swede, who thought Norwegians were stupid, and he told a joke about how many Norwegians it takes to fix a light bulb. But then he said that even though the Norwegians could not fix a light bulb, they could write, and they could compose music, and they could paint. He mentioned Ibsen, and Grieg, and Munch. How many Swedish artists have achieved such international recognition? he asked.

'Why does he keep going on about the Swedes?' Olaf whispered. 'There are Danes at this party, too!'

There are some advantages to having been a downtrodden, colonised country, the Lord Mayor went on. It is countries like that which produce the best artists.

'And the best oil,' said Olaf. 'They even make Volvos now in Oslo, not in Gothenburg. Did you know that? Maybe Gothenburg's cultural renaissance is about to take off!'

Olaf was a Gothenburger, with a lilting accent not unlike that of the Norwegians. He was boyish-looking, with very well-defined features and curly brown hair. His clothes hung loosely, easily on him. A sort of linen jacket. A T-shirt.

He fetched Emily a glass of wine – not her first, her third – and talked to her about his wife and children. 'I have three,' he said. 'I love children, I really love them.'

He laughed when he said this, as he laughed all the time, but his tone changed to one of apologetic confession. So Emily knew what he said was not a boast, but a truth. And she could see that he would love his children, any children, and that they would love him. She could see him playing football, hide-and-seek, she could see him tumbling around the floor. She could see his children racing to meet him when he came home from work or when he came home from conferences – because he did not work, not like Emily. He was full time.

'Oh, you are so successful?' Emily asked.

You could never tell with writers from other countries. You could not distinguish between the successful and the maybes and the ones who would be very lucky to get a review, the way you could at home, where everyone in the literary community could place everyone else in the pecking order as soon as they heard their name.

'I do many odd jobs. I grow vegetables, I pick berries. I fish. And I am poor – poorer than you, probably.'

'That must be awful. For you and your kids.'

'It's not awful. It's fun. I love it. We are happy.'

It's different for you, Emily privately defended herself, as she always did when faced with braver, more committed people. It's different in Sweden, where the state will look after the children if you don't. That means you can take risks that I couldn't.

'I make things,' Olaf was saying.

'Oh? Things?'

He made furniture. As well as writing children's books, he designed chairs and tables. He showed her photographs of the chairs: chairs with three legs, chairs with wheels. 'They've even won prizes!' he said. 'Booby prizes, for the chair nobody can sit on!'

His books had won prizes, too. She saw them in the stall at the conference – books with oddly dressed, strange children grinning on the covers, and stickers saying 'Little Nobel 1995'. Maybe he was not so poor after all?

This suspicion did not put her off him, although she worried about it for half an hour or so. But she walked with him in the park that surrounded the city hall, and along the wide main street. She went with him to Holmenbro, where the ski slopes were, and climbed a tower which gave them a view over several miles of Norway. She walked with him in the woods.

From the first moment she had felt attracted to him. She had felt a strong physical sensation, such as a man might feel, she thought, but which was quite strange to her. The emotional attraction was far from strange, and she warned herself to be careful. She was forty-five. Her hair was bleached, her thighs looked like cold porridge. The flesh on her upper arms dropped like the chin of a cod when she stretched. It is women like you, she told herself, who are the worst. Old fools.

Olaf was fond of her, that was clear. But men could be fond of her as a friend, not as anything else, and she would not know the difference. Her antennae were not attuned to sexual messages, as those of more experienced women can be – at least, that's what novelists suggest. She maintained a dignified friendliness. It was easy for her to ignore the stirrings in her body – she was used to ignoring everything that stirred inside her.

Olaf was not. In the woods near Holmenbro, at two o'clock in the afternoon, on the last day, he spread his jacket under a tree and they sat down. Then, he removed first her clothes and then his.

'Someone will come along and see us!' Emily, on seeing his body, thought about being caught. She'd longed to kiss him for the whole week and now she had to think of the risk, not of the kiss.

'It doesn't matter,' said Olaf, kissing one of her nipples. 'They'll go away again, fast enough!'

'But . . .'

'You're not afraid, are you? You want this?'

'Yes,' said Emily.

His body was hot and silky, twining around hers. He was good-humoured, laughing, but not boyish in his lovemaking. Rather, he was joyfully serious, lightly competent – a poet, a children's writer, a craftsman, what would you expect? He was golden, he fitted her like a glove. We are like gods, she thought, the leaves fondling her back, his body, a boat sailing through her. I am a nymph in the forest. I am a dryad. I am a lynx. I am forty-five.

Somebody actually *loves* me.

What happened was this. The ship's vizor was damaged – the door on the bow which opens to let traffic in. There is another in the stern to let it out. Emily has often used these ferries, called ro-ro ferries, herself, on the way to France or Wales. You drive on, park, drive off. It's so simple. There is one compartment for all the cars and buses and trucks and, in the case of Swedish ferries, trains. This takes up a floor of the vessel. Nobody calls it a ship. You do not even think you are on a ship when you are on one of these ferries. It is more like a town, or a shopping centre. You need never see water, once you come aboard.

The vizor was damaged. In the storm it became more damaged and some water leaked in. Then it broke and a lot of water swept in. When the floor of the car deck was covered by one foot of water the big trucks began to slide. They slid to one side of the ship. The ship turned over. It was as simple as that. Once the listing had begun nothing could stop it. 'Listing ten, listing twenty. We're sinking!' This was the last message the *Estonia* sent out. It was received by the *Mariella*, which was sailing not far off.

Olaf owns a mobile phone.

'I never knew a poet who owned a mobile phone!' Emily teased him.

They spent the whole afternoon and night making love, first in the forest and then in the hotel. They missed the closing ceremony of the conference.

'I'm not just a poet, I write children's books!' he said. 'We need mobile phones, to ring up children.'

'Sure.'

'I ring mine all the time. I'm going to ring them now!'

'Do you think it's a good idea?'

They were sitting in the middle of his bed, naked, drinking wine.

'You ring yours too! What's the code for Ireland?'

'00 353 . . .'

She was saying hello Lydia before she could stop him.

When Emily goes home she sees Lars is on television, reporting on the ferry disaster on the six o'clock news. Although a ferry disaster is not a sporting feature, the television station asked him to cover the story for them, since he is there anyway. The disaster is not a big story in Ireland but it is worth covering directly if it does not cost too much.

Soon after the newscast the phone rings. It is Lars. He asks her to join him in Sweden for a few days, if she can get off. He is getting extra money, and her fare would be paid for by some sports outfit or other that he had worked for. She could come for a long weekend.

She says yes, it's a long time since she's been to Sweden, and she'd like to go, for more reasons than one. She knows she will not see Olaf if she visits Lars and his mother, and in a way she doesn't want to. But she thinks it would do her good to be in his country for a few days.

When she left Oslo she thought about him for a few weeks and then stopped thinking about him. She knew she would never see him again and it is not easy to remain loyal to the memory of a man you will never see again. She had thought he would telephone but he did not. Until yesterday. He rang her at work.

'Hello, it's me, Olaf,' he said.

What is it like, hearing the voice of a man, a man you were in love with recently, on the phone in your office? The objects in the room, the telephones, the boxes of books, shifted themselves and settled comfortably in the yellow September light. Emily closed her eyes and listened to her heart being happy.

'I said I would phone.'

'How are you? Are you well?'

'Yes. I am well. Everything is fine. I am missing you.'

'Yes.'

'You know? It is good to be with my wife and children again. But ...' He giggled. It did not sound as good on the phone as close up, but it was still infectious. 'Are you alone?'

'No.'

'Your colleagues are listening?'

'Yes.'

'Maybe I'll ring you later.'

'Ring me at home. You've got my number at home?'

'It will be all right?'

'Yes.'

'OK. About eleven p.m. You know I love you.'

'Yes.'

'*It* is all right. We do not have to do anything about it. We do not have to do anything about anything any more. I have found that out, now that I am old.'

'We can talk about that later.'

'Goodbye, then.'

She catalogued about sixty books that afternoon. Frances noticed, but said nothing.

How would he phone at eleven? Maybe he would go to some secret place. The bathroom. She envisaged him beside a pile of logs, in an open-sided shed, with the stars glinting icily above him. His ear glued to the phone, his eyes laughing. She saw the forest stacked darkly behind him.

He did not phone at eleven and she was not surprised. It hadn't been possible, because of the family. Or he had forgotten. She did not doubt his intentions. She did not doubt his love. It was genuine, like the promise to call. Genuine, but leading nowhere.

There was no time to give the alarm. Most people on the ferry hardly realised what was happening. Only the very alert made it to the deck, and only the very bravest managed the ninety-foot leap into the sea.

The sea was raging and ice cold, but there were life jackets and rafts. Up-and-down rafts, the reports called them, Lars said. *Op och ner flottar.* Overturned, they meant. Thrown out upside down, or overturned by the waves. Some of the survivors sat on the bottom of overturned rafts for five or six or ten hours. Only a hundred and thirty of the thousand passengers did survive. Lots of people who found a raft died anyway, of cold. And being rescued, when rescue at last came, was not so easy. A helicopter can take one person at a time. That person has to grab a rope, and tie himself to it, while standing on an overturned raft in the raging sea, before he can be hoisted to safety.

Most of the survivors were men, between the ages of twenty and thirty. You had to be young, strong, fit, and courageous. As well as lucky.

She flies on the complicated flight journey from Dublin to Manchester, from Manchester to Copenhagen, and from Copenhagen to Stockholm. From Stockholm she will fly with Lars to Umeå, to visit his mother.

There is a wait of two hours at Copenhagen. She walks around the airport, which is big and elegant, with many restaurants and shops proffering temptation to the traveller – shoes, fine casual clothes, gold and amber jewels. Perfumes, hair decorations. Smoked eels and pickled herrings and cheeses. She loves looking at these luxurious goods, but buys nothing. Everything is outrageously expensive and she and Lars decided, a year or two ago, to resist airport shopping.

She wonders if she might by some astonishing coincidence meet Olaf at the airport. Perhaps he could be on his way to another conference today? By some miracle he could have been in Copenhagen, promoting one of the Danish translations of his books? She laughs at herself for being foolish. Why should he be here? Miracles like that do not occur. Still, she looks at all men who are slim, and dressed in loose, easy clothes, who have dark curly hair. What surprises her is that so many men fit the description.

At the newsagent's she gets a copy of *Dagen's Nyheter* and goes to sit in the waiting area for the Stockholm plane. It is a hushed, silent area, where a handful of well-dressed people wait on the clear blue seats. At this airport there is none of the bustle or haste you feel in London or New York. Instead there is opulence, space, good taste. There is a warm nurturing sense of security. That is the main sensation of Scandinavia, as far as Emily is concerned. A sense of security.

Olaf Andreason, Barnboksforfatter, Göteborg (52)

The newspaper is full of information about the ferry disaster: photographs and theories about why it happened and stories from survivors. In the middle is a centrepiece, listing the names of the drowned.

He had not looked fifty-two. Maybe it is not him. There are so many Andreasons in Sweden, there could be another writer of the same name. It does not say 'children's writer', even. It would say children's writer, if it were Olaf. And she talked to him that day. Wouldn't he have said, 'I'm in Estonia actually'? Or, 'I'm just getting the ferry. I've been to Estonia, shopping'?

Olaf Andreason, Barnboksforfatter, Göteborg (52)
Marit Andreason, Bibliothekar, Göteborg (52)

His wife. His wife was Marit, he had told her that. Marit, and a librarian.

Lars is waiting for her at Arlanda, the Swedish airport. He hardly ever meets her at airports but this time, of course, he has to. There he is, in his new blue raincoat, standing at the end of a long blue corridor. When she sees him her heart warms up, to her great surprise. She feels a gush of love for him, a gush of calm, wifely love. The smile which breaks out on her face is uncontrollable, delighted. She runs to Lars and hugs him un-restrainedly, holding him in her arms for minutes.

'I can't breathe!' he laughs. 'Are you all right? What's the matter?'

'I missed you,' says Emily, closing her eyes. 'I love you.'

★

The papers are full of the story of Sara and Kent.

They had met as they clambered up the sides of the ferry, trying to reach the deck. They promised one another that they'd meet in Stockholm and eat a celebratory dinner, when they reached it. And then they jumped the ninety feet into the sea.

In the water they met again, bobbing about in their life jackets. All night they sat on a raft together, talking and telling jokes, hugging one another for warmth. Other people on the raft had complained. Two died. Sara and Kent kept their spirits up.

Sara was a large, plump, lovely girl of twenty. Kent was a little older.

'We didn't panic,' he said. It was Kent who told their story first, to the TV men. 'We decided to stay calm and keep our sense of humour. And we held on to one another for warmth.'

THE SEARCH FOR THE LOST
HUSBAND

The Scabby Crow went to the witch. And she told her about the girl's magic scissors.

'When she cut her rags the finest suit appeared on her,' she said. 'And she'll give them to me if she can spend the night with the little white goat. And if I get the scissors, I'll cut your clothes and you'll be the best-dressed witch in the whole of the land.'

'Good!' said the witch. 'Tell her to come here tonight and her wish will be granted.'

The girl gave her pair of scissors to the Scabby Crow and the Scabby Crow gave them to the wicked witch.

That night the girl came to the witch's castle. The witch was there, waiting for her, dressed in a lovely new suit.

'Go into that bedroom,' she said. 'And the little white goat will come to you. And he will stay with you until morning.'

The girl went into the room and lay down on the bed and waited. And the little white goat came to the castle. The witch gave him food and drink and then showed him into the bedroom. It was night time, so he was in the shape of a man. The girl jumped up and opened her arms to him. She was overjoyed to see him. And he seemed happy to see her, too. They got into bed together. But the minute he lay down he fell into a deep sleep. The girl did her best to wake him, but nothing she did made the slightest difference. It was all the same to him if she was a man or a woman. He wouldn't wake up.

Just before morning broke the girl fell asleep herself, exhausted. And when she woke up he was gone. She was more depressed than ever. She left the castle and returned to the cottage of the old man and the old woman and told them what had happened.

'Ah, that's the way of her, the ugly old hag!' said the old man. 'She's a divil, may the divil take her, the old bag! I'll tell you what to do. You go there tomorrow, and tell the Scabby Crow that you'll give her your little golden comb, on condition that she makes sure the little white goat stays awake all night.'

THE INLAND ICE

THE HOTEL, AIRPORT, AND FOUR CONCRETE BLOCKS of flats which constitute the settlement of Narsarsuaq are pitched on the sandy plain that runs from the Black River to the Ford of Erik the Red. In the next valley, called the Valley of the Flowers by the Danish tour guides, lie the ruins of an American military hospital, and beyond that low hills, high hills, and the ancient icecap that covers the vast interior of Greenland. Small icebergs float on the fjord, white and jade, blue and silver, dotted like the translucent sails of ghostly ships across the ice-quiet water. They are not jostling each other for space. Down here at the peaceful green bottom of the inlet, miles from the place where the fjord crashes into the Arctic Ocean, and from the glaciers which groaningly belch tons of ice into the viscid water, the icebergs are few and small, harmless as toy boats by comparison with the great battleships which heave and smash further up in a constant icy turmoil.

'I'm going for a walk.' Polly glances at Frank, wondering how he will take this. He is slouching on his narrow white bed, reading some pamphlet which he got from the museum this morning. There is a museum in the settlement as well as the other buildings – an old wooden schoolhouse, fitted out with a photographic exhibition depicting the history of the area; the Ice Age, the Vikings (a model longship, and some woollen dresses and capes, copied from originals hanging in Copenhagen). The Innuit are represented by a ceremonial collar of red beads, a slender, sleek kayak, and some old snowshoes, the kind that look like tennis racquets. Most of the exhibition is devoted to the military hospital, however, which the Americans established here during the Second World War, and to the history of the airport, also established by the Americans at the same time. Bluie West One, the base was called. All the Greenlandic bases were called Bluie, to confound the enemy, a fact which amuses both Frank and Polly. 'Maybe they called the Black Sea white!' he suggested. 'The Red Sea green,' added Polly. 'The Yellow River ... what's the opposite of yellow?' 'Mm. Yangtze?'

'That's all right,' Frank replies now, in his mellow, languid tones, not looking up from his page. His voice exudes patience and charm, qualities which he has not always possessed in as much abundance as he does now. The reason for the change, which has been gradual, is that he is dying. You would not think so, to hear him. You might guess it, if you looked at him, closely, but mostly people don't.

'I'll be back in about an hour,' Polly adds. 'You can ... phone reception, if anything goes wrong.'

Frank is not bedridden, or wheelchair-ridden, but he does not like to move around much unless he has to. He goes on the trips organised by the hotel, but when not on them he stays in his room, reading about Greenland and the Greenlanders. Walking, of course, is out, which is unfortunate since that is the main way of getting around in this area, apart from boat and helicopter.

'I'll be fine. You go and enjoy your walk.'

'OK.'

*

'Greenland,' he said, when they wondered where to go. Polly and he agreed that they should visit a place, or two or three if they could afford to, where he'd always wanted to go. 'Greenland,' he said. 'Egypt. Maybe Lahore, in Pakistan. And I haven't been to Greece,' he said sadly, remembering. 'Or back to Germany in thirty years ... Freiburg. There are so many places. There are so many places in the world I want to be, and now ...'

'Most of us will never see them,' said Polly.

She picks up one of her four holiday books and stuffs it in her bag. *Villette*, the only one she has not read by now, her third day away. She always brings one classic, one new novel, one popular thing that she buys at the airport, and one cultural work relating to the place she is visiting. The classic usually lasts longest, although she has not actually finished the cultural work, *The Saga of the Greenlanders*, as yet, either. It'll have to last until the end of the week. There is nothing in the hotel shop in the line of books, apart from tourist literature and guides to local flora.

She leaves Frank and, passing the giant stuffed polar bear which adorns the lobby, with some trepidation, she steps out into the sparkling white sunshine. The air is like champagne here, or like gin and tonic. It is like nothing she has ever breathed. So much air, so much space, so much ice, means that pollution is non-existent in Greenland, and you can taste that.

She turns left and begins to walk inland. Behind her lies the fjord, and, at the far side, Brattahlið, the old Viking settlement where Erik the Red had set up a sheep farm in the Middle Ages, in a country where even being a sheep was not an easy life. You could see the medieval sheep farms still: the patches of virulent green grass on the darker new grass of the hills marked the spots where they had been.

Frank and Polly had visited Brattahlið yesterday, crossing the fjord on the hotel launch the *Polar Star*. About ten other guests from the hotel had been on the boat as well, along with their guide, a young Danish woman with a blond bob and a red sweatshirt – all the guides, receptionists, and managers at the hotel were Danish, and all the waitresses, cleaners and other menial workers Greenlandic. The guide was shy and awkward, but was helpful getting Frank onto the boat and off it again.

They had met several people on the trip to Brattahlið whom they had not been able to talk to before: the hotel was not all that big, but it was big enough to confer anonymity, or privacy, on its inmates. Besides, most guests stayed for two nights at most, and then moved on to some other part of Greenland. Frank and Polly were the only ones who had booked in for ten days. They had chatted to a little friendly American woman, holidaying alone, who had told them that she lived with her mother in Wisconsin and every year travelled to a different country – this year she was taking in Iceland as well as Greenland. Also a Swedish doctor and his wife, who were celebrating their twenty-fifth wedding anniversary. The doctor had bought a sealskin coat as a present for his wife. Polly had taken a photo of her, wrapped in the shimmering white sleeky fur, against a backdrop of blue and yellow and red wooden houses pitched on the side of a mountain.

'Would you like one?' Frank had asked.

Polly would, but she couldn't bear to spend so much money, almost a thousand pounds, on one coat.

'They are bargains,' the American woman said. 'Absolute snips, and the only bargain you'll get in this place.'

'Are you going to get one?'

'Nope!' She clutched her anorak – it was cold out on the water, even though the sun shone. 'Where I come from, someone'd throw a can of paint at me for wearing that, like as not!'

Then Frank and Polly and the Swedish doctor and the wife in the sealskin coat had talked about cultural imperialism, and how stupid and inflexible some of the environmentalist policies were.

'Half the Greenlanders are unemployed because of boycotts on seal-killing. The seals are eating all the fish!'

'It's the same in Newfoundland,' the American woman joined in. 'Last year some Newfies found seals in their gardens, scavenging in their dustbins – even seals are dying of starvation because nobody is allowed to cull them, keep the population down. It's an ecological thing. Hunters are part of the ecology, that's what those ecologists don't get!'

'We still can't afford one,' Polly said to Frank. 'And it's never that cold in Ireland. I'd never get a chance to wear it really, would I?'

'Ah, you never know!' he said, with his new fresh cheeriness and his firm belief that life was still full of possibilities, which he had always had and which had not diminished.

Frank had a special reason for coming to Greenland, and that reason was to see Brattahlið: the farm of Erik the Red, the church which his wife, Tjodhild, had built and worshipped when she became a Christian, the beach where the first settlers had come ashore. Frank is working on an edition of the Saga of the Greenlanders, has been working on it for many years, and wanted to see the place it described before he finished the work. Even if he didn't finish it, as now seems likely, he wanted to see it.

'You could never imagine Brattahlið looked like this,' he said. 'How could you imagine it? So green, so lush, so pastoral.'

'It is like Mayo, or Donegal,' Polly said. 'Not really all

that lush, but very green, and cold.' It was now called by another name, Quagguarsuk, a name which Frank refused to remember, exhibiting an unusual lapse of his usual good memory of foreign placenames here in this part of Greenland, where, he contends, the Scandinavians were the first to name anything, long ago in the tenth century.

He spent hours walking, slowly, around the stones on the ground which were left from the original farmhouse. Imagine them sitting in here! It was quite big. They must have been frozen half the time! They'd have had a fire. But what did they burn, what did they burn? And what did they eat? No corn. Hardly any vegetables. No wood. Their connections with the mainland – Iceland, and then Norway – were crucial.

Today Polly forsakes the pleasures of medieval history, and walks in towards the icecap. This inland plain is grey for the first mile, covered with an alluvial deposit that lends it a desert-like, moonlike air. But it is not without colour. The most surprising thing about this part of Greenland is that it is pink – carpeted with florescent pink willowherb, whose brilliance is enhanced by innumerable clumps of camomile daisies, white and yellow. Flowers flourish in the climate here, liking the short bright snap of summer with its endless cool sunshine, and thriving in the thin soil which supports little else apart from them, not even potato or cabbage or angelica, the stand-by of other northerners against scabies (the Innuit avoided the disease by eating the stomachs of small birds who had grubbed whatever vitamin C there was from under the snow). They could have eaten bluebells, too – they grow abundantly in the bogland, which stretches from the grey sandy area to the scrubby hills. Also violets, coltsfoot, gentians – a myriad brilliant blossoms. Polly can identify them, because she came here on a guided walk on her first day, without Frank.

She had walked with a couple from Essen, a chemical

engineer and his wife who was dressed in a sort of Gretchen outfit, dirndl, flowery skirt, little black cardigan. Ankle socks and lace-ups, all amazingly inappropriate for a long walk through the bog and hills, a walk to the inland ice. Also she looked about twenty years older than her husband, but probably was not. They were friendly, telling Polly about their seven children at home in Essen, some grown-up and some not, and laughing at one of the other members of the walk, an American from Harvard, called something like Jean or Hilary, some woman's name. The American accompanies the group for part of the walk, but then sets off alone – he is dressed oddly, too, but in the opposite way from the woman from Essen. He wears a helmet with a mosquito veil over his face (not a bad idea – there are plenty of mosquitoes about), lederhosen, huge mountain boots, an alpenstock. He carries a butterfly net with him as well.

'Doesn't he remind you of Helmut?' the wife says, as the little group stand and watch this man from another century walk away from them. 'Helmut is our neighbour at home. He always has everything correct, the correct equipment for everything! That American is just like Helmut!'

'Yes, yes!'

'Get him in the frame!' she says. The husband videotapes everything, and now points his camera at the back of the retreating Jean.

Frank and Polly have had an up-and-down marriage, not a straight run of happiness. Polly is never sure whether this is typical of all marriages, and suspects most of the time it is. At others, she is certain that hers, theirs, is rockier than most, that she and Frank are less compatible than the majority of couples, that their rows are more violent and raging and their range of shared interests very narrow.

And then at other times she has thought the opposite: that they are unusually lucky, unusually happy. There have been oases of calm lasting for weeks, less often months, in the rough terrain of their marriage. These patches have occurred when Polly has stopped demanding that life be happy. This is how it seems to her now. Frank, really, has never asked for much. He has always been calm and content, but then, she thinks, he has been luckier than her as well, in many ways. He has never made the major, increasingly fatal compromises with his own destiny that Polly has made all along the line, almost closing her eyes and picking the path of her life in the dark, as if no choice could have any consequence that mattered, as if all roads would remain open and passable for the duration of her existence and if she turned off one now, it didn't matter, she could always go back again.

Frank is going to have to compromise now. And Polly has realised for some time that choices have consequences, that you usually can't turn back, that it matters what you do with your time because there is only a limited amount of it allotted to you. How could I have chosen wisely? is a question she often asks herself. Nobody ever helped. Frank didn't help her to make decisions. Never seemed to care about her in that deep way that mattered. (What she means is, he let her truckle along with her job as an executive in a public service office, a job which meant something to some people but not to her. I want to be alive! Polly screamed. I want to be creative! Well get out then, he said, get out. But I can't, I can't, I can't. I should never have got in.

Funny. It had seemed so urgent to get a job, to Polly, when she was twenty. Maybe it was urgent at the time, although she can hardly think why. Why? Lots of young people hung out, lived the bohemian life. She was always being told, 'Ah take it! You can change later . . .'

And all along the line there seemed to be good reasons for staying put and putting up with it. After she got married and they'd had their children, she'd had to, because Frank was ill then, too, from the start. His life has always hung in the balance; she's always felt responsible. The children are older, finished college, Polly and Frank have a good shared income. Now should be the time. But now he is going to die. She can't get out now. She's old, almost fifty. There's nothing for her to do but stick it out until sixty-five. And then claim her pension, what she's been working for all these years, like so many of her colleagues. Selling themselves for forty years so that they can enjoy themselves when they are sixty-five.

That's how it seems on bad days, how it has seemed, so that Polly has often found herself awake crying in the middle of the night.

'Who could sympathise with you?' Frank asks testily. 'Being a bit bored is not a real problem. Nobody ever died of that.'

'I know,' said Polly. 'I know, I know. But I thought my life would be so different. I thought it would be, you know, wonderful! I always worked so hard and now it's this. It's just so hard for me to believe that this is my life.'

'Nobody's life is perfect, Polly.'

But she thought others' were better than hers. More fulfilled. More vibrant. She knew that, she could see it on their faces and hear it in the tones of their voices, whereas hers had grown soft, timid, dull. It had grown as grey as the filing cabinets that surrounded her every day, every day except when she was on holidays. Grey carpet, grey filing cabinets, grey brain.

She is at the military hospital. Not much remains. Low concrete walls mark the outlines of the buildings which once stood here. The wards, the operating theatre, the mortuary. Only one building survives intact: the incinerator. It is a blackened chimney, square and not very high, sticking up here from the grey and black landscape.

There are many rumours about the use of the hospital. The official line is that it was never used at all, that the Americans built it but found it impractical to fly injured soliders in to Greenland. The other story is that it was used as a dying camp for those whose injuries were so bad that the authorities did not want them to be at home in America.

Frank believes the first story and Polly the second. The morbidity of it, the underhandedness, the secrecy, appeal to her pessimistic imagination. That's what people do with the injuries that are too horrible to contemplate – they hide them away in the Arctic. Anyway, the hospital, the ruins, look like the guardian of a dark horrendous history. They look as she thinks Belsen must look, or Auschwitz, or any of the ghastly edifices that haunt the imagination of Europe in the second half of the twentieth century, uniting it as well or better than any law or privilege plotted in Brussels.

'You have to stop blaming me!' Frank has said, quietly, despairingly. 'You have to stop blaming anyone.'

'I don't. I blame myself. Can't you see? The enemy is myself. That's what makes it all so hopeless.'

'Well change then.'

'I'm afraid. I'm so afraid.'

'What are you afraid of?'

What is she afraid of? Being cold and hungry. Being poor. That is what she is afraid of. Surely it is not so unusual? Some people choose fun and joy, and hope the other things take care of themselves, and, it seems, they often do. And some choose boredom and security, and hope the fun takes care of itself. And often it does, doesn't it? They get by. It's just Polly who does not get by, at least, not inside her head.

None of that matters.

A voice is coming from the incinerator. American, she thinks, automatically trying to place the accent (she's travelled quite a lot, Polly, for all her boredom). It's east coast, New York, possibly New Jersey. Polite, cultured, upper class. It carries well on the champagne air.

She is too terrified to move. Paralysed from the crown down, a stone frozen to the ground, an iceberg. She has felt like this only once or twice before, when she feared assault, or rape, or murder, at the hands of a strange man in a strange and lonely place: the most numbing physical cowardice she has felt. This is . . . powerlessness. Anything can now be done to me.

He emerges from the top of the chimney. Head, shoulders, the rest of him. A tall, basketball-playing type, twentysomething, black wavy hair, blue eyes, straight nose. Teeth big but not outrageously so, not those gorilla slabs some men have. It's a perfect histrionic face, too good for today's movies, the kind you see in silent films. Jeans, yellow T-shirt, soldier boots. In one hand he carries a pair of nylon stockings. The other hand does not exist: nothing emerges from the right sleeve of his T-shirt.

She breathes again.

Don't be afraid.

I'm not, she says.

He is as familiar to her as her own hand, as Frank. Still, she has not seen him ever in her life. It strikes her that he is one of the figures who occur in her dreams – strange men who do not quite resemble anyone she knows in reality.

I dream about you, she adds.

He is walking closer to her. His skin is slightly spotty, with small white spots like mould on cheese, very few.

Are you going to tell me about your dreams?

No. Rule number one. Never bore a man with your dreams.

Mm. And rule number two?

Never leave a chip pan unattended.

Who told you that?

My mother on the eve of my wedding.

You married a chip pan?

No. Not exactly.

Not exactly.

No.

He's loyal and true then?

Yes, I think so. Mostly.

Once you found an incriminating letter?

How did you guess?

It's that little ridge between your eyes.

A long time ago.

Forget it then.

He's going to die.

So are you.

Soon.

Nobody's perfect.

Being dead . . .

Is worse than not being perfect.

I love him.

Now.

Now.

But not before.

Not so much.

It figures.

You're such a know-all.

I've been around.

You've been around here?

Yeah. You see?

Was it really a camp for the dying?

What do you think?

I think, yes, it was.

Then.

Who are you?

You know me. You dream about me all the time.

So what have you to tell me?

Do I have to tell you something?

Do I have to have an embarrassing conversation with some freaky ghost from a death camp who has nothing to tell me?

It wasn't a death camp.

Whatever.

Things don't have to fit all the time.

That's it.

That's enough.

Erik the Red came to Brattahlið in the year 980 with about forty men. They called the country they came to Greenland, because it was green for three or four months in the summer in the part they settled in. More Icelanders came and a colony was established around the narrow fjords in the south of Greenland. The colonisers were the first inhabitants of this area, and had no contact with the native population of the great country, who lived farther north. For more than three hundred years the Scandinavians stayed in Greenland, speaking Icelandic, farming sheep and cattle, fishing. They maintained close contacts with Iceland and Norway, and their way of life was similar to that in those countries.

Gradually, in the fifteenth century, the Greenland colony lost contact with Iceland, which meant the rest of the world. By the end of that century it no longer existed. Scholars are undecided as to why.

'They're getting a doctor. That Swede.' Frank stooped over her.

'I'm not sick.'

'You've been attacked, haven't you?'

'No.'

'That ghastly American with the mosquito net ... it was him.'

'Frank. It was not him. It was nothing. I just felt a bit weak and he came along.'

'He's a freak.'

'Yeah. Frank, sometimes I think I want to die with you.'

'Suttee. Don't be silly.'

'I know. But what will I do?'

'You don't even ... You fight with me all the time.'

'I wish I hadn't done that. I wish so many things had been different.'

'Well ...'

'It's been such a muddle, hasn't it? Do you think it could have been better?'

'Well, it's better if people try to be happy. Try to be kind to one another.'

'I know. And now ...'

'It's all right.'

'He said, "Nothing fits." '

'Who?'

'The American.'

'Well, he's probably right there.'

They drank some sort of drink at the inland ice. Sweet Martini – the only alcohol Polly got while in Greenland. The tour guide did a little routine: she went to the edge of the ice and broke some off, popped it into the plastic glasses. Everyone, the couple from Germany and the couple from Sweden and the American lady, and others, raised their plastic glasses and drank.

'They export this ice all over the world,' the tour guide said. 'It is millions of years old.'

When you fly over the icecap it is like a field of snow, ridged like corduroy. At the edge it towers over you, like a high mountain of ice, and you see that the little ridges are high hills; it is built in a series of slippery ice ridges stretching for thousands of miles across Greenland. People have walked on it – Innuit hunting, explorers, scientists investigating its depth, its temperature. But it's hard to imagine how.

From a slight distance, or from above, the icecap is as white and glimmering as anything in the world. But when you are close to it, standing beside it, you see that the white ice is full of gravel and sand. It looks dirty, like old snow piled up at the side of a city street. Underneath, however, the ice has formed shapes like stalagmites, and when you peer under you see that they are blue and turquoise, silver, jade, and other subtle, shining, winking colours for which you have no name.

Polly wishes she could say I love you, and undo with that sentence all the millions of mean sentences, the betrayals, the stabs, of her life. But nothing can undo them, and nothing can now transform their marriage, her marriage and Frank's into the blissful union it should have been. There is no time. If there were, it would not happen, anyway. But she says, 'I love you', and Frank smiles, and kisses her, and pats her back gently. 'I love you, too,' he says.

THE SEARCH FOR THE LOST
HUSBAND

The girl took the old man's advice. She went to the Scabby
Crow. And she took out her golden comb.

'Wisha, that's a nice comb you have,' said the Scabby Crow.

'It is,' said the girl. 'And see what it can do!'

She took the pins out of her hair and she combed it. Her hair
was black. And as she combed it her hair turned gold. She
combed and combed and her hair became more and more
beautiful, long and thick and shining like the sun.

'Wisha, I could do with a comb like that,' said the Scabby
Crow, who had very little hair. 'Would you ever give me that
comb?'

'I will give it to you,' said the girl, 'but on one condition.
That I spend another night with the little white goat, and that
he stays awake this time.'

'Didn't he stay awake last night?' asked the Scabby Crow.

'He did not,' said the girl. 'He slept like the dead all night long, and I hardly exchanged a word with him.'

'I'll see what I can do,' said the Scabby Crow.

She went to the castle and spoke to the wicked witch. 'Do you see this comb?' she said. She pulled out the comb and showed it to the witch.

'It is a nice comb,' said the witch. 'And what can it do?'

The Scabby Crow pulled off her hat and combed her few strands of grey hair. And as she combed, her hair grew long and thick and turned to gold. She had the most beautiful, shining hair you ever saw.

'I'd like to have that comb,' said the witch.

'You can have it,' said the Scabby Crow, 'if you let the girl spend the night with the little white goat. But this time he'd better stay awake.'

'Very well,' said the wicked witch.

THE WOMAN WITH THE FISH

A NEW WOMAN HAD COME TO WORK in the English department, replacing Maggie, who was on maternity leave. Everybody was talking about her. There had been no new staff for ages and most people on it, apart from Maggie and the secretaries, were men. The new woman was small and fair-haired, and so far had worn the same thing every day: a blue jumper and blue jeans. This was not so interesting. What was interesting was that she also wore, when she came into the department in the morning and when she left at six o'clock, a large blue beret, made of thick stodgy felt and resembling a chanterelle in shape. In addition, she owned a pet fish. The fish lived in a glass bowl on top of her filing cabinet.

Michael noticed her the first day she came in, as he noticed all women who came to the department for any length of time. He was pleased that she had joined the staff. He told himself that she was probably a nice person, meaning that she was good-looking enough to be a pleasant companion and not too good-looking to be a threat. He made a mental note to befriend her at the earliest opportunity. This would be a kindness to her. He knew she would appreciate and no doubt need the friendship of a man like him, a nice man and a modern man, a man who was a supporter and lover of women, but never a womaniser: a man who, in his unique new way, was God's gift to women. He was one in a million.

But he did not talk to the new woman at all for a whole week. Once, on the Friday, he met her in the lift on the way down. She was going home, laden with her briefcase and the fishbowl, wearing the mushroom hat. He was slipping out to meet a friend for a drink, and planning to come back and finish the lecture he was working on later. When the lift hit ground he picked up the fishbowl, which she had laid on the floor, and handed it to her.

'Better not forget him!' he said, with a smile.

She returned the smile.

After that he did not talk to her for another week.

Michael had been working in the college for two years. He was employed as a tutor, and was working on a Ph.D. on Irish women poets of the nineteenth century. Before, he had been a schoolteacher, of English and Irish, but he had been delighted to give up teaching when the opportunity for different work arose. Lecturing seemed to him to be a more challenging and glamorous occupation. When someone asks you what you do, and the answer is 'I'm a lecturer', or 'A lecturer, actually', the response, Michael thought, was a nod of admiration, a silent What a clever and important fellow you must be; whereas, when the answer was 'I'm a teacher', people thought, Oh good, someone who is as harmless and dull as me.

Ever since he had been a little boy, Michael had wanted to be considered a step above the run of the mill. He knew he was several steps above it. He knew, in his heart, that he was at the top, the match of kings and presidents, company directors and brain surgeons. But knowing in his heart was never enough. Others had to see it, too. And they wouldn't, while he was a teacher, especially a teacher of Irish, the language so many Irish people scorn and despise.

But Michael had loved teaching children, and so far his new dream was turning out to be very dull. Half the time he spent correcting other people's lousy English. It was astonishing how bad students were at writing, spelling, punctuation, or logical thinking. The rest of the time he spent trying to communicate the excitement and importance of literature to people who were less sensitive to the beauty of books than a cat is. Half the class never bothered to turn up to lectures at all. Work on the Ph.D. progressed at a snail's pace. Sometimes Michael despaired of ever finishing it.

He was barely forty. Already he had a teenage daughter and two boys aged ten and twelve. His wife had been in his year in college and the year they graduated she had suggested to him that they get married. He hadn't wanted to – young men didn't, according to custom, at that time. Marriage was an institution that women coerced men into, it was commonly believed. But he had been attracted to her, or in love with her, and he did not want to lose her or do the ignoble deed. Her parents expected him to do the right thing, since he had been going with her for three years. Wasting her time, they would have said, had he pulled out at that stage. That was what people said. He would have been wasting her time on her, the time she should have been using to get a husband, just as she had used her time in college to get an education and then get a job. Whereas a man's time was somehow different. For him those three years would not have been wasted had he not got married. He would have scored a victory and totted up experience, and moved on to other things.

She – her name was Maureen – got pregnant on the night of their honeymoon. She never had a job herself. At the time it had seemed correct for her to stay at home and be pregnant, and paint the flat, and then stay home and mind the baby, and then stay home and be pregnant again and mind the two children and then paint the house and make curtains and plant shrubs in the front. Michael had approved and had felt proud to be a breadwinner and a father.

Then. But times had changed. Now it was not fashionable for women to stay at home. The trendiest, best women had jobs and earned as much money as their husbands. Michael liked to be in the fashion where things like this were concerned. Maureen was now taking a Back to Work course. Too late, Michael sometimes thought. Like many women in their late thirties who have spent their lives in the gentle prison of the home, she was full of cheerful expectation. She did not realise the cruel realities of the business world. A plump, soft, faded prettiness was all the armour she possessed, along with her pathetic optimism. Even her clothes were subtly incorrect – too timid and too ladylike for the sharp-edged modern world, the world Michael inhabited. By now, Maureen and he seemed to belong to different generations. He felt himself to be much younger than her in mind and spirit, even in body, although in chronological terms she was his junior by almost a year.

He believed he loved her and always said so if she asked. But since he had come to work in the college he spent little time with her. He liked to come in at ten in the morning, to work on articles and his Ph.D. Nevertheless, he stayed very late. He found it difficult to finish any piece of work: he was a perfectionist. In consequence he seldom saw his family at all. His wife did not often accompany him to social functions. She had to stay home and babysit. In general he avoided events to which he would have to bring a partner. He claimed to dislike parties but the truth was he did not like to parade his wife in front of the other university wives, who were all size tens with glossy ashen coiffures. He liked his wife's body when he was at home, though. It was lovely to curl up on the sofa with her, or to curl up in bed. At home, look is not as important as feel. And Maureen felt good. Familiar and warm and reliable. He trusted her. She had always loved him and always would. She was more mature than him in character and was good at giving him advice and encouragement, praise and endorsement. Besides, she was an excellent cook.

He considered his marriage happy and liked to congratulate himself privately and not so privately on having made such a success of it. He had never been unfaithful to his wife, even though he was extremely fond of women. She was so understanding that she even understood this. It was a joke between them, in fact. She laughed when one of his friends phoned, when he spent hours chatting to them, or even when they called around on Sundays, the only day he was at home, to go for a walk with him.

When the woman with the fish, whose name was Anna Muller, had been working in the department for two weeks, he went to her room.

'I'm Michael,' he said. 'Remember, we met in the lift? How are you both settling in?'

'We're surviving.' She looked up from her computer.

'Well, I've been here for two years and I haven't cracked it yet. It takes time,' he said. 'By the way, I read that article on Forgotten Women. It was really good.'

'Thank you.'

'We need much more of that sort of thing in this college,' he pointed out. 'It's dreadful, the way women writers are simply ignored as a matter of course.'

Anna had heard this comment a thousand times. She had made it a thousand times herself. But Michael managed to make it sound fresh and original. He mentioned a book that had been published five years previously, and asked her if she'd read it.

'No actually.'

'I've got a copy somewhere under the bed. I'll root it out and bring it in tomorrow if you like.'

'Thank you,' she said. 'That would be great.'

He gazed into her eyes for a minute as she said this. But before he left he stared for a while at the fish. His eyes and the silver glasses that framed them glinted. The fish, whose name was Anton and who was a big guppy, began to swim frantically around the bowl, as if it could feel itself being observed.

Michael did not come to Anna the next day. He was in. She saw him in the canteen. She kept thinking he would probably come over. But he did not. Nor did he come to see her on the following day. But on the third he came and handed her a paperback volume.

'Oh!' – she was overwhelmed with relief – 'thank you so much.'

'No trouble,' he said. He did not mention the delay, but glanced at his watch. 'Found a good place to eat yet?'

'I go to the canteen. Or I bring a sandwich.'

'Me too. But today I've left them on the kitchen table. My wife just rang to tell me. I'm like that. Can't be let out on my own. Would you like to join me for a tomato soup in a pub outside?'

'Oh well,' said Anna. 'Why not?'

She put on her coat and mushroom hat.

'When do you feed him?'

'Anton? Just before I go in the evenings. Six o'clock. That's dinner time for him.'

'And weekends?'

'I bring him home. Or I have done so far. But now that he's settled in I might leave him. He'd be all right for a few days.'

'I could feed him for you if you like, at weekends. I'm always in on Saturdays.'

'That would be great.'

'Where do you keep his stuff?'

'Second drawer of the filing cabinet actually.'

Over lunch he found out that Anna was married too. Her husband was a businessman, working with a multinational computer company. She did not know precisely what he did, but he was away a lot, at least once a fortnight, in London or Boston, where the company headquarters were. She lived in Donnybrook – he made a note of the address. She'd worked in an American college in the past, and her ambition was to bring women's issues into prominence in this one.

He told her he was a feminist and was planning to teach a course on the suppressed female literature of de Valera's Ireland. He told her he believed women were better human beings than men, more intelligent and understanding and thoughtful. In particular, he had noticed how much better his daughter was than his sons. 'My daughter put her arms around me today and said, "Daddy, everything will be all right, don't you worry!" The boys wouldn't do that in a million years.'

'They are younger, aren't they?'

'It won't be different when they are older.'

Anna found herself having to defend the masculine sex in general, which she thought most amusing.

He asked her if she had children and she told him about her miscarriage. He wanted to know everything about it. When it happened? Where? How? How long she had spent in hospital and how many consultations she had had afterwards. Had she needed therapy, or any other form of treatment? He asked if she was trying to have another baby and she said yes. Yes. He told her that he was thinking of being sterilised, because his wife got pregnant every time he looked at her.

'Gosh!' was all Anna could say aloud, and the word she said in her mind was 'Yuck!' The very word 'sterilisation' nauseated her, although in general she approved of all modern developments in the area of contraception, as in all areas of life.

'You haven't . . . been done, yet?' she asked, trying to mask her consternation.

'No,' he replied drily, pulling back from her as he spoke and stiffening his back. 'Where do you go on your holidays?'

Three days later he had lunch with her again and on Friday asked if she'd like to go to the pub for a quick jar when she'd finished work. She would have liked to but she could not. She had to go to a reception with her husband.

'Drat!' he said. It was one of his strongest exclamations. He abhorred vulgar language. 'I'll see you on Monday then. I'll feed him for you tomorrow.'

'Goodnight,' she said softly, and sadly.

'Goodnight, love,' he said, even more softly.

Had she heard him correctly? She wasn't sure. But she hugged herself briefly when she got into the car. All evening a warm glow filled her, and her reception chatter was leavened with a vivacity which it usually lacked. Her husband complimented her on her good humour and appearance.

The next week Michael had lunch with her every day. After lunch he asked her to walk with him in Stephen's Green, and she did. On Friday he began to fret about the weekend. He asked her to telephone him in the department on Saturday, just to say hello, and she promised to do so. But she did not do this. Her husband never left her side, all day. At about four o'clock the phone rang. When she lifted it there was no one there. She knew it must be him and felt remorseful for letting him down. It was such a little thing to ask, one phone call, and she had failed to give it to him.

On the following Monday he kissed her. They were in the Green again, on the path that runs along the east side, from the Shelbourne corner to Earlsfort Terrace – it is the shadiest and quietest of the paths. He had checked beforehand to make sure the coast was clear.

'Do you know what is happening to us now?' he asked in his most serious tone.

'Yes,' said Anna, simply and firmly. She guessed he was about to declare his love.

'It's as if a sack has come down and covered our heads, isn't it?'

'Yes,' said Anna, in a darker voice. Her heart sank. She had no idea why and she did not know what he was talking about. It was a trick of his to use striking, concrete metaphors of that kind, which sometimes seemed brilliant and uniquely accurate and which sometimes seemed utterly meaningless.

The next day her husband went to London on one of his trips. She let Michael know he was away.

'Oh good,' he said cheerfully. 'I can ring you at home.'

'When will you ring?'

'Oh, about ten o'clock or so.' He smacked his lips at the close of the sentence, with a little sucking sound.

Anna supposed that he really would not ring at all, but would take the opportunity to call on her in person. She tidied the house and bought a bottle of white wine to put in the fridge. She also bought some cheese, French bread, and a fruit-cake. She had noticed his liking for sweet things.

At half past ten he had not arrived.

She put a Mozart symphony on the CD player, guessing that he would arrive at any moment. She curled up on the sofa with her legs tucked under her and sipped a glass of wine.

At half past eleven she went to bed. She was crying and her stomach felt as if it had been kicked about by a rugby team. Her whole inside felt like that.

At ten to twelve the phone rang.

'Hi!' he said.

'Hello.' She sat up in bed. Her body slipped back to normal. It was as if it had been an object pressed into the wrong container, by accident, for a while. And now it had been taken out and put back in its own box.

'It's lovely to hear your voice,' he said in his caressing one. 'Isn't the telephone marvellous?'

He did not mention the time, or the delay, but asked her many questions and let her talk on and on. He asked all kinds of silly, enjoyable little things. What was her favourite food? Did she like *Father Ted?* On what side of the house was her bedroom situated, the road or the back?

At lunch the next day he pressed his knee to hers all the time they were eating, and he kissed her in the porch of the pub, quickly but so passionately that they both shook afterwards and could hardly walk back to the college. Anna asked him to phone her at home again that night and he did. They talked for three hours in one of the most absorbing conversations Anna had ever had. This, she felt, was the essence of true communication. This was the best talking experience she had ever enjoyed in her entire life.

The third night he came to see her.

He wanted to see everything in the house and examined objects closely, picking up books and ornaments and observing them in the light. He did not eat or drink anything, however, nor did he go to bed with Anna. Instead he sat with her on the sofa and kissed her for hours. She hadn't done anything like this since she was eighteen.

'What are we going to do?' she asked, at about three a.m.

'Do?' He patted his lips tenderly.

'About us.'

'What can we do?'

Anna considered it might be useful to go to bed, for one thing, or to find a flat and live together, for another. But she did not voice these thoughts, knowing that it is unwise to push a man in matters of love. She could see how deeply in love he was and knew that, given time, he would realise what they had to do.

He came down with a bad dose of influenza the next day. This Anna learned from the departmental secretary – he'd phoned in sick. She waited for him to telephone her but he didn't. Three days passed. Anna became frantic. She could not concentrate on her work, she could not sleep, she could not talk to anyone. It amazed her that nobody seemed to notice her turmoil, which threatened to swallow her up like a whirl-pool. It became so overpowering that she phoned him at home. A woman who sounded young and vulnerable, child-ish, answered. Anna banged down the receiver, terrified.

The next week Michael did not come to college: term was well over and the examinations already marked. On Tuesday he telephoned Anna. He told her he was on holiday in Mayo, and also that he had got a new job for next year, at another institution. It was not as prestigious as the one he was leaving but better paid, and he felt the work itself would be less demanding, leaving him more time for his own projects. He had not been ill at all last week, but negotiating and being interviewed. 'It's just as well, I think. Don't you agree?'

'You mean we won't see each other again?'

'What is the point in making one another miserable?'

Anna knew she could never be more miserable than she had been during the past ten days. But she felt beaten. She could not argue with him on the phone – the departmental secretary was sitting in her room. 'I suppose that's right,' she said. 'Good luck with the job.' There were no exclamation marks in her speech, on that occasion or for a long time afterwards.

Anton the fish died. He had been putting on weight, since Michael tended to overfeed him. Anna came in one morning and found him floating on the surface of the water. She threw him into the wastepaper basket and at lunch time went to the pet shop and bought a goldfish. It flashed like an amber gem in the water.

As he had anticipated, Michael found the new job easier. He taught only five or six hours a week and had plenty of time to read and write. 'The Hidden Ireland: Irish Women Poets of the Celtic Revival' was finally beginning to take shape. Michael worked hard at it. Anna he pushed to the back of his mind. As far as he was concerned, he would never see her again. She had been a nice friend, but no better than a dozen of other such friends he had had over the past several years. They all had to go, in the end. That was the way life was.

But after a month or so he began to think of Anna again. In particular, he remembered her house, which he had seen only once. He pictured her walking through its rooms, which were sparsely furnished and elegant. He saw her hoovering the plain white floors, or arranging white flowers in a vase of eggshell blue. He imagined her going to the fridge and taking out plates of cheese and caviare and wine and other delicacies, and putting them on the plain wooden table for that husband of hers. Muller. His grandfather had been German, she thought. Thought! She did not even know for sure. That was typical of her. She was so clever in some ways and in others so insecure. All her knowledge quivered and shook on its basis of sand. She was seldom sure of anything.

She had not telephoned. This surprised him. Usually when he dropped a woman in this way she plagued him with calls for a while. In such cases he would be friendly but indifferent, making and breaking appointments, feeding that woman a diet of uncertainties and disappointments until, eventually, she would abandon him in despair, sometimes after a very long time. But Anna had not phoned even once. He found himself wondering, quite irrationally, if she were still alive.

Six months passed. Now there was not a day when he did not think of Anna. He did not think of her all the time, of course. His work was very preoccupying. He was constantly talking to people and had made many new friends, including a few women friends. But the image of Anna popped into his mind many times every day. Anna in her blue beret. Anna with her fish. One evening he was drinking a pint of stout with his colleagues. Anna had been on his mind more often than usual that day and he had to talk about her.

'Did you see that piece by Anna Muller in *Hibernian Studies* last month? On the deconstruction of quotidian discourse among females.'

One of his companions, a medievalist, shook his head. The other, who specialised in Swift, said no.

'It was so original in its thinking. She's an excellent scholar, isn't she?'

'I love these salt and vinegar crisps,' said the Swift scholar. He munched loudly and the pungent smell of salt and vinegar and other crisp flavourings flooded the air. 'I've always loved them ever since they came out. Are you old enough to remember when there were no salt and vinegar crisps, just cheese and onion?'

'Not really.' Michael was, but he felt nauseated. He stood up. 'I'm off,' he said in his short voice. 'Got to get some sleep.'

The next morning the very first thing he did was to ring Anna. But she wasn't in. He left a message on her answering machine asking her to contact him at the earliest opportunity. She did not phone.

The following day he went back to his old university, and marched straight up to Anna's office. It was only half past nine when he got there, but she was in.

'Christ!' she exclaimed when she saw him. She wore a black

skirt and jacket and looked thinner. Her hair was longer than before. 'What are you doing here?'

'I had to talk to you. Will you talk to me?'

'When?'

'Right now.'

'I'm sorry. I'm in the middle of something.'

'Will you have lunch with me?' His voice was wheedling like a little boy's.

'Yes,' she said, and sighed.

He smiled. They arranged a place and time.

'I missed you terribly,' he said, over his tomato soup. 'I just have to see you.'

'I missed you, too,' she said. 'I've been thinking of you all the time for months.'

'Will you see me again?' His face crumpled and his eyes were wet with tears.

'All right,' she said.

'Tomorrow?'

'All right,' she said.

They met at her house. Muller was in London again.

After kissing him Anna sat on the sofa and started to cry.

Michael stared at her, miserably. He decided to let her cry. He knew what she was crying about: strength of her love for him, its clandestine nature, the need for lies and deceit to cover up something that seemed so good and beautiful.

'Don't cry,' he said, after a while. 'Don't cry, dear.'

He knew that at some time this love would end. But he did not know when this would happen and he did not think it would happen soon. There was no point in telling Anna this. She would not believe him. She was deeper in love with him than ever. She worshipped him – he could see this, without vanity, as a strange and frightening fact.

He moved towards her and caught sight of himself in the

mirror. His hair had been falling out more rapidly than usual over the past week, thanks to the stress. It had receded noticeably, and the grey hairs were becoming very numerous. He looked at Anna, who was ten years his junior. She was slim and light and girlish, but soon she too would show signs of ageing. Her beauty would wither.

He pitied her profoundly. She loved him too much. He did not understand why women did this, women whom he simply wanted to befriend. They fell in love with him, or with some ideal of him to which he could never measure up. They needed him to be kind and gentle, understanding and warm. And when he failed them they continued to love him, like stupid goldfish. Indeed, they loved him even more, fondling his failings as they had fawned over his virtues. And he had never loved any of them. He had never loved even his own wife.

And now when his hair was receding and he was fat and forty he was in love for the first time. It seemed to him that he and Anna were soul mates. They were a perfect match. Their minds were one mind and their bodies fitted together like two sides of one fruit.

'Stop crying,' he said. 'Stop crying and let's talk. Let's talk about what we are going to do.'

'What are we going to do?'

'What can we do? There's Maureen and Muller and Nathan and Emily and Patrick.'

'And there's us. This is so good. It is so important.'

They sat on the sofa and talked about what they would like to do and what they could do and what they could not do.

It seemed to Anna that they were just on the brink of making a decision. And that decision would change their lives utterly and make them perfectly and wondrously happy. She could catch a glimpse of the new life just around the corner from the decision, a life of bliss, where physical and spiritual, temporal and eternal, blended into one simple being. The life there would be like a glass of clear cool water, unruffled, lovely.

And what Michael saw was that it would end. It would all have to end, and Anna would have to take the consequences. But the end was too far away to see and he was too deeply in love, at the moment, to look for it. All he knew was that the most complicated part was just beginning.

THE SEARCH FOR THE LOST
HUSBAND

The Scabby Crow told the girl to go to the witch's castle.

And she went that night, for the second time. And the witch showed her to a bedroom. The girl sat on the bed and waited.

After a while the little white goat came to the castle. Again he was in the shape of a man. And the witch offered him food and drink, but this time there was no sleeping draught in the drink. The little white goat ate and drank. Then she showed him to the bedroom.

The girl was waiting for him with open arms. And he fell into her arms and they went to bed together. And this time he did not fall asleep. They made love all night long and they had a blissful time.

When morning came he turned into a goat again.

'Will I ever see you again?' she asked.

'I am under a spell,' he said. 'If you can persuade that witch to lift the spell, I will be a man all day as well as all night. And your children will be restored to you again. And everything will be fine.'

'Why did you take my children away from me?' she asked.

'I don't know,' he said. 'I was under a spell.'

And he went away.

She went back to the old man and the old woman.

'How did you get on?' they asked.

'The best,' she said. 'He came to me and he stayed awake this time. We had a lovely night together. But I don't know what to do next. He is under a spell, and my children are under a spell, and unless that old witch lifts the spell I will never have him again.'

'You should have told me that in the first place,' said the old man. 'But I'll tell you what to do. You bring that tablecloth to the Scabby Crow, and tell her you will give it to her if she can persuade the wicked witch to lift the spell from the little white goat, and all the rest of them. That's all you have to do.'

'I should have thought of that myself,' said the girl. 'It's so simple.'

'Better late than never,' said the old man.

HOW LOVELY THE SLOPES ARE

THE CUSHIONS OF WOODLAND that scatter the plain are dark green and bright yellow. The pines are the green bits, the birches the yellow. Bronwyn has seldom seen so many leaves of this identically clear yellow colour. Where she comes from autumn foliage is an oily palette of blending pigments – kaleidoscope rather than mosaic, every shade of brown and orange, red and gold. In Sweden the trees form a neat patchwork: green and yellow, yellow and green, lightly draped across the landscape between brilliant lakes and ribbons of silver river. It is all so typical, she thinks, in its neatness and its symmetry and its prettiness.

When people in Ireland think of Swedish stereotypes they often picture curvacious blondes. They think 'sex'. Where did this image come from? Think Volvos, Bronwyn says, instead. Look at their heavy reliable bodies, their square, conservative shape. Observe that the style of a Volvo changes less often than most other makes of car. (There is only one kind of car that changes less often than a Volvo, and that never changes at all.) Examine, also, its price tag.

The plane descends. Her ears, especially the left one, react badly. It is so painful that she panics, and fears, irrationally, a burst eardrum. She's never had a problem like this before.

Why is it starting now? But by the time they've landed and taxied to a halt, the pain has diminished. By the time she is in the terminal, queuing at the passport control, it has faded to the merest buzz.

No burst eardrum after all. She turns to Erik. But Erik, who has not, in any case, heard her complaints, because he was engrossed in his book while she was making them, is not at her side. He has already vanished through the gate marked 'Nordic Citizens', while Bronwyn has to pass through the one called 'Foreigners' – Sweden has not yet joined the EU. Bronwyn is surprised that he is gone, but she feels another lift of spirit: this is Erik's airport, Erik's country. For once he is the expert and she is the foreigner, the disempowered one, rather than the source who knows everything from the whereabouts of the children's underpants to the location of the city morgue, and its telephone number. She anticipates her little holiday in Sweden with pleasure. It will be so relaxing to be a foreigner with a native spouse, instead of a native with a foreign one. Of course, there are disadvantages, and this queue is one of them. It's moving very slowly. Some woman from Belfast is having trouble with her passport and is holding everyone up.

The other people in the queue are also Irish, like Bronwyn, but she does not feel like one of them. Who can they be? They have permed hair, and their faces are thin and peaky, like the faces of people who smoke too much and don't get fresh air very often. The favoured outfit among them is a black leather jacket with tight jeans, mostly with a pink or yellow jumper sticking out under the jacket. Their shoes are pointy-toed, silly black boots.

A club, she decides. Members of some community club, over on the extremely cheap mid-winter, mid-week flight. Bronwyn and Erik are with a club too – the Irish–Swedish Club. Its members look different from the people in this queue, though. They have creamy skin and smooth, shining, straight hair. Their clothes are muted classics – beige coats, neat tweed skirts or trousers. Always discreet and quiet, as they approach their home ground, they seemed to Bronwyn to become smug. That was as close as they would get to being excited.

The Irish queue is bubbling over with mirth and pleasure at being here. But Bronwyn feels worried about them: how will they cope with the silence, the shyness, the *savoir-faire* that awaits them? How will they cope with the cold? None of them have decent coats. They are armed with shopping bags, plastic bags of cigarettes. It's not Manchester or London, she wants to tell them. It's not Spain or France.

She's ashamed, too. These people, people who look more like her than any of the Swedes, are brash and noisy. They giggle, they scream, they joke in their Belfast and Dublin and Portlaoise accents. They're making a show of themselves before they're even past passport control.

They're getting impatient, as well. The Belfast woman is taking her time. Two women with white plastic bags and carrot perms wink and slip over the Nordic Citizens gate. Poker-faced, they show their purple passports to the fat bespectacled man who sits there. He glances at them humorously and winks as well. They go through. Then all the Irish people, from Belfast and Dublin and Portlaoise, go to the Nordic Citizens gate. The official lets them all through, glancing perfunctorily at their passports. Another stereotype bites the dust, thinks Bronwyn, who is the last to do the illegal thing. She is becoming more Swedish than the Swedes themselves. Or maybe she was always like that.

They have come to Sweden to visit Erik's mother, who lives in Uppsala. That's where Erik used to live, too, when Bronwyn met him about ten years ago. She was on a post-graduate scholarship, doing a doctoral thesis on women in the Icelandic sagas. Erik was a lecturer in the department of Nordic Studies. He was the most vibrant and enthusiastic scholar Bronwyn had ever met, the sort of teacher who infected every student, at least those who were at all impressionable or sensitive, with his own great love for his subject. It is not that he had any pedagogic tricks. (He did have a few – you can hardly teach for twenty years without having a few – but they were not very good.) But he had what was much better: knowledge and love. If you know the literature you teach inside out and if you live by it, your students will love you.

And if you are tall, muscular and handsome, well, that helps, too. Bronwyn fell in love with Erik within a month of arriving in Uppsala. And he fell in love with her about a year later – a great deal of patience, suggestion and manipulation had been necessary, but in the end it had worked.

'You love me still, don't you?' asks Erik. They took the airport bus from Arlanda to Uppsala, and now they are walking over the iron bridge which spans the Fyris, the broad silver river which races over rocks and stones through the city, rushing and wild as a mountain river, although they are far from any mountains. The iron bridge has been painted postbox red since they last saw it, and it provides an excellent foil to the greyness of the sky and of the water on this dim October day. But it seems disconcertingly bold for Uppsala, one of the world's most discreet cities. What is the Commune trying to do?

'Yes,' Bronwyn yawns. They were up at four a.m. this morning. 'Of course I do.'

She has visited Uppsala many times since her marriage, and the sight of Karen's apartment building on the bank of the river fills her with a comforting mixture of intense familiarity and exoticism. She forgets most things about it until she arrives there. And then, suddenly, every detail is as intimate as her own front door – the brass handles on the thick doors, the russet marble floor with fossils flattened into some of the slabs, the narrow green lift, called by a name anyone would love, *hiss*. It is the same with the flat itself, and Karen. She has not seen her for almost two years, but as soon as she comes to the door it is as if they had all met yesterday.

Karen is a thin, tall woman, with an open countenance, spectacles, a thick grey bob pinned over her left ear with a silver slide. The image of Erik, a feminine version. She dresses in the non-descript, loose-fitting, almost dowdy clothes which are always *de rigueur* in Uppsala, university city, arbiter of good taste and humane values, soberly intellectual, judiciously democratic. Karen is of the city. Everything, from the rimless glasses to the slight uncomplaining stoop of her shoulders proclaim it: the latter you might imagine to be a scholarly stoop, but it has been caused by many years of bending over children. Karen is a retired paediatrician. And she still bends, trying to accommodate her height to the doorways of the flat, which are too low for such a tall woman. The flat is too small, as well; it inhibits her flowing, liberal style of movement. It is a *trea* – kitchen, bedroom, sitting room, all crammed with furniture which once sat in a large apartment.

They come into the kitchen and Karen immediately begins to chat and ask questions. Of course she speaks Swedish. Bronwyn understands and responds as well as she can. She learned Swedish when she was here, long ago, before she was married. But now she is used to speaking it with one person only, namely Erik. His accent, his personal intonation, are the only ones she really understands well. When Karen and her neighbour Axel, who has dropped in to be part of the welcoming committee, start to chatter she feels a misty veil descend and separate her from them. They make signs to her through this veil but they do not touch her.

When Bronwyn first met Karen, Karen lived in Stockholm. She was married to a man who was not Erik's father, from whom she was divorced when Erik was ten. (She'd had an affair, Erik explained. His father could not forgive her. The man she married was not the man she had had the affair with.) They lived in a large apartment in an old part of the city, Kungsholmen, in an old, grand house. In that apartment there was a grand piano in the entrance hall, an enormous fragrant log fire at one end of the long dining room. The furniture which crowds Karen's aparment now had sat comfortably in the spacious rooms in Stockholm, and large, dark, mysterious oil paintings of hares in snow and huntsmen in forests had hung on the walls.

Karen's husband died twelve years ago. She moved here then, and has fallen into the habits of widowhood. She seems to Bronwyn to be more immersed in the ordinary details of life than anyone she has ever known, and to be happy with that absorption.

Erik suspects that Bronwyn is wrong about this. He thinks Karen is having some sort of affair with Axel. Bronwyn cannot believe it. She can't believe that two people with grey hair and wrinkled skin, with sagging flesh, could bother about sexual love. 'Don't be too sure!' Erik laughs. He is older than Bronwyn and has grey hair himself. But Bronwyn is sure, dismayingly sure – not that no one could be attracted to Axel, who is crisp and trim although he is seventy-four, but that Karen, however beautiful (for her age), is past it.

They sit in the kitchen, drinking coffee and eating rye bread and cheese, and talk about how Erik and Brownyn will spend the two days, and what they will eat and drink. Questions such as does Bronwyn like prawns and should they have the salmon with bread or potatoes are raised and answered, timetables for buses and trains are discussed, shops which should be visited, exhibitions which are worth seeing, museums which are still open.

The kitchen is painted a deep yellow, which gets deeper and more buttery each time they visit. There is a smoke-coloured wooden sofa, with a striped seat, against one wall. The table, spread with a white lace cloth, is under the window. From the window you can see the courtyard, with its trees and play-ground which is seldom used. Apparently there are few chil-dren in this apartment block, but on every street in Sweden there is at least one playground. It is a country that cherishes children.

Karen discusses films. Or rather she discusses how she will celebrate Axel's birthday, coming up in a week's time (Axel has gone home by now). Dinner, she thinks, in a nice restau-rant in the old town, and then some sort of show. The problem is that Axel is not fond of the theatre and he doesn't like films much, either, especially Swedish films. 'Always down at the bottom of everything!' says Karen, wrinkling up her nose in disgust. 'Diving for the deepest most horrible places in the psyche!'

Bronwyn, who likes those films very much, is surprised at the acumen of the remark. It has never struck her that Karen knew about that deep and horrible place, where Bronwyn spends quite a lot of her time. In fact, she has never credited Karen with having any deep emotion. The indisputable facts of the two marriages and the suspected two affairs amaze her. Passion and Karen. The equation doesn't convince. She seems so matter of fact, she seems to thrive on the surface. Of course, plenty of practical people, living on the surface, fall in love, or, even more often, inspire it. You don't have to be a neurotic Bergman type for that at all. The question is, do they experi-ence love in the same way as the others? Love, and the lack of love?

They have prawns and brown bread for lunch, and blueberries which Karen picked on her summer island in the archipelago during the summer. Her freezer is full of plastic butter boxes filled with blueberries, raspberries, redcurrants, and blackberries, all picked by herself and Axel, berry by careful berry, in the summer sun, and stored just as meticulously for the dark winter, already well under way in October.

Karen regales them with stories of her childhood. She talks about the big house in the Swedish countryside where she herself, and later Erik, were born. It was a wooden house on the shore of a lake, with a large garden full of flowers, fruit trees, every kind of vegetable. Bronwyn has heard about this house so often that she feels she has been there, too. She knows Karen's room and Erik's room and the apple attic with the wonderful smell (Erik usually mentions Goethe at this point, because Goethe found the scent of apples inspiring). She knows the veranda, where they ate meals during the summer, and she knows what they ate – pike, perch, other fishes they don't know the English for, and good sauces. 'Mother made excellent sauces!' Karen says. 'She was a great cook. Sauces are the most important thing, for food, don't you agree?' She goes on to catalogue a number of these sauces.

Karen's mother went to market every Saturday on the train which ran on a single track through the cornfields at the back of the house, like a train in a Lego set. She returned, laden with fish, meat, chocolate, coffee. (All the fruit and vegetables eaten in the household she grew herself.) This was her one outing of the week. Saturday at the marketplace in town. Sometimes Karen accompanied her. More often she was out in the woods, boating on the lake, swimming. Hunting pike in the flooded autumnal fields. Tobogganing down one of the rare slopes in that flat wooded landscape. Skiing. She, and later Erik, went to school on skis, across the fields, three or four miles.

Bronwyn thinks this sounds idyllic. She sees the glittering white landscape, the dark trees laden with snow. She sees the ice gleaming on the lake. 'It wasn't so much fun,' says Erik. 'I had to get up at six a.m., and it was cold and dark. And I had to pass a dog who barked at me. I hated that dog so much!'

After lunch Bronwyn escapes and walks into the city centre. She wanders along the racing river, overhung with yellow trees, and down through the medieval parts of the city, which are painted ochre, and look more eighteenth century than medieval to her. She goes to the square.

She wantes to buy lovely Swedish things as Christmas presents – glasses, candlesticks, scraps of needlepoint or lace. She hopes to get some Christmas decorations, as well, but it is too early for them. They have not been laid out in the department stores. She tours a few of them, and sees very little that attracts her. Then she finds a tiny shop on a side street, a toy shop, a nonsense shop, stocking oldfashioned foreign toys made in China or Korea. There are clockwork mice, tin chickens in eggs, kaleidoscopes. The shop is scented with herbal candles, hung with musical mobiles. In one corner is a large, exquisitely furnished doll's house.

Bronwyn spends a lot of time looking at the doll's house, and then more time examining clockwork toys which are displayed on a big table at the back of the shop: frogs, tortoises, pigs, chickens, geese, all sitting on their own in cardboard boxes with keys sticking out of their backs. She winds up the toys and watches them hopping or skipping, or lifting spoons up and down to their mouths. The musical mobiles play 'Someday over the Rainbow'.

Finally she selects two mice and two hedgehogs – identical – for her two children being looked after at this moment by her mother at home in Cork. The mice run around the floor and the hedgehogs sit up and beg. The girl at the counter asks her if they are presents and Bronwyn says, yes, presents. The girl takes the tiny boxes and wraps them carefully in silver paper and red ribbons, finishing them off as exquisitely as boxes of precious gems.

Opposite Karen's block of flats is a row of houses. They are low, two-storey houses, yellow and white, with miniature decorative chimneys on their pitched, shingled roofs. You can see into most of them from Karen's kitchen: flat candles flicker on the tables in the dark mornings, and the rooms are furnished with warm, honey-pine furniture, red and blue striped rugs, wooden toys.

When Bronwyn was living in Uppsala she used to look through windows like those windows, and wish she was inside. Walking alone on cold streets, the glimmering lights of homes tantalised her with visions of love and calm and everlasting content. She believed that behind those glowing yellow windows were delightful, cheerful families, and she wished she was a cheerful young mother, in dungarees and clogs, making bread among the flickering light. She wished she had a child in a red and yellow jumper, the kind of child she saw all the time cycling along the paths in the park, or trailing along the side of the road with a chain gang of other children from some kindergarten, all clutching a rope held by a teacher. (In Uppsala, the kindergartens seemed to spend their whole time going on outings, like multicoloured ducks waddling across meadows in search of ponds.)

At this time she was spending most of her days in the big library, the Carolina, immersed in study. She was fired up so passionately by her thesis that she could hardly sleep at night. Her head was full of ideas about *Laxdaela Saga*, her main text. When she was in the library, or when she was with her fellow students in their common room, she shared their ambitions:

nothing in life mattered except continuing to do research, no ambition was thinkable except the ambition to be a lecturer, to stay in the environment of the university.

Bronwyn wanted that. But when she saw the blond children playing on the coloured swings, and their cheerful, lovely mothers and fair-haired, grinning fathers she wanted to be like them as well.

She had had to choose and she chose Erik.

She had two colourful, brilliant children. She had a house with wooden floors and pine furniture and flat candles glimmering on the table, a house with a mildly Swedish flavour in the centre of Cork.

Erik had his library, his career, an expanding curriculum vitae. He learned more and more languages, wrote more and more books, won more and more acclaim. Bronwyn read novels and taught part-time in a school. She decorated her house. She played with her children. Her admiration for Icelandic literature diminished over the years, because she was too lazy or too preoccupied to keep in touch with it. Her admiration for Erik was sometimes as great as it ever had been, and sometimes non-existent. He did not change.

The cathedral, library and castle are perched on a hill in the centre of Uppsala. The library and castle are built of huge grey blocks of granite, but the cathedral, a great Gothic monster, is composed entirely of minute red bricks.

Bronwyn goes inside. In the porch, children's crayon pictures are pinned to the wall on one side. On the other is a small bust of Plotinus, and this is more surprising than the children's pictures. What is Plotinus doing in a Lutheran cathedral, or in any cathedral?

The huge dim body of the church is almost empty of people and sound, but it is filled with the special ecclesiastical air –

candlewax, wood, the smell of age – that medieval cathedrals usually have. Bronwyn looks up at the distant vaults of the roof: they are sweeping and vast, but tiled with myriad tiny tiles of blue and gold, made to imitate the sky. There is a Byzantine influence, probably, but there is a Swedish aspect to the ceiling, too – it is simple, Protestant, unostentatious. It represents the heavens, but it is down to earth.

Earth.

Bronwyn wants to look at the tombs. She wants to stare at the rich sepulchres which hold the bones of kings and queens: Gustav Vasa, Charles the Twelfth, the mother of Queen Kristina who loved her husband so much that when he died she kept his corpse in her bedroom for months (she was a necrophiliac, Erik comments, like the fellows in Snow White).

The occupants of the sepulchres have been modelled in gold and laid to rest on top of their tombs. Long noses, stiffly folded dresses, small heads banded by tiaras or weighed down with crowns, lie side by side in the chancel. In the immense silence Bronwyn stands and stares, trying to imagine the time that has elapsed since the bodies were placed in the tombs and the gold-en images sculpted. Five hundred years. Six hundred years. This immutable golden woman with deep large eyes, two burnished braids of hair gently smoothed over her breasts, was alive six centuries ago, living with the man whose graven image still lies beside her. They rode on sleighs in the snowy woods, they ate fish and blueberries, they made love. And for six centuries they have been lying here under quiet images of themselves. Not feeling, not knowing, not caring about anything.

The silence is so vast and deep you feel you are lying in it. You feel it enfolding you like a rich dark velvet wrapper, and you smell it as it passes into your lungs, into the blood in your body.

Why has Bronwyn come to the cathedral? Not to think about death. What she is seeking is something else, harder to put your finger on. Enormousness. She wants to grasp the enormousness of time itself. She feels she should be able to expand and stretch her mind to accommodate the idea of it, to feel the stretch of six hundred years or a thousand years, just as her eye can accommodate the height and width of the cathedral, and her whole body become an ear for its silence.

That's why she came. She hopes that if she can fully experience the ideas that the cathedral encompasses, in its colossal spaces and its intricate details, she would have a nuclear explosion of the mind. She would be on the way to freedom and joy.

But she can't do it. She can't take it all in. She only succeeds in stretching her hand toward this experience, getting a hint that it might, under different circumstances, be possible to achieve.

Looking at the high mosaic ceilings, at the millions of tiny blue and gold tiles fixed over the arched nave, puts thoughts in her head, all right, but they remain thoughts. They do not have the power to affect her spirit.

She leaves the cathedral, nodding at the bust of Plotinus as she goes. And when she steps out onto the gravel path that leads from the church to the silent park she is feeling much the same as she felt going in. Except that now she is more aware than ever of the black blanket that is locking her mind, shutting out space and light. She thinks she is a clock that has stopped, its cogs stiff and rusty.

Nevertheless, she breathes more deeply than before. Her lungs have responded to the largeness of the cathedral, and there is a surge of oxygen in her blood.

'I wouldn't mind going to IKEA,' Bronwyn says on the second morning.

'Your word is my command,' Erik says genially. But Bronwyn winces. It's a joke, but one of these true jokes that are inspired by hurt. Their relationship has reached the stage where he is scared to death of her. She must have whatever she wants. Every single thing. Then maybe she will become happy. Maybe she will become loving. Maybe she will stay.

Nobody wants that much power.

Erik has a sore foot. All the rich food has sparked off his arthritis. But he insists on accompanying her, anyway. He knows where the shop is – on the outskirts of the town, on the road to Märsta.

Karen fumbles with a bus timetable but can't figure out which bus they should get. She shows him the place where the shop is on the map and gives him the map.

'We can easily walk,' says Erik.

'Can we? It looks far away.'

'It is no distance. You need a walk.'

'Yes, I do.'

'Do you love me?'

'Yes I do.'

They start off on the familiar way across the river, past the grey buildings with their discreet, dull shop fronts: Apothek, Systembolaget, Domus. They continue past the medieval houses, the yellow houses, towards the station.

Uppsala is a mixture of very dull, fifties architecture and very picturesque medieval buildings, all looking as if they have been *in situ* for ever, nonchalantly and most casually assembled in the vicinity of the cathedral. There is nothing higgledy-piggledy about it, though. Even the narrowest, most olde worlde parts look unruffled and ordinary. They've been there for a long time, but they are not going to make any sort of song and dance about that.

This is the kind of thing Bronwyn would like to talk

about. But Erik is never interested in such idle speculation. He has the unassuming self-possession of the city. It is his city. He has lived and studied here, worked here, been a professor up on the hill, close to the cathedral, in the university where Linnaeus and Celsius and many of the great scientists of Europe worked, easily, one senses, and quietly, classifying the plants of the world or finding a way to measure heat, as if such activities were natural, child's play. There seems to be no fuss or stress in Uppsala, no messing – although this cannot be entirely true.

Erik, for instance, although he is one of the world's great experts on *Njal's Saga*, can be a bit of a messer. He is not good at calculating distance, for one thing, or of guessing what would make a pleasurable walk. The way to IKEA takes them along a straight busy road, dissecting factories and warehouses. On this intensely grey day, with winter ominously sitting over the city like a dark cold blanket waiting to descend, it is not a pleasant place to be. True enough, Bronwyn is interested in looking at the solid factories, big and rich and famous – Volvo and Statoil and Hellman's. The buildings are huge, and there are hundreds of them stretching as far as the eye can see. This is what supports the cultural heart of Uppsala, then. The cathedral and the libraries and the thousands of students. It takes all this industry, as well as the rich flat plain with its yellow clay and yellow corn, to establish and keep going a true centre of learning. In Cork, industrial estates look as if they were built last week and will soon tumble down into the marshy green fields where tinkers' horses run wild, where all such estates tend to be built.

Where is IKEA? They have walked for miles. Erik takes out the map. Now they are in the middle of a roundabout. The road has become a tangle of motorways marked Stockholm, Märsta, Knivsta. Cars race around them as they stand like fools at the centre. Nobody else is walking here. Nobody ever walks in places like this.

'It's this way,' says Erik.

They get off the roundabout and walk along one of the motorways, which seems to turn off into bleak farmland quite soon. There is no path now. They plod along in the squelching yellow clay which is heaped up on the side of the road. Bronwyn steps into something black, softer and stickier than the clay. It clings to her new boots and emits a sickening chemical odour.

Out here the sky is enormous. Over the flat landscape it broods like a monstrous beast, its grey ferocity stretching for miles above great grey fields.

'No!' sighs Erik, when they have plodded for ten minutes. 'We should be down there!' He points to another, bigger motorway, underneath.

'We can't go down!' Bronwyn is beginning to whine. She glances at her watch. It is almost lunch time. They have spent half of one of their two days in Sweden walking through an industrial estate, along a motorway.

'Of course we can!' He puts one leg over the crash barrier. Between them and the motorway is a bank about twenty yards long, covered with rough grass and scutch. Below, the trucks and cars race relentlessly.

'I'm not going there!'

'Why not?' Erik is genuinely puzzled.

'I'm just not!' She listens to the trucks roaring. 'I'm not dressed for it.' Bronwyn is wearing her cream winter coat, a small brown hat, patent boots. She is dressed as she thinks a fashionable lady should dress for a Christmas shopping trip to a foreign city. When she bought these clothes she was thinking of coloured lights in a dark street. She was thinking of coffee in a fine old café. She was thinking of a walk to the theatre on a starlit night.

'Don't be silly! It's quite easy to go down!'

Erik begins to descend. Bronwyn begins to cry.

Then she begins to scream. 'You're so stupid!' she yells. 'We should have got the bus!'

He climbs back up. 'Well we didn't,' he says patiently. 'Do you want to go back to the station and get it now?'

It's two miles back to the station.

'I don't want to go back to the station! I don't want to go anywhere! I'm sick and tired of being here, and I'm sick and tired of being married to you! You are so useless!'

'We're there again, are we?' Erik looks weary.

'Yes, we are there again. This is your place! You should know how to handle the buses. You should take responsibility. I can't know everything in Sweden as well as in Ireland.'

'You know I'm not good at directions. If you're so damn clever why can't you find the shop? Here's the map.'

The sky is grey. The temperature is three degrees above freezing. Erik looks very grey, very lined, in the harsh light. The trucks roar along the highway.

Bronwyn tears up the map and flings it over the crash barrier. 'I hate you!' she screams. 'I really do!'

Erik jumps over the barrier and picks up a few scraps. 'That's Mama's map!' He is cross, for the first time. 'You madwoman!' He looks as if he wants to hit Bronwyn. His face is purple with rage and he grits his teeth.

When he goes purple she is afraid he will get a heart attack. That is another hold he has on her: if she screams too much, he will get a heart attack. It doesn't stop her screaming, but it makes her feel guilty for doing it.

She stalks along the road, running away from Erik, crying. She wishes she were dead. Her frustration is barbed wire in her brain, pressing in on it. If she had courage, she'd fling herself under a train – there is a track running alongside this road.

She can imagine being crushed to death by a train quite easily –
the sharp, cold wheels cutting through her. All that stops her is
physical cowardice.

'You're hopeless!' she screams at the top of her lungs. 'You
can't do anything! You can't fix anything! You can't find anything! You're no good, anywhere!'

The twin spires of Uppsala cathedral are on the skyline. She
is on the motorway, shouting like a fishwife at her husband,
telling him he is hopeless.

'That's enough,' Erik says, in his grimmest voice. 'I've had
all I can take.' His face is ashen, or iron. 'When we get home
we can make arrangements to separate. I can't have you ruin-
ing my peace of mind and my concentration for ever.'

Bronwyn stops crying. She walks towards him.

'Do you understand, you devil? I'm sick of living life as if it
were a Bergman film. Life should be peaceful and pleasant.
People should try to be kind to one another, instead of . . .
We will separate. As soon as we get back to Ireland.'

Bronwyn feels like a leaf falling from a tree. 'Do you mean
that?' She is almost smiling, with relief.

He grimaces. 'Of course I mean it. I am at the end of my
tether. Don't you realise there is only so much anyone can
take?'

'Yes,' says Bronwyn. She is thinking of Gunnar, in *Njal's
Saga*, who asks his wife, Hallgerdur, to lend him a hair for his
bow, to save his life. And she refuses him, reminding him of
the time he slapped her face. 'You will not be asked again!'
Gunnar says, in his grim, heroic, Icelandic voice. It is one of
two lines in *Njal's Saga* that Bronwyn still remembers. 'I'm
sorry,' Bronwyn adds. 'But it's the only thing to do.'

She stares at him and he stares back.

'Will we really do it?' Bronwyn says.

Her mind settles itself, spreads itself calmly across her

heart like a newly woven silken sheet. The sky of the future broadens overhead, wide white roads stretch to a bright horizon. The buzzing in her head stops.

If they are apart, she can start everything again. She will be normal and kind and cheerful and pleasant. She will turn herself inside out and be a new person. She will live the way other people live, happy, laughing people, occupied with the Christmas baking and the children's piano lessons. She will resume her studies and find intellectual fulfilment. She will be herself, and be happy. She actually believes all this, that all it takes is a cut down the middle of her life, and, like a worm, she will wriggle off and live the perfect life that is now being denied her.

'Yes, you bloody madwoman, of course we'll do it.' He laughs one of those grim Icelandic laughs and shakes his head. 'Let's shake hands on it!'

On the motorway they stand, husband and wife, about to part, and shake hands.

'Now that's settled!' Erik laughs again. He seems amused, and also relieved. 'Let's be friends. Let's be civilised for our last day here, and not upset anyone any more.'

'Oh yes!' Bronwyn gasps. You will not be asked again.

She looks at Erik and feels a surge of affection for him. She admires his tall thin body, his head held lightly and jerkily, like a boy's. She likes his green coat, his shock of grey hair, Karen's hair, falling untidily over his forehead. 'We should be friends!' she says.

He seems now such a kind person, such an interesting and knowledgeable person, such a wise and special person. It would be good to be his friend.

'So, will we go home or what?'

'What do you think?'

'Why don't we go to IKEA, anyway?' asks Erik. 'Look, there's a taxi!'

And a taxi appears, the first taxi they have seen all morning. Erik hails it. But it sails right past. However, one minute later another taxi pulls up beside them.

'Aha!' smiles Erik.

'Yeah!' smiles Bronwyn. 'The good old efficiency!'

They sink into warm plush seats. Bronwyn feels she would like to sit in the taxi all day, enjoying the smooth comfort of it. Erik chats to the driver and in minutes they are at the entrance to IKEA.

They go in.

First they treat themselves to coffee and pastries. While they are having this, they look with pleasure at the other people in the shop and talk about them in low English whispers.

Then they get a trolley and walk around the store.

It is a cathedral, a wonderland of household equipment. Sofas and beds and shelves and lamps. Curtains and towels and duvets and bolts of fabric. Candlesticks and tablecloths and wooden toys. Everything is wooden, everything is lovely, everything is cheap. They ooh and they aah. They pick up things and feel them and put them down. They pick them up again.

Bronwyn buys a candlestick shaped like a toy horse, a set of blue table mats, three metres of material for curtains. Erik buys picture frames and fixtures for bookshelves, and considers a toilet-roll holder in white pine. They buy two hobby-horses and a dinosaur, and a collection of coloured file boxes for the children. When they reach the checkout they have to buy two big sacks to hold all their purchases.

'Do you love me after all?' Erik asks, as they wait at the taxi rank.

'Yes,' says Bronwyn.

In the taxi she thinks that this is true, as true as anything else she might declare. It is certainly as true as 'no', more true than 'maybe'. I love you. I love you not. I love you.

The boxy Volvo, silent as snow, warm as the sun, sails along the grim highway towards the twin spires of the cathedral. More lines from *Njal's Saga* visit her mind, spontaneously and unbidden, as is the habit of proverbs and saws, or any of the old scraps of traditional wisdom we have heard and which whirl invisibly in the air around us all the time, choosing their own moment to descend to our consciousness, like angels bearing featherlight gifts of truth.

They rode down to the Markar river, on their way to the ship. Gunnar's horse stumbled, and he had to dismount. He glanced up the hill to his home.

'How lovely the slopes are!' he said. 'More lovely than they have ever appeared to me before. Golden cornfields and new-mown hay. I am going back home, and I will not go away.'

THE SEARCH FOR THE LOST
HUSBAND

She went to the Scabby Crow. And she spread the magic tablecloth on the ground. It was covered with every kind of delicious food and with goblets of the finest drinks in the world.

'That's a lovely tablecloth,' said the Scabby Crow. 'I wouldn't mind having one of them myself.'

'It's very handy,' said the girl. 'I'll give it to you if you can persuade the old witch to lift the spell off the little white goat and my children.'

'It won't be easy to do that!' said the Scabby Crow. 'But I'll do my best, so I will.'

She went to the castle of the wicked witch. And she spread the tablecloth on the table there.

'Look at this!' she said. 'What do you say to this, now!'

'It's a great tablecloth,' said the wicked witch. 'Tell that girl she can spend the week with the little white goat, if she lets me have that cloth.'

'That's not enough,' said the Scabby Crow. 'A week isn't enough. She will part with the tablecloth only if you lift the spell off my son and off their three children. And off my daughters, too, while you're at it.'

'I couldn't do that,' said the witch, 'for any tablecloth.'

'Very well,' said the Scabby Crow. 'I'll take it back to her. At least she's got the cloth.'

'Can I have another look?' asked the witch.

The Scabby Crow spread the cloth again. And all the most beautiful foods and the finest wines appeared on it.

'I can't resist it,' said the wicked witch. 'I'll lift the spell tonight. Tell her to come here, and bring the cloth with her.'

That evening the girl came to the castle of the witch. And the little white goat came. And the Scabby Crow came.

'Give me the cloth,' said the witch.

'Lift the spell,' said the girl.

The witch took a magic wand out of her dresser. And she hit the little white goat a belt of it. And he turned into a fine young man.

'You'll never be a goat again!' said the witch.

She hit the Scabby Crow a belt of the wand, and she turned into a handsome woman.

'You won't be a Scabby Crow again for as long as you live!' said the witch.

'My three babies!' said the girl. 'Where are they?'

The witch shut her eyes and breathed deeply. Then she hit the air with her wand, three times. And the three little boys appeared on the kitchen floor. They laughed and danced around, one more beautiful than the other. Their mother hugged them and wept with joy to see them.

She gave the magic tablecloth to the wicked witch. The

witch combed her golden hair, and flounced around in her lovely suit, and spread out the tablecloth and ate and drank to her heart's content.

'And now,' said the handsome young man, who had been the little white goat, 'we can get married, and live happily ever after.'

The girl looked at him. 'I don't think I want to,' she said. 'You have led me a merry dance, up hill and down dale, and through briars and brambles and bracken and thorns, through rivers and lakes and ditches and puddles, through thick and through thin and in and out. And I think I have had enough of you.'

'I was under a spell,' he said. 'None of that was my fault.'

'I don't care,' she said. 'I've had enough of you. I'm tired, running around in circles, chasing you to the ends of the earth.'

'But you love me! You can't live without me! You've proved it by your relentless hunting down of me, your dauntless passion!'

'I am weary of ardent ways. Passion is so time consuming, and it makes me so unhappy.'

'It's not fair. You were the one who instigated all the passion. You were the one who followed me. I asked you to stop, time and again.'

'It's true. But you were the one who came to my doorstep, day after day, fawning all over me until I fell in love with you. And as soon as that happened, off you went!'

'It was too much for me. You exaggerate everything so much!'

'I didn't start it.'

'I'm sorry.'

'I hate it when men say I'm sorry. What good does saying sorry do?'

'I'm sorry.'

'Goodbye to you now. I'm going home to my father and my mother, and I'm bringing my dear little children with me. And we'll have a bit of fun, playing together and laughing, and I'll love them more than I ever loved you or anybody else. And maybe I will find another husband, who will be kind to me and my children, and who will look after all of us and not lead us around in circles. Because it's time for me to try another kind of love. I'm tired of all that fairytale stuff.'

With that, she called her children to her and they set off. They walked over the land at the bottom of the stairs, and they climbed the stairs and they came home to their own country.

And the girl returned to her old home. And there was a young farmer there who was happy to marry her, even though she had three children already. And she married him and they lived happily together for many years.

And as for the little white goat, I do not know what became of him.

That is my story. And if there is a lie in it, it was not I who made it up.

All I got for my story was butter boots and paper hats. And a white dog came and ate the boots and tore the hats. But what matter? What matters but the good of the story?